Awaken

Book 1

The Kat Kritchley Chronicles

Claire Buss

Tales from the Seaside
The Blue Serpent & other tales
Flashing Here and There

Anthologies
Underground Scratchings, *Tales from the Underground* anthology
Patient Data, *The Quantum Soul* anthology
A Badger Christmas Carol, The Sparkly Badgers' Christmas Anthology
Dress Like An Animal and *Afraid of the Dark*, *Haunted*, The Sparkly Badgers' Anthology
Someone, *Mrs Latimer Had A Fat Cat And Other Cozy Mystery Poems*
The Last Pirate, *Tales from the Pirate Cove* Anthology

Chapter 1

Kat stood at the bus stop in the rain. She'd forgotten her umbrella and her hair was plastered to her head, rivulets of water running down her face and neck. *Of all the days,* she thought, *it had to be the day of my interview.* She'd been too busy making sure her mum had taken her tablets and her brother had got on the bus to school to remember to pick up that stupid umbrella.

The bus finally arrived, and it was packed. Kat squeezed her way on, doing her best not to step on anyone's toes or drip on anyone's knees. As the bus pulled away, Kat tried to see where they were going, but the windows were steamy from all the bodies and it was difficult to tell where she was. She'd not taken this bus route before and she didn't want to be late as well as soaking wet to her job interview, so she'd memorised the route. It was five stops.

Scrambling off the bus at what she hoped was the fifth stop, Kat stood in the drizzle, trying to get her bearings. Sampson Close, the appointment letter had said. She spied the street sign and began hurrying to her destination, going through the standard interview questions in her head. She had to get this job. The rent was well past due.

As she entered the immaculate foyer, a pristine receptionist looked disdainfully down at Kat's bedraggled appearance.

"May I help you?"

"I have an interview at ten. My name is Kat Kritchley," replied Kat with what she hoped was a confident smile.

"Take a seat." The receptionist pressed a button and murmured into her headset that the next candidate was here. Then she completely ignored Kat.

Looking at the material covered sofas in the waiting area, Kat decided against sitting and fervently wished there was some way she could stop the rainwater from dripping off the edge of her coat and bag. She was creating small puddles on the floor.

"You can go through," said the receptionist, pointing to a door on the left.

Kat uttered her thanks and tried to ignore the desperation butterflies flapping around in her stomach.

Ten minutes later and Kat was back at the bus stop with tears on her face to match the raindrops that were still falling. The interview had been a disaster. Apparently, appearance was critical and her explanation as to why she'd forgotten her umbrella had brought into question her attention to detail. That, coupled with the fact she had no previous experience in selling luxury candles, had sealed her fate. Crossly Kat kicked at a stone. If they didn't think she had the right experience, then they shouldn't have asked her for an interview.

Deciding not to wait for the bus, Kat plodded on down the path, heading into town. She might as well double check with the temping agency she'd signed up to last week, to see if there was anything available. Whilst the clouds matched her mood, they held off from raining again and Kat arrived once more in an office foyer, this time a good deal drier.

"Hi, how can I help?" Another receptionist, but this time, she was bright and bubbly.

"Hi, it's Kat. Kat Kritchley? I signed up last week. Just thought I'd check in, see if there were any jobs going."

"Right, okay. Well, we ring you when we get something that matches your profile." The girl's smile grew even wider. "Have you been contacted via phone?"

"Er, no. No, I haven't." Kat could feel the hot prickles of embarrassment causing her to blush.

"We'll let you know if anything pops up, okay?" Another huge smile before the receptionist's attention was diverted by the shrill sound of an incoming call.

Shoulders slumped in defeat, Kat pushed the agency door open and returned to the rain. Huddling in the office doorway, not wanting to step out into the miserable weather again, she looked in her bag for her purse and checked the contents. She had about a pound in change. Not really enough for anything, but then she remembered she had a full coffee bean card for McDonalds so she could get a free hot drink. Feeling slightly buoyed, Kat marched off toward those golden arches debating whether to spend her last pound on some small fries.

The fries won and Kat sat in the corner of the restaurant with her meagre meal and a hot chocolate and pondered her next move. Rummaging in her bag, she pulled out a dog-eared letter, opened the envelope, and began to read. It was pointless, really. She already knew the contents off by heart. It told her mother than unless the overdue rent was paid by Friday, the family would be evicted and fined an additional hundred pounds in late fees.

Kat's hands trembled as she refolded the letter to put it away. Her mum and brother were counting on her to get a job. Well, her mum was. Her younger brother didn't really understand the nitty gritty of daily life. It was part of his autistic charm. Completely oblivious to anyone and anything else unless it directly affected him, in that particular moment.

What was she going to do? She gazed out of the restaurant window, watching the rain belt down even harder, and a flash of light caught her attention. She looked but couldn't see where it came from. There it was again. On the third flash, she saw where the light show was coming from. It was a bulb in an outside fixture, flickering. Kat stared at the building. She didn't remember seeing it before. Peering hard, she could just make out the name above the windows. Magus Employment Services.

Kat's heart leapt with excitement. It sounded like another temping agency. She hadn't been to this one. Maybe they would have something for her. Downing the last of her now cold hot chocolate, she shoved the eviction notice into her bag and hurried out into the rain. She ran across the square and grinned up at the flickering light before pushing open the door to the agency. It was a thick wooden door with a large brass knocker and Kat felt a tingle as she passed over the threshold.

Once inside, Kat looked around with interest. She was in a dimly lit passageway with a hatstand and an umbrella box. There was a darkened staircase on the right and a cosy glow emanating from the end of the hallway. As Kat walked along, she trailed one hand on the wall. It seemed to hum underneath her touch. She took her fingers away in wonder. Must be the result of old wiring, she thought.

The corridor opened onto a warm and inviting reception. There were four large leather armchairs, arranged around a fireplace with a small coffee table in their midst, covered in magazines. A fire flickered lazily in the grate. On either side of the fireplace were shelves dense with books. Kat's eyes darted from cover to cover. There was a real mixture of genres, authors and eras. Classics rubbed shoulders with newer volumes. And there were multiple books about dragons.

There was a small cough behind her.

Kat spun around guiltily. She had been admiring the bookcase and savouring the smell of the old books, having completely forgotten why she was there. A young woman sat at an ornate desk with an old-fashioned typewriter before her. She had piles of auburn hair arranged in a messy bun on her head and startling green eyes that looked brightly at the soggy and slightly bedraggled Kat.

Before Kat had a chance to introduce herself, the lady picked up the handle of a highly decorative rotary phone and dialled several numbers.

"Your noon appointment has arrived," she said in a melodious voice.

"Oh, no, I don't have an appointment…" Kat tried to explain, but a door on her left creaked open by itself and the receptionist gave her an encouraging smile.

"Go right ahead."

Kat looked doubtfully at the door. Desperation overrode the bizarreness of the situation and she tentatively walked through the doorway.

She had never been in a more unusual office before. A huge telescope stood in the large bay window, pointing up to the sky and planets she didn't recognise hung suspended from the ceiling, spinning gently in elliptical patterns. Another fireplace warmed the room and its green flames licked the grate hungrily. Kat's head whipped back to the fire. The usual colours danced, no green to be seen.

Feeling a little unnerved, she redirected her attention to the other person in the room. He wasn't paying her any attention. A mop of dark hair with speckles of silver here and there was bent over a pile of paperwork. She could see a pair of half-moon spectacles atop a slender nose with a neat moustache. The man was impeccably dressed in a three-piece grey suit with a plum coloured cravat. Kat glanced down at her old school skirt and shirt ensemble. There was no money for a smart interview suit, and she had a hole in her right shoe, so one foot was colder and wetter than the other. She shifted slightly and could hear squelching. She hoped fervently that the man wouldn't notice.

"Katerina, please, take a seat."

His voice was deep, warm, and welcoming. Kat moved to one of the seats arranged in front of the man's large wooden desk. The chairs were high-backed with red velvet furnishings, matching the upscale quality of the rest of the furniture. She noticed an ink well and a quill. Then her brain caught up with her body.

"How do you...?" she stammered as she faltered, only half-sitting in the chair.

The man steepled his hands and looked over them at her, waiting for her to finish taking her seat. She sat, but did so with mounting trepidation.

"I understand you are looking for employment. We would be delighted to offer you a contract. I think you will find the particulars acceptable." He flourished a large piece of parchment and laid it gently before her.

Her curiosity piqued, Kat glanced down and saw a beautiful manuscript in front of her with delicate calligraphy and intricate patterns decorating the page. There was her full name and the name of the agency. It stated she would work reasonable hours to complete temping contracts that suited her skill set until the end of each assignment. She would be paid... Kat gulped and peered closer at that information. It was more than three times the national minimum wage.

"Is this a dream?" she murmured in wonder, then attempted to pull herself together. She pushed the contract back slightly and looked directly at the man across the desk.

A hint of amusement danced in the dark, almost black eyes that looked at her over his glasses.

"Who are you?" she asked. "How did you know my name?"

"Where are my manners? I am Xavier Magus, pleased to meet you." He held out his hand.

The clock on the mantle ticked loudly as Mr Magus watched Kat, and she tried not to be unnerved by him. She slowly extended her own hand in kind and Mr Magus clasped it with both of his own. His hands felt warm and somehow safe. Gently, he let hers go.

"Is your fee unacceptable?" he asked.

"What? No, it's beyond generous." Kat tried to marshal her thoughts so she could come up with a pertinent question. "Don't you need to test my skills, look at my resume or ask me questions about my experience before you give me a job contract?"

"Do you have a resume with you?"

"No, but I can email one over if you like."

Mr Magus winced at the mention of the word email, and Kat realised that was another thing that seemed odd about this place. No modern technology, not even the phones.

"We just need a signature. If you don't mind." Mr Magus was holding out the quill from his desk. A drop of blue ink fell from the nib and landed on the corner of the contract. Kat automatically held out her hand to take the quill and stop it from dripping any more ink on the paperwork.

This is mad, she thought to herself as she signed her name on the dotted line. Although the more she considered it, it wasn't much different to signing up with the other agencies in town. They'd just made her fill in exhaustive personality questionnaires and undertake several exams on the computer to demonstrate her skills. Signing her name with a quill was so much easier. Kat looked up with a grin.

"When do I start?"

The door to the office opened. By itself.

"Amelia will set up your first contract. Thank you, Miss Kritchley." And Mr Magus proceeded to completely ignore Kat's presence. She picked up her bag and squelched out of the office, realising that her feet were feeling slightly less soggy than before. The door closed behind her.

Has to be on some kind of timer switch or motion detector, thought Kat, although that technology didn't match the rest of the premises.

"Did you want to go get some lunch? It will take me a little while to set up your contract."

Kat blinked in surprise at the receptionist. Despite having eaten the small bag of fries not that long ago, her stomach rumbled in appreciation at the idea of more food.

"Are you Amelia?" she asked.

"Yes, that's right."

Kat held out her hand. "I'm Kat. It's great to meet you."

Amelia's eyes flashed golden so quickly Kat thought she must have imagined it. The receptionist looked down at Kat's hand as if she didn't quite know what to do with it. Finally, she extended her own. Kat was too relieved at the fact the gesture had been returned to realise Amelia hadn't physically put her hand in Kats. Instead, Kat grabbed the other and shook it warmly, ignoring the tingly vibes that went shooting up her arm.

"I hadn't planned for lunch. I've got nothing with me. I don't mind waiting." Kat realised she was gabbling, but she felt her own panic rising at the thought of trying to while an hour away in the rain when she had no money and no place to go.

Amelia held out a crisp, white envelope.

"Oh, didn't Mr Magus tell you? This is your signing bonus. All our employees get them so they can purchase the right equipment and wotnot for their first assignment. The Agency has a reputation to uphold and unfortunately, shoes with holes in them don't fit in that category."

Kat flushed with embarrassment. It wasn't that Amelia had said anything in spite. Quite the opposite. Her tone had been understanding, tinged with concern.

"Take this and come back in an hour," said Amelia. "Then I'll explain your first assignment."

"I've got a job already?" Kat couldn't keep the disbelief out of her voice.

"Of course." Amelia shrugged as if it were no big deal. "Run along, now. You're losing your lunch break."

Obediently, Kat turned and walked down the hallway, letting herself out of the thick wooden door. The outside world assailed her sense with sound, noise and a chilly breeze. The agency interior had cloaked all of that and, truth be told, Kat thought she preferred it that way. *Get it together, Kat,* she reassured herself, trying to focus her mind after the bizarreness of what had just happened. She took out her phone to call her mum, but remembered she didn't have any credit left. Phone contracts had been one of the first things to go when they'd tightened their belts. She quickly typed a free text explaining that she'd found a job, and she'd fill her in when she got home, then she began walking towards the large reduced price department store. It was the best shop for cheap shoes nearby. Thinking she ought to check her newly available funds, Kat opened the envelope and then stopped dead in her tracks in amazement.

A fat wedge of notes sat unapologetically within the envelope. If these were ten-pound notes, there must be a couple of hundred pounds easily, but they didn't look quite like tenners. She pulled one out and registered the fifty-pound sign. Her heart was pounding, blood thudding in her ears. A quick thumb through the remaining bills showed they were all fifties. She could pay the rent. She could buy some food. Hell, she could buy a pair of shoes. A pair of shoes that she liked and not just the only ones in her price range that fit her feet. A giggle escaped. She couldn't help it.

Glancing behind at the agency door, Kat shook her head in wonderment. She could just never return. They were putting an awful lot of trust in her to do the right thing here. A passerby jogged Kat's elbow, bringing her back to the fact that she was standing stock still in the middle of town with an envelope full of fifty-pound notes in her hand. Hastily, Kat closed the envelope and shoved it into the inner pocket of her bag, carefully zipping it up and then wearing it cross ways across her body. It might be a grandma move, but there was no way she was going to risk a bag snatcher. Not now.

Smiling broadly, Kat went into the nearest fashion

store to check out the shoes. She didn't mind that her tummy was grumbling in protest. She could grab a sausage roll or something on the way back to the office.

Forty-five minutes later and Kat had a new pair of trainers and some smart-looking court shoes. She was hoping that one or the other would be suitable for whatever the new job was. She'd had time to nip into the bakers and grab a couple of sausage rolls; two normal, two vegan. She wanted to bring something back for Amelia, but she had no idea whether the woman was a meat eater or not.

Kat returned to the agency and practically bounced into the reception area. Amelia looked up serenely.

"Ah, you're back."

"Yes. I brought you a sausage roll. I didn't know whether you would be getting out for lunch or not. I've got vegan if you'd rather?" Proffering the bags in the grandness of the agency surroundings, Kat keenly felt the inadequacy of this meal, but Amelia's eyes were glittering.

"You brought lunch? Just for me?"

Kat nodded. Happiness rolled off Amelia as she reached up to grab the vegan sausage rolls. A small part of Kat sighed in relief. She didn't mind those, but faced with the real deal, she preferred that.

"I shall make us some tea," announced Amelia happily, and she disappeared through a door on the right.

As Kat tucked into one of her sausage rolls, she could hear Amelia humming to herself as she boiled a kettle and got the cups ready. What Kat had not been prepared for was a full tea tray with teapot, milk jug, sugar cubes and a plate of dainty biscuits.

"Let's go through the placement, shall we?" asked Amelia as the tea brewed.

"Yes, of course. And I think you made a mistake with this. There's way too much money in there. I brought shoes so I would be prepared for the job and some lunch, but I've got receipts for everything, and you can take it out of my paycheck if you need to." Kat proffered the envelope back to Amelia together with several receipts.

Amelia put a hand to her mouth and gasped softly. "You kept the receipts. Oh, you're my new favourite human." The realising she'd spoken aloud, Amelia pushed the envelope back at Kat. "It's not wrong. Standard starting bonus. All our temps get one. Think of it as incentive pay."

Incentive pay? Thought Kat. Incentive for what?

Amelia opened one of her desk drawers and pulled out a brown file, laying it carefully on her desk. She rested her hands on it for a moment before opening it and seeing what was inside. Kat tried to get a peek, but Amelia closed the file very quickly. Her nostrils flared widely.

"I'll play mother, shall I?" Amelia leaned over to pour the cups of tea.

"Is there something wrong with the placement?" asked Kat, petrified that she might lose this job before she even started it.

"Not at all. I just thought we ought to be fully refreshed before we get stuck in."

Kat wasn't sure she believed her, but she took a tentative sip of the hot tea and was amazed at how lovely it tasted. She closed her eyes and inhaled the aroma.

"This is a good cuppa."

"I'm so pleased you like it." Amelia reopened the file and exhaled loudly. "The placement is on the other side of town, working for the Luciano firm. Have you heard of them?"

"Aren't they the biggest solicitors in the city?"

"That's right. Filthy blood suckers, the lot of them. It says here they need something to go in and handle some filing for a few days. Nothing too strenuous, but it seems their last intern just stopped turning up for work and they've hit a backlog."

"And I'm getting paid thirty quid an hour to do filing?" Kat arched an eyebrow at Amelia, her brain whirring at the weird comment that they needed something to go in and do the filing. Surely that was a typo.

"Plus hazard pay." A guilty look flashed across Amelia's face.

"Hazard pay? Why would I need hazard pay?" The hairs on the back of Kat's neck rose. Things were getting a little weird.

Amelia stared at Kat for a long moment and murmured paper cut softly before pulling herself out of her reverie.

"Look, the Luciano's are very old-fashioned and are sticklers for dress code in the workplace. Do you have anything else you can wear?" Amelia asked with kindness in her voice.

Kat was about to cover for her lack of wardrobe options by pretending she did when she realised she was sick of pretending she had what she did not, so she just shook her head mutely.

Amelia seemed relieved. "Great. You go home, tell your family the good news about the job and get that rent paid. I'll come pick you up at five thirty pm and take you over to the retail outlet past Narrow Bridge. We can go clothes shopping and then check out that cute Italian place. I hear their garlic bread is the best in town."

"Oh, I couldn't. My Mum and brother will need me…" Kat faltered. As much as she liked Amelia, she didn't want to dump her life story onto her. She barely knew her. Then she frowned. "How did you know we hadn't paid our rent?"

"References," said Amelia breezily as she began collecting the empty teacups. "I'm afraid I simply must insist on the clothes shopping. We'll be two hours maximum, I promise."

Kat was torn. Part of her knew she should stay at home and perform her dutiful daughter duties, but the other half of her that was starving from real-life interaction was jumping up and down, begging her to take Amelia up on the offer. Besides, she really liked her. Maybe they could become friends.

"Okay, but just the two hours. I can't be too late back."

"Wonderful. Now, off you pop. I'll pick you up in a couple of hours." And Amelia flashed another bright smile at Kat before she returned the tea tray to the kitchen.

Kat stood in a daze and gathered her bags, her head spinning about everything that had happened. She had the presence of mind to tuck the money envelope away safely again before leaving the agency and making her way to the bus stop. It was still raining, but this time, Kat didn't care one bit.

Chapter 2

"Kat? Is that you?"

"Yes, Mum."

"How was the interview?"

"Hang on!" Kat shrugged out of her wet coat and hung it up to dry. Then she put her soggy shoes in the bin with a flourish and couldn't help but smile at the thought of wearing new shoes. She flicked the kettle on and headed through to see her mum.

"Hiya, love."

Kat gave her mum a hug, dumping her bag on the floor by the sofa.

"So, how did it go?" Kat's mum leaned forward in her wheelchair, eager to hear what had happened.

"I didn't get the job. I did text you, didn't you get it? Do you want tea?" Kat was bustling around, picking up empty cups and glasses. Her mum could just about get her wheelchair into the kitchen and out again, but it was a tight squeeze, and it made carrying things tricky. She couldn't balance a tray on her knees because she didn't have any. Kat's mum was a double leg amputee.

"I didn't hear my phone." She patted Kat's arm as she passed by. "Oh, I'm so sorry, love. What about the rent? Have we got enough to scrape through?"

"Hang on, I've got more news. Just let me make the tea and I'll tell you all about it." Kat was bursting to tell her, but she was also still finding it hard to believe. She hummed cheerfully under her breath as she clattered about in their poky kitchen.

"Here's your tea," said Kat, handing her mum her favourite cup. It was one Kat had painted years and years ago. A pattern that was now faded somewhat, but her

15

mum refused to replace the mug.

"Come on, spill the beans."

"So, I forgot my umbrella this morning," Kat began.

"Oh, no!"

"Yeah, and I was soaked at the bus stop. Honestly mum, when I got to the interview I was literally dripping in the reception. I think they took one look at me and decided there and then."

"They don't know what they're missing. It's their loss. You would've been brilliant at that job."

Kat smiled at her mum for the kind words, but she was pretty sure she would have sucked.

"After that humiliation, I thought I'd walk into town and see whether there was anything at Admin Angels yet."

"That's the temping agency you signed up with, right?"

"Yeah."

"And they had a job."

"Nope."

Kat's mum looked so crestfallen that Kat hurried to tell her the rest of her news.

"I found another temping place. It's called Magus Employment Services, and they were expecting me. Which was a bit weird because I'd never seen them before or made an appointment or anything like that. But they hired me on the spot and, get this, they gave me an advance. I haven't even had a chance to count it, but can you believe it?" Kat had fished out the envelope of money from her bag on the floor and was showing her mum the contents. "Mum? Are you alright?"

Kat's mum had gone deathly pale.

"You tell them thank you, but no thank you and you give that money back. Every penny. It's not safe."

"Mum, what are you talking about? How do you know about Magus Employment Services?"

Two spots of colour appeared on her mother's face, and she leaned forward.

"Katerina Kritchley – you will return that money and refuse their job offer."

Before Kat had a chance to reply, the front door opened, and her brother walked in. Both Mikey and Kat had dark black hair and pale blue eyes. Apparently, they took after their father, as their mum was a mousy brunette.

"Dolores. Katerina." Mikey greeted his family as he stood in the doorway of the living room. His autism meant he found it difficult to read social situations and respond accordingly. It also made him feel more comfortable to call his mum by her name.

"Hey, Mikey." Katerina smiled at her brother. As always, she ached to give him a hug, but she knew if she did, it would be like hugging a statue. Occasionally, he hugged her out of the blue and she treasured those moments.

"I'm hungry." He looked expectantly at the two women in the room.

Kat grinned and fished out the bakery bag with the other sausage roll she'd saved since lunchtime. Mikey took it and headed upstairs to his room.

"Mum, I'm taking this job. We need the money. I'm getting picked up at five thirty by the receptionist. She's really nice and has this gorgeous auburn hair…"

"Amelia," said Dolores softly. Kat stopped talking.

"How did you know her name?"

"Please reconsider this, Kat. It's not safe for you to work at Magus." But before she could say anymore the doorbell rang.

Kat went to open the door, her mind in turmoil at how her mum knew who Amelia was. It took her a moment to register who was standing in the doorway. Slimey Simon, their landlord, with two men built like brick walls looming over him.

"Rents overdue."

"I've got the money."

Simon smirked. "It's five hundred pound plus a late fee of two hundred quid, or these nice men will help you leave."

Kat felt like she'd been punched in the stomach. "We're only a couple of days late with the rent. You can't be serious."

Brute number one cracked his knuckles.

"Okay, okay. I said I've got the money." Kat was still holding the envelope with all the money inside. She hadn't had a moment to count it, so she fervently hoped there was enough in there. She counted out fourteen notes, angling the envelope away from the men at the door. There was still a lot of money left. Kat wanted to giggle, but tried to keep the smile from her face. Handing over the cash, she was gratified to see the shock on Simon's face. He didn't say anything, just grabbed the money and walked away.

He was half-way down the path before he turned and yelled, "Don't be late next month!" Kat slammed the front door in response. Her mum was waiting for her in the corridor.

"You shouldn't have paid him. You need to give that money back to the Magus Employment Services and…"

"And what, mum? We get evicted? Where are we going to go? You're in a wheelchair, for god's sake." The two women stared at each other. Kat reached out a hand. "Mum, I'm so sorry. I didn't mean…"

Dolores rolled backwards, away from her daughter.

"No. You're right. There's nowhere else all of us can live right now. So maybe I should wheel myself into the old people's home down the street and your brother can go into care then you would be free to do whatever the hell you like!" She tried to reverse back into her room, in the lounge, but got stuck in the door frame.

Mikey reappeared on the stairs. "I'm hungry."

Kat sighed. Her brother would continue to state that he was hungry until he was fed. When he was little he used to whine and cry and shout and demand, often using wordless noises and pointing two fingers to his mouth. Now he was a teenager, he'd learnt to just state what it was he wanted.

"I'll see what we've got," Kat put a smile on her face for him, but he was oblivious to the argument he'd walked into. Kat glanced at her mum as she walked past, but Dolores was ignoring her and trying to manoeuvre herself back into her room. "Help Mum, would you Mikey?"

Dolores began to protest, but Mikey was already heaving and twisting the wheelchair, providing that extra bit of turning circle needed.

Kat left them to it while she looked for something for her brother to eat. There was a little milk in the fridge but nothing else. The freezer had half a bag of Brussel sprouts. Who knows where they came from – nobody liked them. And there was a tiny bit of breakfast cereal but no bread and a solitary instant noodle pot on the shelf.

"Jesus," whispered Kat. She knew they were running low on food, but she hadn't known it had got this desperate. The last few nights she had been filling in job applications at the library computer, so she'd missed dinner. A pang of guilt shot through her. She should've been here to go shopping for her family. Her mum couldn't do it and sending Mikey to the shops would result in him coming back with whatever filled his head. Potentially unedible. Besides, he was terrible with money. He could not grasp basic arithmetic.

She grabbed the noodles and put the kettle on. Then checked the time on the kitchen wall. It was a quarter past five. Amelia would be here soon.

"Right. Mikey, here are your noodles. I'm going out soon and I'll bring back some dinner. Tomorrow I'll go food shopping, get some stuff in the cupboards."

"We shouldn't use that money," muttered Dolores.

"Thanks to that money, the rent has been paid for another month and I'll be able to put food in the fridge. I can't see the downside, Mum, I'm sorry, but this is the best thing that's happened in... in... in forever."

Dolores slumped her shoulders in defeat, then gave her daughter an imploring look.

"Please, be careful, the Magus Employment Services is not the knight in shining armour you think it is."

Kat really wanted to get into why and how her mum knew Amelia and the agency, but she didn't have time. She grabbed her bag, put the envelope of money in it, and pecked her mum on the cheek. She held Mikey's hand briefly, then walked out of the house. Holding hands was how you hugged Mikey. He wouldn't tolerate anything else. Doing her best to blink back the tears, Kat looked along the road. She realised she had no idea what kind of car Amelia drove.

A black BMW slid silently to a stop and Amelia stepped out of the passenger side.

"Ready, Katerina?"

"It's just Kat. I don't usually go by my full name."

Kat said as she hurried over to the BMW and slid inelegantly into the car.

"Sorry, my mistake." Amelia tapped the driver on the shoulder and told him to take them to the shopping precinct on the edge of town. "It's open late and we'll have plenty of time to kit you out. We can shop, then eat." She looked Kat up and down. "If that is alright?"

Kat's stomach growled in answer and blushed again.

Amelia smiled. "Okay. First, we'll eat, then we'll shop."

"It's so nice of you to do this."

"Oh, Mr Magus has very high standards when it comes to his employees. He likes all our staff to exude a certain level of professionalism and he believes much of that comes from the way you are presented." Amelia glanced at Kat. "I'm not trying to make you feel bad, you understand?"

"Yes, of course. I get it. The agency is very elegant, but I don't think wearing good clothes will hide the fact that I'm not that elegant."

Amelia patted her knee. "Don't you worry. You'll be great."

"How many other employees are there at the agency?"

"Well, there's Flynn, but he's on assignment, so you won't meet him yet." Amelia patted her bun. "And then there's you. Our new recruit."

"Oh, what happened to the person before me?"

Amelia looked out of the window. "They moved on."

After that, there was no more conversation forthcoming from Amelia and Kat's head was whirling with questions she was too nervous to ask, so the pair travelled in silence to the retail park.

Chapter 3

"Shall we eat first?" Amelia smiled encouragingly at Kat, who looked around at the brightly lit food court in awe. She couldn't remember the last time she'd been surrounded by so much choice.

"Um yeah, ok. But we can just get a sandwich or something though, if you like." Kat hoped Amelia didn't want to eat anywhere too expensive. Yes, she had the envelope of cash with her, but she also knew she had to do some food shopping, pay the overdue utility bills and buy some suitable clothing — whatever that meant.

"Oh no. Oh, no no no. I'm ravenous." Amelia smiled toothily and Kat had the merest glimpse of a lot of very sharp teeth. "My treat. Let's do that Italian. Get some garlic in you."

"Garlic?"

"Oh yes, it's great for the circulation and you do look a bit peaky, you know. Come on." Amelia strode off confidently towards the Italian restaurant in the far corner of the food court, with Kat hurrying to catch up.

Kat tried to see her reflection in the glass, but she was just a black and white blob. By the time she'd caught up with Amelia, the redhead had already snagged a table and was chatting to the server. Kat slid into the empty chair a little self-consciously. The server passed her a menu, but all his attention was focused on Amelia, who appeared to be glowing slightly. Kat blinked, and the glow disappeared. *Must be the lighting,* she thought.

"Lovely," said Amelia, as the server bustled off. "He's going to bring us some wine and water and some bread – I do so love bread, don't you?"

Kat nodded, not really sure what to say. Everyone

loved bread, didn't they?

"Order anything you like; the agency is paying for it."

"Oh no, surely I should buy dinner." Kat wanted to at least make the offer, but secretly she was pleased she didn't have to dip into her supply. Immediately, she felt guilty. She hadn't even done any work for the agency and already they'd bought her new footwear, paid her rent and given her cash for groceries. Now they were paying for her dinner. What sort of temping jobs would she be doing?

While they waited for their food to arrive, Kat decided to ask a few questions.

"How long have you been working for the agency, Amelia?"

"Oh, feels like forever. You know how it is."

"Do you like working there?"

"It's very rewarding."

Kat smiled, but inwardly she was frustrated. Where was the office gossip? She tried another tack.

"Can you tell me more about the place I'll be temping at tomorrow?" She took a sip of her water. She'd never really drunk wine and didn't want to embarrass herself in front of her new employer.

"Luciano's? It's the oldest solicitors' firm in town, been here since the beginning. They tend to hire internally, so it's a little unusual that they've asked for external help, but I believe it has something to do with the job. Filing. It's very... mundane."

Kat nodded to herself. She supposed filing was pretty mundane, but for what Magus Employment Services were willing to pay her, she didn't care.

Amelia smirked to herself as she picked up her wineglass.

"Clearly they think filing is beneath them, but you and I both know it's completing the boring jobs well that keep things running smoothly." She was prevented from saying anymore as their dinner arrived. A simple cheese and tomato pizza for Kat and a huge bowl of spaghetti carbonara for Amelia with a hefty side of garlic bread.

The pizza was cooked to perfection and there was a contented silence while the two women ate. Amelia kept pressing her garlic bread on Kat, but after she refused for the third time, she just left it on the side of the table.

With a full stomach and a touch of drowsiness after having eaten properly for the first time in a while, Kat sighed happily.

"Let me settle the bill and we'll get cracking." Amelia left Kat to gather her things as she went in search of the server. Not sure whether to stay or go, Kat opted to walk out of the restaurant and stand in the doorway. There was a good-looking bloke leaning on a pillar directly opposite. He had a shock of black hair and was wearing a leather jacket. Kat blushed when she realised he was watching her. She'd never seen him before in her life. Feeling exposed, she dithered about going back inside, but Amelia finally arrived and linked arms with her.

"Come on, let's get you a couple of outfits. What do you prefer, skirts or trousers?"

"Um, I don't mind."

"Excellent. We'll try both."

Two hours later and a somewhat stunned Kat was sitting in the BMW on her way home, surrounded by shopping bags of various sizes. Amelia had been on a mission and Kat now had new underwear, perfume, makeup and something called a capsule wardrobe which contained more clothes than Kat thought she'd ever owned before. Amelia had even brought an evening dress, just in case, she'd said. What had made the whole thing more surreal was that Amelia paid for everything. At least the agency paid for everything. It was too generous.

"Amelia?"

"Yes, dear."

"This is my paycheck, isn't it?" Kat gestured to the bags.

"How'd you mean?"

"I mean… no-one pays for all this upfront. And all that money you gave me earlier. It's all too much. Just how dangerous is this temping job?"

"You'll be fine, as long as you follow the rules and wear this." A very serious faced Amelia passed over a necklace. What looked like a black arrowhead dangled on a slender chain. "Thrice-blessed obsidian. It's the best we can do as a deterrent. Ah, we're here. Do you need help with those?" She pointed to all of Kat's shopping.

"Um, yes, please. If you don't mind."

"Not at all, not at all." Amelia helped Kat gather everything together and saw her to the door of her house. "Now, don't forget. Eight am sharp at Luciano's – they're sticklers for promptness. Wear the blue suit, it really brings out your eyes. Call me if you have any problems." She pushed a business card into Kat's hand. "Good luck!"

Feeling utterly overwhelmed, Kat let herself into the house, called hi to her mum, but didn't go and see her, laden as she was. Kat managed to carry all the bags upstairs to her room in one trip and dumped them on her bed. She checked the time. It was eight pm. The corner shop would still be open. She could run down and buy a few bits for tomorrow – just to tide her mum and brother over, and then she could go food shopping after work. A frisson of excitement swept through her body. She'd done it. She'd got a job. It might be the weirdest job in the world, but she'd done it.

Kat ran lightly down the stairs.

'Mum? I'm going to run to the shop, get some essentials. Anything you want in particular?'

She waited for a reply, but the curt negative told her that her mum was still cross with her. Deciding to buy her some chocolate biscuits and then cheer her up with a fashion show afterwards, Kat headed out. She'd never been so happy to buy bread and milk.

Chapter 4

It was five to eight in the morning. Kat stood outside two incredibly imposing dark black doors. The windows on either side were clad in black. She couldn't see inside. There were no cars in the carpark and the entire building seemed swathed in a greyness. Tentatively, she knocked. The sound echoed ominously, making her shiver.

Just as Kat was thinking about knocking again, one of the doors inched open.

"Hello?" she called, but there was no response. She peered into the slim opening, trying to see what was inside and, in doing so, pressed one hand on the ajar door. It swung noiselessly the rest of the way open. *Ok, that's weird,* thought Kat. Unnerved, she stepped across the threshold and tried to make out what she could from the dim lighting within. She was standing in a large hall. There was no way it could ever be described as a hallway. The ceiling stretched far above her head so she could only barely make out bulbous shapes that she assumed were chandeliers, none of which were lit. There were two vast staircases curling up the sides of the hall, one on the left and one on the right. The hall itself fell back into thicker gloom. A small light caught Kat's eye, and she walked cautiously to what looked like it could be a receptionist's desk. There was no one there, but a small bell sat forlornly on the counter. Looking around again to double check she truly was on her own, Kat dinged the bell. The sound echoed throughout the hall and she cringed inwardly.

"Yes?"

A voice behind her made Kat whirl around in surprise. A young looking, tall, thin man with oiled black hair and the palest complexion she'd ever seen stood there. He was dressed in black; black suit, black shirt, black tie – even black eyes. Kat blinked. Black eyes? *Must be contacts,* she thought.

"Um, hi, I'm Kat, the temp. From Magus Employment Services. Here to do the filing?" Kat wished she knew more about her assignment, but those were all the details Amelia had given her. After witnessing the grandness of the reception area, she was heartily glad of the new clothes she was wearing. Her washed-out school uniform would definitely not have cut it here.

"This way." The man turned on his heel and stalked across the floor, not making a sound.

Rude thought Kat as she hurried to keep up with him. He led her through a concealed side door into more gloomy corridors with what looked like empty offices. There were stairs, some more corridors and identical doors until finally, he stopped in front of one set, painted white with the words *Records Room* displayed.

"You will work in here. The documents that require filing are in the blue boxes. The filing cabinets work on an alphabetical system. Here is the key to the room. Lock yourself in. Do not come out unless I come to collect you and escort you out." He held out a key in such a way that she could take it without touching him.

"What if I need to use the bathroom?" asked Kat, trying not to panic at the thought of locking herself into a records room.

A look of disgust flitted across the man's face.

"Amenities have been made available." He unlocked the door with his own key and stood behind it as it slowly opened enough for Kat to enter.

She took a tentative step forward, then relaxed as she

walked into brightness. There were floor-length windows running down one-side of the room and the morning sun was just beginning to peep in.

"Look the door, Miss Kritchley."

Kat jumped at the command, shouted through the door, and hurried to comply. She wondered briefly how the man knew her surname, but realised Amelia must have given him all her information.

"Er… what time do I finish?" she called, but there was no immediate reply. Kat dithered whether to unlock the room and chase after the mystery man who brought her here, but before she could decide, there was an audible sigh from outside.

"I will collect you at five pm. Remember, stay in the room."

Fair enough, thought Kat, and she turned back. There were at least ten blue boxes of documents waiting for her and the filing cabinets stretched backwards down the length of the room. She wandered down one aisle, noting the number of cabinets devoted to each letter. Recalling what Amelia had said about the company, they'd been here since the founding of the town, so of course they would have a lot of paperwork. At the bottom of the room there was a kink out from the wall, which revealed a toilet and small kitchen area. Kat noted the new paint smell and peered inside the toilet – all brand new. Further exploration of the kitchen area had her smiling widely. There was running water, a kettle with cups, tea and coffee as well as milk in the fridge. She opened a cupboard expecting it to be bare but instead found biscuits. *Best job ever,* Kat thought as she happily made herself a tea, grabbed the biscuits and headed back to the filing.

By four thirty, she'd had enough. The paperwork

was confusing at best, she didn't know if she was supposed to file by client name or case name and it had taken her a while to figure that out. There was no phone line in the records room and even if there had been, she had no idea who to call. Her mobile had poor signal, and she didn't think she could eat another biscuit even if she wanted to. She'd only managed to clear one box of filing, which meant she would be coming back for another nine days at least. Tomorrow she needed to remember to bring lunch with her.

Kat watched the clock hands move ridiculously slowly. By the time they were almost at the five, she was standing by the doorway, bag and coat in hand, straining to hear anyone moving outside. At five pm precisely, a voice spoke.

"You may unlock the door." It was the same man as earlier, for which Kat was grateful. She didn't know him in the slightest, but at least he was a semi-familiar face in this odd building. Wordlessly, she did as he asked and let herself out of the room. Again, he stood behind the door. "I trust you had a productive day."

"Yes, thank you. I think it will take me another week or so to finish everything, though."

The man had started walking away, so Kat dutifully followed.

"That will be acceptable." He led her back the way they had come that morning, but now, instead of empty offices, each one seemed to be occupied. The man walked too fast for Kat to take everything in, but one thing she did notice was that everyone who worked here was very pale.

"Do you keep long hours?" she asked in an effort to make conversation.

"We find the night brings us everything we require."

30

Huh, thought Kat, trying to ignore the prickly feeling on the back of her neck. As they rounded a corner in the hallway, she glanced backwards and was surprised to see every office door open with every inhabitant stood watching her.

"This way, if you please, Miss Kritchley. No time for dallying." The young man picked up his pace and while he seemed to glide across the floor, Kat was half running to keep up with him.

The two of them practically jogged down one of the large staircases. Not the way they had come this morning, but Kat was glad to be out of the side hallway and the offices. Arriving at the front door slightly out of breath, Kat turned to thank the man for his help, but he had deliberately turned his head away from her.

"Good evening. Be here tomorrow promptly at eight am and don't wear that perfume." He held the door open for her, again concealing himself behind it as Kat left the building. The door slammed shut on her heels and she took a moment to regain her composure.

Kat pulled her shirt up towards her nose and sniffed herself. She smelt fine. Normal. She couldn't even tell she was wearing perfume. *That was beyond strange,* she thought, and she began the walk back to town and then home.

Chapter 5

Kat arrived home to a dark house. All the other houses in the street had lights blazing from merry looking windows.

"Hello? Anyone home?" Mikey should be back from school by now and her mum hadn't been out since she lost both legs. She said she couldn't take people staring at her like some kind of freak.

"In here, love."

With relief, Kat headed into the living room and saw Mikey on the floor, his face illuminated by his touchscreen. He charged it every night without fail, so the power would last all evening. Her mum was sitting in the dark.

"What happened?"

"The power went out about lunchtime. I tried to ring the electric company, but the phone line is dead as well." Dolores laughed softly. "That's what comes from not paying your bills, I suppose."

"Oh mum! You've been sitting in the dark since lunchtime? Why didn't you call me?"

"I didn't want to bother you. First day of your new job and everything. How did it go?"

"It was fine, Mum. Look, let me just sort this out." Kat fished her mobile phone out of her pocket. She'd put some credit on it at the shopping centre. Leafing through the pile of bills on the table, she found the electric bill and started making calls.

Two hours later they had electric and the phone line was back on and because it had been such a nightmare getting through to a real person to get the bills paid and the supply turned on, Kat had thrown caution to the wind and ordered a Chinese takeaway. Her mum alternated between making yummy noises and then declaiming whether or not they could really afford it.

"Just enjoy your kung pao chicken, mum. It's not every day, is it? We deserve a little happiness."

Mikey had already demolished his special toast and plain noodles – the only things he would eat from the Chinese. Luckily for Kat, the takeaway had remembered her and her brother and had been only too happy to supply the noodles plain. Not everywhere was so accommodating.

Fully recovered from being power-less, Dolores asked Kat again about her day.

"Honestly, Mum? It was weird. They locked me in the records room, which had its own toilet and kitchen, and I wasn't allowed out until five pm when I was escorted from the premises. I didn't see anyone going in but coming out, they were all there and it was like they'd never seen another person before."

"Where are you temping again?"

Kat glanced at her mum, her own mouth full of spring roll but surprised at the urgency of Dolores's tone. She waved her hand while she finished eating.

"Luciano's, at the other end of town? Why?"

Dolores stiffened.

"You leave, this instant. Don't go back, it's not safe."

Kat laughed.

"Don't be silly, Mum. It's just filing at a solicitors' firm. If anything, I might die from boredom."

"That's not funny. Don't ever joke about dying. That's what your father used to say and look at what happened to him. Give me your phone. Now!"

Kat handed it over without thinking. Her mum never

talked about dad.

"Amelia? Dolores. What are you playing at sending my daughter over to Luciano's?"

Horrified, Kat tried to get the phone back, but somehow her mum deftly kept her at arm's length. How did her mum know Amelia?

"She wasn't aware what she was accepting. Danger money's no good to her dead, is it?" And Dolores hung up. She turned to her daughter and glared at her fiercely. "Tomorrow morning, you march down to that agency and turn in your notice. Tell them we'll pay them back every penny, but you are not to work there anymore. Do you hear me?" She was breathing heavily by the time she'd finished.

"No." Kat's voice was quiet yet emphatic as she held her hand out for her phone. "I'm not an idiot. I realise something weird is going on. It's a creepy place and the agency being there across the square from McDonald's and me never noticing it before. How they've swooped in at the last minute and saved our bacon. We have somewhere to live, thanks to Magus Employment Services. We have electric and food in the cupboards, thanks to Magus Employment Services. So they want me to work a week and a half at some weird solicitors. Fine. What are they going to do? Eat me?"

"They may well," said Dolores, too softly for Kat to hear her.

"I'm going to call Amelia and apologise. I've got to be up early in the morning again so I'm not late for work. Are you alright getting Mikey on the school bus?"

"Kat, please!"

"No, Mum. This is non-negotiable. For the first time, I feel like I'm doing something with my life. I'm not about to throw it all away because you don't like where I'm temping. Suck it up, it's my future." Whirling in anger, Kat left the room and stomped upstairs to her room. She slammed the door behind her and threw herself onto her bed. But she didn't feel like crying. She was too angry. She didn't know why her mum was being so funny about this job.

She dialled Amelia's direct line, but there was no answer. It just rang and rang and rang. No sophisticated answer machine technology either. Dammit. And she didn't have Amelia's mobile number. Or even know if Amelia had a mobile number. She'd have to ask next time she was in the office. And she would call first thing in the morning to apologise for her mother.

Realising that in her anger she had never asked her mum how she knew Amelia, Kat pulled her laptop over and logged online. Maybe she would be able to find something.

Chapter 6

The next couple of days went by without incident. Kat had spoken to Amelia and apologised for her mum, which Amelia had brushed off as nothing to worry about. Relieved, Kat had continued to arrive for work at eight am sharp, was escorted to and from the records room and locked in, finishing at five on the dot.

Her online searches had proved fruitless. She hadn't managed to find anything about her mum and Amelia or her mum and Magus Employment Services. In fact, she hadn't found anything about the agency at all, which was strange given their high brow appearance and apparent limitless funds.

Her mum maintained a disapproving, frosty silence, making it impossible for Kat to ask any questions. She knew if she gave it enough time, her mum would thaw eventually, but it was taking a lot longer than usual. On the other hand, Mikey was thrilled that they could now afford to buy Cadbury's chocolate mousse, which in his considered opinion was the only one that tasted nice.

It all started to go wrong on Thursday, when Kat slept through her alarm. It was only the slamming of the front door that woke her and when she checked her phone bleary-eyed; she saw it was eight thirty-four am. Mikey had just left for school.

"Argh!" she yelled as she leapt out of bed. Without thinking, she grabbed the clothing closest to her, pulled in on and ran out the door, shouting at her mum for not waking her up. She legged it down the street, rummaging in her bag for mints to help with the fact that she hadn't brushed her teeth. A scrunchie made short work of her unbrushed hair and she arrived puffing and panting at Luciano's at ten past nine. Kat knocked and then bent over, hands on her knees, to catch her breath. It was then that she realised she'd chucked her trainers on with her black trousers and blue jacket. The same black trousers that she'd spilt last night beans on toast on. *Dammit!* Kat tried in vain to scrub the stain off.

As usual, the door half opened but the young thin man was not waiting for her. Instead, Morticia Addams or someone who could give Morticia a run for her money was looming in the hallway. Kat had thought Jeeves, as she'd nicknamed him, was tall, but this lady must have been at least seven feet tall.

"Sorry I'm late. I'm the temp, here for the filing," panted Kat, not quite having got her breath back.

"I know who you are. Hard to forget that odour."

Kat frowned. Okay, so she hadn't had time to jump in the shower this morning, but she was pretty sure she didn't smell funny. She waited, but the woman didn't move.

"Shall I make my own way to the records room?" Kat asked, her glance darting around the hall in case Jeeves was lurking in a dim corner.

"What fun that would be. I'll give you a minute's head start. No peeking." And fake Morticia put a lily-white hand over her eyes and began counting softly under her breath.

A little freaked out, Kat quickly walked over to the staircase. She didn't think she could remember the side route up to the records room, but if she got some height and made her way to the right floor, she was fairly certain she'd find it sooner or later. Her footsteps echoed loudly and fake Morticia swivelled her body, tracking Kat by sound. Kat started to walk a little faster, but took her eyes off the woman in the hall as she concentrated on not tripping up the stairs. When she glanced backwards, there was nobody standing there. Instead, she heard a delighted giggle in front of her and whipping her head around, she was gobsmacked to see fake Morticia right there.

"Not that quick, are we?" The woman ran her tongue across sharp white teeth and leant forward, hands like claws about to grab Kat when Jeeves appeared out of nowhere and inserted himself between the woman and Kat.

"Walk away, slowly, Miss Kritchley, and lock yourself in the records room." Without looking at her, he passed the key backwards to Kat.

Wordlessly, she took it and quickly walked away from whatever was happening on the staircase. Her heart was thudding in her chest and she tried not to walk too fast, but fear was rapidly taking over any common sense and by the time she made it to the corridor where her white doors were, Kat was sprinting. Her hands trembled as she pushed open the door, entered, and hurriedly locked herself in. Was it her imagination or was there a faint thump on the door? The sound of someone not quite getting there in time. With jelly legs, Kat went to make herself a cup of coffee with extra sugar.

The longer she stood in the kitchen, the more she was able to make the encounter seem normal. The woman was obviously a rich client of Luciano's, a bored housewife perhaps looking for a little light entertainment while her husband thrashed out the legalities of another trade deal or some such. That's all it was. She wasn't going to do anything sinister. And she had clearly started moving as soon as Kat wasn't watching her, which was why she got up the stairs so quickly. Jeeves knew her. She must have tried to play these games before. But even with all her rationalisations, Kat felt scared.

Three times she checked the doors were properly locked before she could get her head into the filing process. She worked right through lunch, trying to get as much done as humanely possible before she had to go home. By the time five pm rolled round, there was only one box of filing left. Right on time, there was a soft tapping on the door.

"Time to go, Miss Kritchley."

Nervously, Kat unlocked the door and waited for Jeeves to pull it in front of him while she stepped out of the room. The dim corridor gave her the shivers, and she stuck as close to her guide as she could while he walked her out of the building. For the first time since she'd come to work there, Jeeves paused before he opened the main exit.

"I trust you now realise how important it is for you to arrive promptly at eight?"

Kat nodded, not trusting her voice.

"Then I will see you here tomorrow. On time." He held the door open for her and Kat hurried outside, for once not waiting to get her bearings, instead immediately walking as fast as she could away. Pulling her mobile from her bag, she saw two missed calls, both from Amelia. In her haste this morning, Kat had forgotten to take her phone out of silent mode and then, trying to lose herself in the filing, she had neglected to check it for messages.

"Hi, Amelia? It's Kat. Look, I'm really sorry about being late this morning…"

"Hello, Kat. Don't worry about that. I need you to come into the office. There's been a change of assignment and you haven't been dropping in your time sheets. I can't pay you if you don't submit your time sheets. Can you swing by now? I'll pop the kettle on."

Kat remembered how wonderful the tea had been before and quickly agreed, changing her walking direction. She didn't notice the Morticia look-alike watching her from the shadows. Nor the young man in a leather jacket watching them both.

**

"Sit, sit. Make yourself comfortable. I'll warm the pot." Amelia smiled broadly at Kat as she came in. Her hair was down today, and it cascaded like lava down her shoulders, glinting with specks of gold and amber in the red.

Kat sank gratefully into one of the armchairs by the fire and her stomach grumbled loudly. Amelia reappeared with toasted crumpets, smeared with butter and a plate of scones with strawberry jam.

"I thought we might have a little something, in case I've disrupted your dinner plans."

"Oh, this is so lovely, thank you Amelia," gushed Kat, tears threatening.

"Oh no, have I offended you?"

"No, not at all. It's just been a busy week and I'm still mortified about the phone call from my mum. She had no right to speak to you like that. I'm so sorry…"

"Nothing to be embarrassed about. Your mum is worried about your safety. It's only natural."

Kat sank her teeth into a buttery crumpet and forgot everything for a short while as she savoured the deliciousness. Amelia busied herself with making the tea, and it was almost like Kat was having tea with a friend.

"So, I've taken the liberty of filling out your

timesheets for you. All I need is a signature at the end of each day." Amelia held out the pages.

"I'm so sorry. I didn't know I was supposed to do a time sheet."

"Not to worry. It probably got forgotten in all the excitement."

"Do you have any spare, blank ones I could take with me? Or maybe I could use the photocopier?" Kat glanced around, but there was still no sign of such modern equipment in Amelia's office. Instead, she felt a slight fizzing to her left and when she looked, there was a folder of blank time sheets available.

"You can have those. That should keep you going for a while. Make sure you fill one in and drop it back to me daily. It makes life easier, should anything untoward happen."

The office door crashed open and Mr Magus stalked out. Impeccably dressed in a pinstripe suit this time, but still with a dashing purple cravat.

"Amelia, did you know there's a bloody va… er, varmint running around outside?" Mr Magus changed what he was going to say when he noticed Kat. "Ah, Miss Kritchley. Still alive, I see."

Kat opened her mouth to say something, but couldn't think of a suitable response.

"Flynn is on external monitoring, Mr Magus. I'm sure he will deal with the… varmint." Amelia smiled brightly at her boss, her eyes widening slightly, trying to tell him to go away in the nicest possible way.

"Yes. Fine. Very good. Carry on." He disappeared into his office.

"Varmints?" Kat asked curiously.

"Nothing for you to worry about, my dear. Now, let's get back to your assignment at Luciano's. They've

41

been pleased with your filing endeavours. I understand you are practically finished?"

Kat nodded, cautiously. She wasn't sure whether that was a good or a bad thing.

"They want you to fill in at Accounts for a brief spell. It's nothing too strenuous, just data entry. Do you think you'd be up to that?" Amelia asked with a touch of concern in her eyes, and Kat wondered why it felt like she would be doing a lot more than entering some data. "We'll be increasing your hourly rate to cover the risk factor of temping in the offices and the young man who has been escorting you to the records room will be working alongside if that makes you any more comfortable."

Kat swallowed. She wasn't sure how comforting Jeeves was to her. On a scale of scaring the bejeesus out of her and being almost pleasant to be around, she supposed he scored about half-way between the two. Questions swirled inside her head and before she could stop herself, they started tumbling out.

"Risk factor – what risk factor? And how can you possibly increase my hourly rate? It's already more than generous. Why was Mr Magus so surprised to see me alive? What are you not telling me?"

Amelia watched Kat without answering her as if she were waiting for something.

Kat had a moment of clarity. She'd been meekly going along with everything weird that had happened since she walked through the door of Magus Employment Services. She'd accepted more money than she'd ever seen before in her life to go file paperwork in the creepiest workplace ever. The more she thought about it, the more this sounded like a really bad idea. She took another swallow of her delicious tea. "Yes, of course I'll do the data entry. How hard can it be?"

Kat seemed utterly unaware that all her questions had gone unanswered, and that she had capitulated so completely.

Amelia smiled sadly at Kat and handed over a new contract for her to sign. Hand-written, it was hard to decipher every word, so Kat just signed at the bottom.

"When do I start?"

"Tomorrow at eight. Don't be late." Amelia tinkled with laughter, but a shot of dread ran through Kat's stomach as she remembered what happened the last time she was late.

Chapter 7

Kat stood for ten minutes, shivering outside Luciano's. She'd been determined not to be late again, but in her haste to leave home on time, she'd run out the door without her coat. It was unseasonably chilly.

As always, the door inched open, and she pushed inside, eager to be out of the cold. She was met with Jeeves.

"So glad you could make it on time today. I take it Amelia explained the change in job?"

Kat nodded, and the man glided away. She hurried to keep up. This time, they stopped halfway down the corridor of offices and Jeeves unlocked a door, opening it to show two desks facing each other with large accounting books, one on each desk.

He paused, waiting for Kat to enter the room.

"Which desk do you want me at?"

"Either is fine," replied Jeeves, as if he were bored by the entire idea.

Kat plumped for the left desk and draped her bag over the back of the chair.

"Where are the computers?"

"Here at Luciano's we pride ourselves on following the old traditions, where possible. And hand accounting is one thing the partners refuse to update. Hence the need for a temp from time to time." Jeeves didn't sound too impressed with the partner's decision. "My name is Maxwell, by the way."

"Great to meet you, Maxwell. I'm Kat." She held out a hand, but Maxwell looked at her wrist with an odd look on his face. After a few moments, it became obvious that he wasn't going to shake her hand, so she retracted the offer and sat down. "What is it you want me to do?"

Maxwell dumped a large stack of invoices onto her desk. "Enter these into the outgoings column."

Kat looked around for a pen and her heart sank when she saw the expensive-looking fountain pen. She'd used those in her secondary school and had always ended up with ink all over her fingers and her work. She resolved not to let that happen here.

Maxwell was already sitting down and working on his own accounts book, so Kat took a moment to peruse the large one in front of her. It smelt earthy and rich, like it had stories to tell, and it wasn't at all dusty or musty. Clearly, the book was regularly used and despite the old-fashioned method, this was a relatively new accounting book. Kat read back over some of the entries to make sure she knew how to enter the records. Nervously, she opened the fountain pen, picked up the first invoice and began copying the pertinent information.

Maxwell stood up abruptly, making her jump, and locked the office door. He glanced at Kat watching him.

"For security," he explained.

They worked in silence. The only sound was the scratching of their pens on the paper. Kat's stomach began growling louder and louder and she sneaked a peek at her phone. It was twelve thirty.

"Are we stopping for lunch?" she asked.

Maxwell tutted and stood.

"You can eat here. I will be back in half an hour. Please clear up your mess." He unlocked the door, then relocked from the other side.

Kat hadn't noticed before that the windows of the office were in fact smoked glass. She couldn't see Maxwell clearly now that he had left the room, only his shadow. She realised there were several shadows passing by, which made her shiver at the memory of fake Morticia. Reaching into her bag, she found the slightly squished peanut butter sandwich she'd packed earlier and began munching straight away. Her thoughts turned to dinner and what she might cook tonight. She felt inspired and started looking for a piece of paper she could write a quick shopping list on.

The first two drawers she opened were empty, but the third one contained a brown file. Curious, Kat picked it up and looked inside. There were at least fifteen invoices and late payment demands from the city blood bank. Leafing through them, Kat realised these were recent, within the last couple of months.

What was a solicitor doing with invoices for a blood bank and, more importantly, why weren't they paying them? Kat resolved to ask Maxwell when he returned, but just in case she forgot, she took photos of them. At times, she had a memory like a sieve and if there were photos on her phone, it would remind her to raise the issue.

At one pm exactly, Maxwell re-entered the room. Kat could see a cluster of shadowy shapes behind him and he seemed to have difficulty fully closing the door on his return. It locked with a sharp click and Maxwell's nose wrinkled.

"Your diet might need to be more substantial than a peanut butter sandwich."

Kat was floored. How did he know what she'd eaten for lunch? He put a coffee cup on her desk.

"I thought you would appreciate a beverage. It's hot chocolate. I wasn't sure what you like."

"That's really kind. Thank you so much." Kat was so surprised, she completely forgot to ask about the unpaid invoices and instead took a sip of the delicious drink.

The shadows continued to pass by the windows, sometimes in blobby groups and other times in single file until Maxwell announced it was time to go. Kat had made it perhaps a third of the way down her pile of paperwork. Hand entry was a slow process, plus she was terrified of making a mistake.

"Put this on over your coat." Maxwell handed Kat a voluminous black cape. It completely covered her from tip to toe. She felt ridiculous. "Trust me."

He unlocked the door and stood to one side to let Kat out, then flanked her down the corridor briskly. There were other people around, and Kat lifted her head to see who they were.

"Eyes down. Do not make eye contact!" hissed Maxwell urgently, and he quickened the pace. In no time at all, they made it to the front door and before she knew where she was, he had whipped the cape off and propelled her through it.

Kat shook her head. This was the weirdest job she'd ever done. Ever.

Walking through town, Kat fished out a time sheet to fill in so she could drop it in on her way home. She pushed open the door to Magus Employment Services and heard raised voices.

"It's not fair. We should at least tell her the risks."

"She signed the contract."

"She didn't read all the small print."

"That's not our fault."

It was Amelia and Mr Magus.

"Dolores has lodged an official complaint."

"Dolores already paid for her removal from our community. There was nothing in that agreement that said we must turn the children away if they came to us."

"You activated that light charm, didn't you? You knew she was desperate for a job and you lured her here."

Mr Magus's reply was muffled, and Kat couldn't catch it properly. Her heart was racing and her hands were clammy. What did they mean Dolores paid for removal and when did her mum lodge an official complaint – and to who? What was that about luring with a light charm? Kat understood the words, but it didn't make any sense.

"I just think that sending her to the vampires for her first assignment is too risky. They've got her in Accounts now. Maxwell is doing his best to keep the others away, but it's hard for him as well."

"Pfft. We send our staff wherever help is needed, and this will be good for Katerina. It should trigger her manifestation. She will need us when that happens. Better that we are already a part of her life beforehand. Besides, Flynn is on guard duty."

"I just think we should give her all the facts. She's utterly unproven and inexperienced in our world. What if she gets eaten?"

"Amelia, do you wish to file a formal complaint?" There was an edge to Mr Magus's tone. "Are you declaring?"

"No."

"Then I suggest you carry on with your tasks and I shall go back to mine." There was a door slam, and it sounded like Mr Magus had returned to his office. Kat was frozen in place. She was unsure if she should move forwards or leave. Her head was spinning. Vampires. Manifestation. Being eaten. But vampires? What the hell did that mean? Her timesheet fluttered to the floor and her legs carried her out of the building. She didn't know where she was going, but she needed to move. She didn't spot the young man with dark hair, wearing a leather jacket, once more observing her from across the square.

Half-way home, it began raining, but Kat wasn't paying attention. She was still in shock at what she'd heard and didn't realise initially she was getting cold and wet. It wasn't until she began shivering that she started to take in where she was. If she went down that street, it was a shortcut home. Kat picked up the pace.

A tall, pale girl crossed her path, making Kat flinch as she thought of fake Morticia. Of course, she was a vampire. How could she be anything else? Kat felt cross at her own stupidity. And obviously her mum knew something about it all, otherwise she wouldn't have gone on about Kat leaving and it being dangerous. But vampires!

Since her mum's accident, the Kritchleys were isolated. Visitors were scarce and with Mikey to manage plus school, Kat hadn't really thought about how alone they were. If a pack of vampires turned up to finish them up, would anyone even notice?

Kat hunched her shoulders against the rain and hurried home. Mum would need help with dinner and Mikey. But she couldn't shake the sensation that someone was watching her.

Chapter 8

"AAAAAAARRRRRRGGGGGGGHHHHHHHH!"

Kat's heart fell as she walked through her front door. Her brother was having an episode. There was nothing anyone could do when he was like this. You just had to leave him alone and let him scream out his rage. It was unsettling and Kat worried about the neighbours. He hadn't had one for a long time.

She quickly went to her mum in the living room. All memory of their fight forgotten and forgiven.

"How long?"

"He's been going about ten minutes. Should wear himself out soon." Dolores sighed, looking older than her years. "Maybe you should go see him, just so he knows you are here."

Kat nodded and gave her mum a brief hug. She went up the stairs and cautiously opened her brother's bedroom door.

"NOOOOOOOOOOOOOOOOOOO!"

"Hey Mikey. What's going on?"

But Mikey wasn't back yet. Sometimes when he was on the verge of a meltdown, it was possible to reason with him and bring him away from the scary feelings that overwhelmed him, but not today. All Kat wanted to do was give him a huge hug, but that would make things worse, so she gently backed out of the room and left him to it, heading back downstairs. Hopefully, he would allow them to comfort him when he was finished.

"Yeah, he's not done yet."

Dolores nodded. "Do you want a cuppa?"

"I'll do it." Kat busied herself in the kitchen, trying to block out the noise her brother was making when her stomach grumbled. She tried to remember what she'd been inspired to make for dinner, but it had completely gone from her mind. Taking tea and half a packet of chocolate biscuits into her mum, she sat down.

"Mum, things are getting really weird. I popped into the agency on my way home to drop off my time sheet and, and... I heard... stuff. They said you'd lodged a formal complaint?"

This time, Kat wasn't angry that her mum had interfered. She was confused and still trying to process the vampire comment. All the weirdness that had been accumulating over the last couple of weeks now felt smothering.

"You should not be working at that place. You are not safe." Dolores pulled her cardigan closer around herself. "I will do what I must to keep my daughter safe, even if she won't listen to me." A half smile played upon her face as she looked at Kat.

"It always seemed a little too good to be true. All that money. You put up with a bit of strangeness, right?"

Kat's phone pinged. It was just an email notification, but as she swiped open her phone, Kat was reminded of the images she'd taken at work.

"Hey mum, look at these. Why is a solicitor's paying, or rather not paying, a blood bank? It's a bit odd, isn't it?"

Dolores grabbed Kat's phone and began swiping through the images.

"You have to tell Amelia immediately. And you don't go back there. It's not safe."

"But why Mum? I'm hand-writing figures into an accounting book. Boring is the word I'd use." Kat tried to make light of it, but she felt sick to her stomach remembering the conversation she'd walked into at the agency and the freaky nature of Luciano's.

"I mean it, Katerina. This is serious. You stay away from Luciano Solicitors and you quit your job with Magus Employment Services."

Kat had never heard this level of fear and urgency in her mum's voice before. She wanted, more than anything, to tell her about the rest of the conversation she'd overheard. To have her mum tell her that vampires didn't exist and to stop being so silly, but she was afraid that if she brought it up, her mum wouldn't be able to.

Before she had the chance to reply, Mikey appeared in the doorway.

"Hungry."

"What would you like for dinner, Mikey? Anything you want." Kat decided this was something she could do. She could buy her brother whatever he fancied for dinner.

"Noodles. And special toast," he replied.

"Excellent!" Kat beamed. Chinese takeaway was a firm favourite in their house. "What you after, Mum? Kung Pao chicken and rice?"

"We haven't finished talking about this, Kat."

Kat didn't say anything, just waited for her mum to confirm her dinner order.

"Fine. Yes, please. And get some ribs. We may as well have ribs. It is a final supper of sorts."

"Okay, I'll run to Shanghai Gardens and get the order in. Be back soon." She held out a hand to Mikey and was relieved when he gave it a small squeeze.

It was still raining when she left the house, so she hurried down the road to the Chinese takeaway on the corner, not noticing she had a follower. Opening the door to the restaurant, she was surprised to be followed inside by a young man with a shock of black hair. She hadn't heard him approach, but he nodded his thanks for the door and went to look at the menu. He looked familiar, but Kat couldn't quite place him. Obviously, she'd seen him around somewhere. Shrugging, she greeted the girl behind the counter.

"Hi Ursula, you okay?"

Ursula nodded and smiled sweetly. "Hello Miss Kritchley. Hope family well? What you like to order – usual?"

"Ummm, sort of. Can I have prawn toast and plain noodles for Mikey, please? Then I want some capital ribs, Kung Pao chicken and egg fried rice and… let's have some Singapore noodles and yellow cashew chicken, please."

Ursula repeated the order and pushed a bag of prawn crackers across the counter to Kat as she paid for the meal. Taking a seat, Kat's attention returned to the young man who had followed her in. He was dressed all in black, wearing a leather jacket. Kat listened to his order. She was always interested in what other people chose.

"Could I have chilli beef and special fried rice, please? Thanks."

He had a very melodious voice with warm notes to it that made you feel like you'd been verbally hugged. Kat smiled to herself, and Ursula positively beamed.

"Thank you, Mr Magus. Take a seat. Be ready soon."

Kat blinked. Magus? That was the same name as her boss at the agency. She looked at the man with renewed interest. He caught her gaze and smiled, coming over to sit next to her.

"Hi. I'm Flynn. We've not met yet, but we work at the same place."

Kat's heart was hammering at being spoken to by such a good-looking stranger. She managed to smile and nod while she marshalled her thoughts.

"You're Mr Magus' son?"

"Yeah, for my sins." He laughed, which put Kat a little more at ease. "I hear you're working up at Luciano's. How's it going?"

His instant likeability made Kat throw caution to the wind.

"Honestly? It's been a bit weird. There's this vibe over there that's really hard to shake, and I found something odd today. Here, take a look at this."

Kat took out her phone and showed Flynn the photos she'd taken earlier that day, figuring that they worked for the same agency so she ought to show him what she'd discovered.

"Do you mind?" He asked as he took the phone and quickly sent the images to himself. "Sorry, but these are important." He looked directly at her. "You've got my number now."

"I... er... thanks." Kat knew she was blushing and scrambled to get on top of the conversation. "What's so important about those invoices? Do you know something?"

"I know a lot of things," Flynn replied with a laugh and then stood up as Ursula called his order. "I'll see you around."

"You're not going to tell me it's not safe?" Kat was a little annoyed that he clearly knew something and wasn't sharing information.

"Oh, I think you can take care of yourself." He replied with a grin. "Besides, I won't let anything happen to you." His gaze softened as he looked at her, making her feel even more self-conscious.

"Miss Kritchley, your order ready." Ursula broke the moment and Kat automatically turned to look at her upon hearing her name. There was a swish of movement as the door opened and Flynn was gone.

"Thank you," murmured Kat, and she carried the Chinese home, deep in thought.

"You look like you've seen a ghost," laughed Dolores, not entirely joking. "I got plates out."

Kat handed out the silver takeout trays and smiled at her brother's delight in his simple food order.

"I just met... someone."

"Flynn?"

Kat turned to her mother in shock. "How did you know?"

"He has that effect on people. Don't take his charm personally. He's not interested."

"Mum!" Kat was blushing furiously. She sat down and scooped out some food onto her plate, studiously ignoring her mother's amused glances. This day had gone from weird to weirder.

After everyone had finished eating and Kat had cleared everything away, she sat down with her mum. Dolores brought up the subject of work again.

"Kat, dear..."

"Mum, I'm not going to quit my job. It's the best thing that's happened to us in a long time. Even if it is the weirdest." She felt determined to get to the bottom of things.

Dolores bit her lower lip. She held out a hand to her daughter and Kat took it and gave it a squeeze.

"I can't change your mind, can I?"

Kat shook her head.

"Kat, there's a lot you don't understand about Magus Employment Services, about Amelia and Mr

55

Magus."

"But you do, don't you? Did you used to work there or something?" Kat was half joking but stopped smiling when her mum nodded.

"Magus Employment Services is where I met your father. It was a long time ago, another world." Dolores glanced at the only photo of Kat's father she allowed to be displayed. He looked very distinguished in a smart suit, standing outside a gothic-style building with a cheeky smile and a twinkle in his eye.

"You never talk about him," Kat said softly, hoping to prompt her mum to reminisce a little. She only had vague memories of him, herself. He died when Mikey was a baby.

"Kat, promise me you will be careful. Extra careful. Be vigilant of your surroundings, keep yourself safe. Please, please don't take any risks. Magus Employment Services isn't worth your life."

"Mum, I'm not going to die!"

Dolores ignored her daughter's comments. "What do you know about Luciano Solicitors?"

"Um, they're weird. It's in that big building at the far end of town and I have to be locked in every day. I was doing filing for them in their records room but now I'm working in accounts. And you know what, there's no computers, so everything has to be done by hand. It's going to take a while to finish, I think."

"Anything about the people who work there?"

Kat frowned at the odd tone in her mum's voice.

"Well, I've only met Maxwell. He's nice, I guess. He doesn't say much, but he did bring me a hot chocolate today, which was unexpected."

"He did?"

"Yeah. Oh, and you know the other day when I was

late, I got there and there was this scary-ass woman at the door. She looked just like Morticia Addams and…"

"Veronique. She is one of the partners in the firm. You stay away from her, do you hear me? If I can't stop you from going to work, then at least keep away from that… woman."

"Okay." Kat was a little surprised at her mum's insistence, but seeing as fake Morticia or rather Veronique scared the wotsits out of her, she wouldn't have to try too hard to stay away from her. She changed tack.

"How do you know Amelia? Isn't she like my age or something?"

"Or something. Let's just put it that way." Dolores shifted painfully in her wheelchair but waved away Kat's motion to help. "Just don't get too involved with it all, Kat. Stay safe. Keep your distance."

Kat could see her mum was getting tired, so she just nodded. A thousand questions were swirling in her head, but they could wait another day. Tomorrow was Friday and after that, they'd have the whole weekend together. Kat was hoping she could convince her mum to come out with her and do a bit of retail therapy. It had been ages since they'd done anything like that.

Chapter 9

Kat hurried to work. Raining again. At least this time she had remembered her umbrella. The door opened for her and she stood for a moment in the hall, adjusting to the gloom, rain dripping onto the marble floor.

Maxwell glided over to her and looked pointedly to an area on her left. Kat glanced and saw an umbrella stand. She quickly put hers in it.

"Sorry about the rainwater."

"Someone will clean it up." Maxwell turned and waited for Kat to walk to their office. He never went in front. He always followed behind her. Not that she ever heard his footsteps.

With her mum's urgent warnings swirling around in her head, the back of Kat's neck was prickling even more than before.

Maxwell wasted no time locking them into the office and getting the large accounts books out. Kat sighed as she looked at her pile of invoices that need inputting. She was sure it was bigger than yesterday. Despite the oddness of this contract and how she came to be there, she still wanted to do a good job. Kat found her place in the book and began writing in the next entry. After a few minutes, she glanced up to check if Maxwell was absorbed in his own entries. He was, so she began studying him.

He had inky black hair and near translucent skin. There was a certain ethereal quality to him, as if he belonged in a torrid love story rather than in a dingy office. Kat couldn't see his eyes as he was bent to the task in front of him, but she remembered they, too, were dark. *So he never goes out, and he has dark features, probably Italian or something,* thought Kat. Goes without saying, given the name of the place, really. Then a stab of fear shot through her stomach as she realised he wasn't breathing. Panicking, she looked down at her work and with trembling hands tried to complete the entry she was working on. Her brain was racing to normalise what she thought she'd seen. Maybe he was breathing so shallowly she couldn't see his chest moving or hear the air going in and out of his nose. She peeked another look. Maxwell was still engrossed in his work. Kat stared hard at his torso, trying to make out if it was moving at all.

"Is something wrong, Miss Kritchley?" Maxwell asked without raising his eyes. "You've been staring at me for the past four and a half minutes. You do know staring is considered rude, don't you?"

"I, um, sorry, but…" Kat flushed, trying to find the right words.

Maxwell looked up at her, his black eyes pinning her to her chair.

"You know," he said, flatly.

Kat shook her head in protest.

"Do you have any questions?"

"I… how… I mean, I mean… are you really a, a vampire?" Kat felt foolish the second the words left her mouth. Her overactive imagination would get her in trouble again.

Maxwell regarded her for a moment.

"I have no plans to bite you. If that's what you're worried about. The same cannot be said for the other members of staff here at Luciano Solicitors." Maxwell's gaze flitted to the smoky glass windows. "That is why you are escorted and locked in. And why you must begin work and finish work at the exact times I gave you. To keep you safe."

"Why do you need me at all? Can't one of the other, er… vampires do this?" Kat's brain still wasn't prepared to accept that vampires were real, that she was actually talking to one and that they were having a conversation about being one.

"This kind of work is menial, and many vampires believe menial work to be beneath them."

"But not you?"

"I am here merely for your protection. Doing *this* staves the boredom."

"Right." Kat couldn't think of anything coherent to say in response. Her inner voice was screaming about vampires draining her dry and to get the hell out of there, but her sensible voice told her to enter the next invoice. The normality of office work won, and she returned to her books.

Several times a question occurred to her, but as she worked up the courage to ask Maxwell, she psyched herself out, not wanting to know the answer. In the end, she decided to go and grill Amelia about it after work. Her stomach grumbled, and glancing at her watch, she saw it was lunchtime.

"I will be back in an hour. I trust you have sustenance."

Kat nodded.

"Please lock the door behind me."

"Why do you always do that?" asked Kat.

"Do what?"

"Leave the keys with me."

Maxwell smirked.

"Anyone could take them from me, and then where would we be? A free lunch and a rather large *human* resources bill."

Kat's arms goosebumpled as Maxwell left the room. She hurried to lock the door behind him, hands shaking and heart thumping. She jumped as her phone rang shrilly in the quiet office. It was Mikey's school.

"Hello?" Kat's shoulders slumped as the women from West Chesterton School explained Mikey had had one of his episodes and would she come and collect him. "I'll be there as soon as I can," promised Kat, not knowing exactly how she was going to pull that off.

With a sinking heart, Kat grabbed a piece of paper and wrote a brief note for Maxwell. She hoped this meant she hadn't lost the temping job, but when Mikey had a meltdown, no-one could do anything with him and even the support staff at his school were unequipped to deal with him. Kat would have to pick him up and walk him home. She shoved her phone into her pocket and grabbed her coat. Unlocking the door, Kat felt a frisson of fear but pushed it to the back of her mind. Nothing mattered now except her brother. The office door shut with a resounding slam that made Kat jump. She quickly hurried down the corridor before anyone had time to think about investigating the sound and hoped she travelled unnoticed. Kat had almost made it to the large entrance hall when, out of the shadows, Veronique appeared.

"My dear, off so soon. You simply must stay for lunch."

Kat yelped in surprise and took a couple of steps backwards.

"I can't stay. I'm sorry. My brother needs me. I have to go, but I'll come back later to finish up."

Veronique arched an eyebrow and ran her tongue across her ruby red lips.

"Yes. We would like to finish you up later."

Kat took another step backwards, then flinched as she bumped into something. Whirling around, she saw two more vampires had appeared. A man and a woman, both pale, both fixing her with a hungry gaze.

"Look. I know what you are. Stay away from me or I'll…"

"Or you'll what? Cry? Shout for help?" The man took a step forward and Kat hurried backwards, then remembered Veronique was behind her, so turned again and yelped once more when she realised the vampire had closed in. Kat now stood in the middle of a ring of three with no idea what to do next.

The front door banged open, and sunlight spilled into the entrance hall. A smoke bomb landed by Kat's feet, giving off the strong pungent smell of garlic and forcing the vampires to cover their faces. Whilst they were distracted, Kat legged it for the doorway and almost collided with Flynn.

"What are you doing here?" she cried as they both dashed for the sunshine outside.

"Keeping an eye on you. What on earth made you think it was a good idea to leave the office?"

"How did you know I was working in the office? Or that I'd left?" Kat rounded on him. "Are you stalking me?"

"Come on, we'd better get you away from here before one of them decides to brave the sunlight."

Kat looked back nervously.

"Do they not burst into flames, then?"

Flynn barked a laugh.

"No. It's like instant sunburn though, and they can't see very well, so they tend to avoid bright sunshine."

"But the garlic is actually a thing?"

"Not especially. It just smells really strong." He

laughed again. "It will take them ages to get the stink out of their clothes."

Kat couldn't laugh. She was overwhelmed.

"Thanks for the help in there. Tell Amelia I'll swing by the office in a bit. I've got to go get my brother." She hesitated, torn between staying and needing to go.

'Sure, sure. I can let Amelia know. She was worried about you and I was between assignments. It's no bother. You go. They won't come out after you at this time of day. Don't worry.'

Kat gulped. She hadn't even thought about vampires coming after her. She really, really needed to talk to Amelia about forms of protection. Perhaps she had more amulets, like the one Kat wore, although it hadn't seemed to do much earlier.

Kat smiled briefly at Flynn, then hurried off. If she was quick, she might make the number six bus and get to her brother's school within the next half an hour.

Chapter 10

"Hi. I'm here to pick up Mikey, er, Michael Kritchley. I'm his sister, Kat."

Kat was out of breath as she spoke to the school receptionist. She'd run from the bus stop to get here as quickly as possible.

"You'll need to sign him out. Mrs Marshall will bring him to reception."

Kat ignored the offhand tone of the receptionist. She knew it wasn't personal. The woman had to deal with problem children and their parents all day long.

Kat searched in her bag for something to divert Mikey's attention when he arrived. Her hand closed round one of his trains and she still had a chocolate bar left over from her lunch that she'd not yet eaten. Her stomach protested about that loudly.

"Hi Mikey." Kat was careful not to get too close to her brother. He was avoiding her gaze and was currently sucking the lapel of his coat.

Mrs Marshall handed over his school bag.

"Picture day," she said, as if that explained everything.

"I'm sorry, what?" Kat tried to keep one eye on her brother whilst listening to Mrs Marshall at the same time.

"It was school picture day today and we think it was all too much for him. He was out of routine. There were new people, and it was noisy. When he came back from the main hall, he was displaying self-soothing actions and we felt he was on the verge of a meltdown. The teaching assistant took him out of the classroom so he could read, but it was clear that he wasn't going to integrate back in successfully." She leaned into Kat. "Then he had a little accident, so we thought it best he came home."

Kat sighed. That wasn't good. Mikey had managed not to wet himself at school for the last couple of months. They'd gone through a bad patch a few months back when a new pupil had joined his class, but Kat had hoped they were past it now. She opened his school bag and saw the familiar blue plastic bag within. It held Mikey's wet clothing.

"So, he hasn't actually had a meltdown?" she asked the teacher.

"No, but the Special Educational Needs team felt it was best that he take the rest of the day off. They felt it wasn't productive for Michael to stay in the classroom."

Which meant they didn't want him disrupting everyone else, thought Kat bitterly. Then she told herself off. The school had been wonderful with Mikey. There was no way Kat and her mum could afford for him to go to a private special needs school, the fees were too high so they'd been very open and honest with the local primary school about Mikey's needs and had spent some time highlighting trigger points and how to handle his behaviour. On the whole school had been good for him, but there were times when they erred too much on the side of caution. Kat couldn't really blame them. Mikey had had a meltdown in the dining hall when he first started, and the depth of his condition had unnerved the teaching staff considerably. He was usually such a sweet, kind boy.

"Thank you. Have a nice weekend." Kat smiled at the teacher before looking at her brother. "Mikey, shall we go home?"

There was no reply. She held out the train.

"Do you want to hold this for me?"

Mikey looked at the train and made a grab for it.

"Woo woo," he said softly under his breath and walked out of the reception. Kat hurried to catch up with him.

"Come on. Let's go home."

It was a long walk. Mikey got distracted by leaves on the floor, the sound the lamppost made when he dinged it on the way past. He walked into people's front gardens and tripped over the pavement, making his school trousers all muddy. It took forty-five minutes to make the twenty-minute walk home, and by the time they got to the front door, Kat was simmering with anger.

Mikey was refusing to walk through the gate.

"Mikey, come on, please. Let's just get in the house."

He shook his head mutely and began kicking the front garden wall. Kat took a step towards him and he took two steps backwards.

"Mikey, come on. I don't want to play this game. I want to go inside and have a cup of tea."

There was no response. Then Kat remembered the chocolate bar.

"Hey, do you want this chocolate bar? If you come inside, you can have it before dinner."

Mikey took his time, considering the deal. Finally, he nodded and slinked past Kat, through the garden gate. He began yanking the door handle up and down aggressively.

"Hang on, I've got my keys. Don't do that, you'll break it."

Fumbling with her the door, she got it open and Mikey pushed past her into the hallway. He kicked his shoes off and dropped his coat on the floor.

"Hey. Pick this up or no chocolate."

Throwing his sister a black look, Mikey picked up the shoes and coat and went upstairs with them. He came thundering back down as their mum wheeled out of her room.

"You're early."

"Yeah. The school rang, asking me to pick Mikey up. They were worried he was going to have a melt-down. Picture day apparently."

Dolores nodded sadly.

"What about your job? Are you done for the day?"

"I need to go back to the agency and hand in my timesheet. Amelia said I have to do it every day. And I'd better check and see if I've lost my placement or not."

"That won't necessarily be a bad thing," Dolores commented before calling out to Mikey. "Hands!"

He stomped into the downstairs toilet and began washing his hands noisily.

"I promised him this." Kat handed over the chocolate bar to her mum. "Are you alright with him if I go sort out this work stuff?"

"Yes. We can watch some TV, can't we?" Dolores fought the urge to hug her son. It was hard for both of them not to give Mikey hugs and kisses, but unless he gave you one, it was pointless to try, as he refused to accept them.

"Okay, I won't be long. See you in a bit, Mikey, be good!" Kat held out her hand to him, their version of a hug, not expecting anything back, and was surprised when he lightly brushed the tips of her fingers with his own.

He looked at her directly, holding her gaze.

"Be safe." Then he turned and went into his mum's

room to change the TV channel.

Kat frowned. What was all that about? He'd never told her to be safe before. Putting it out of her mind for now, she hurried outside and down the road, back into town and the agency, hoping she still had a job.

Chapter 11

Kat pushed open the door to the agency. She was beginning to feel like she belonged there and got a sense of satisfaction when she arrived. It was a bittersweet emotion.

"Amelia? I've got my timesheet."

"Hi Kat. Give me a minute and I'll put the kettle on." Amelia was sitting at her desk, admiring herself in her compact. She had on a pair of beautiful sparkly earrings that dangled and glittered in the light. There was a matching necklace lying on the desk. "Actually, could you?" She held out the necklace, and Kat hurried over to help do up the clasp around Amelia's neck.

"Amelia, are these diamonds?"

"Yes, I think so. Aren't they gorgeous?"

Kat was momentarily speechless. The jewellery was exquisite. It must have cost a fortune.

"Where did you get them from?" She asked, guessing Amelia would tell her about a lunchtime shopping trip.

"They were a gift from a secret admirer." Amelia was still looking in the mirror.

Wow, thought Kat. She'd never ever had an admirer, let alone knew anyone who could afford such expensive gifts.

Amelia sighed happily before snapping the compact with a click. "I love sparkly things," she said. "Did you want some tea?"

Kat nodded. The tea at the agency always tasted so good. She went to stand by the fireplace while she waited for Amelia to brew it. The warmth made her feel lovely and toasty.

"How was your placement today?" Amelia asked, bringing the tea tray over.

Kat sank into an armchair.

"Um, I had to leave early. I hope that's okay. My brother had an episode at school, and they're not equipped to deal with him, so I had to go pick him up and bring him home." She glanced at Amelia, who was nodding sympathetically. "I mean, I'm the only one who can do it. My mum, she can't and... it doesn't happen very often, and I promise I'll make the time up somehow." Kat was on the verge of tears. She hadn't meant to cry, but she was feeling very emotional.

Amelia patted her arm.

"Don't worry, Luciano Solicitors want you to continue your placement. They've said it's been delicious having you work there." Amelia waited to see if Kat would say anything. She didn't. "Flynn tells me you found some odd invoices?"

"Yeah. Unpaid invoices for um... well, for blood."

Amelia sipped her tea and regarded Kat over the rim of her cup.

"There's some things we should tell you." She began.

"If you're about to tell me they're all vampires, I kinda figured that one out already." Kat wanted to say more, but Amelia carried on.

"Yes. We do cater for a unique clientele and usually our workforce is better equipped to deal with such supernatural employers. Not that you don't have wonderful potential, dear."

"So why did I get the job, then?"

"Mr Magus has faith in you. And Maxwell is looking after you, isn't he?"

Kat huffed a laugh. Here she was sitting, taking tea

in an old-fashioned building, talking about her vampire work placement as if it were an ordinary Friday afternoon.

"Shouldn't we be worried about these unpaid invoices? I mean, vampires. They need blood, don't they?"

"Yes."

"And if they're not paying their supplier, then…"

"Quite."

Amelia wasn't giving anything away and Kat could barely believe how calm the conversation was given the subject matter.

"Maxwell came to us, concerned that an ancient faction within their organisation is making a power play. He wanted a temp so he could volunteer to be their protector and move around the different departments."

"Am I bait?"

"No. Of course not, dear. You're providing an important service."

"You want me to spy on them?"

"Not spy per se. And do be careful, no unnecessary risks. We don't want anything to happen to you." Amelia smiled. "Just let us know if there is anything strange going on."

"Stranger than a bunch of vampires running a solicitor's firm? Okay. I'll look into that."

Kat sipped her own tea, considering her next question.

"Why didn't you tell me all this when I walked in here on my first day?"

Amelia stretched sinuously and locks of auburn hair curled down her neck. There seemed to be a slight sheen to her skin and Kat was certain her eyes gleamed in the firelight.

"Would you have believed it?"

"I'm not entirely sure I believe it now," murmured Kat.

"The tea helps." Amelia smiled.

Kat looked at the cup in her hands that was half empty and realised she didn't care that much about vampires at all.

"Are you drugging me?" She tried to sound incredulous, but it came out more casual, as if she were asking for the time.

"It's just a... well, it's like a brain relaxer. Takes your focus away from stressful situations and allows you to perform at your peak. But it's very exclusive – employees only."

Kat nodded. Somewhere in the back of her mind she knew she needed to be aghast at the tea, the vampires, being left in the dark, working for this peculiar agency, her mum knowing Amelia but honestly, she was just enjoying the company and the fireplace.

Chapter 12

An uneventful weekend led into Monday morning. Kat's mum hadn't wanted to go out, so Kat had done all the shopping by herself. It was strange buying food and topping up the electric and gas cards and still having spare cash. She had brought her brother some new clothes as he'd had a recent growth spurt and splashed out on some perfume for her mum. She couldn't shake the guilt that her mum didn't want her spending this money, but Kat couldn't deny the relief at not having to scrimp and scrape every single penny.

Arriving bang on time at Luciano Solicitors, Maxwell let her in the usual way. But instead of leading her to the Accounts office, they turned right, not left.

"We're working in Stores today. Amelia briefed me on the invoice situation." Max sounded put out at not being notified in the first instance. "Today, we will be working on inventory. Stay close, stay quiet, and do exactly as I tell you."

Max unlocked a set of doors and led Kat down into the basement. She tried to quell the fear building in the pit of her stomach.

"I can't lock you in here and I can't prevent anyone else from coming down here, so don't wander off, no matter what you hear," said Max. His serious tone did nothing for Kat's nerves.

The lighting was muted, and it was chilly. There was a long line of refrigerators containing bags of blood, but not all of them were full. Max handed Kat a clipboard.

"We'll check blood supplies first, then go through the valuables."

"Valuables?"

"Some of our members have been around for centuries, Miss Kritchley. They've amassed wealth. Wealth that cannot be out on display. It raises too many questions."

Down here, Max looked paler and his eyes darker. He was more menacing, and Kat thought she could see the points of his teeth just below his upper lip. She never noticed his fangs before.

They began cataloguing the blood supplies. It was straightforward enough. Each fridge had an inventory list on the front, so it was a matter of counting and tallying. They all matched, but only three of the fridges were fully stocked.

"How long will this last?" Kat asked the question she wasn't sure she wanted the answer to.

Max glanced up and down the fridges.

"About a month, depending on whether current employee levels stay the same."

Kat swallowed any further questions. She decided she didn't want to know how many other *employees* were off site as it were.

"Are you alright to continue working? I don't need to take any breaks, but you humans require greater upkeep."

"I'm fine." Kat had no desire to eat down here in the stores, and the sooner they were finished, the better.

Cataloguing the valuables was fascinating. Kat couldn't believe the amount of fine paintings, ceramics and jewellery that was being kept down there. She was in awe of the amassed wealth. They were almost finished with the diamond collection when Kat noticed an empty display case.

"What should be in here?" she asked.

"What do you mean? Is it empty?" Maxwell moved

so fast, he took Kat's breath away and she stumbled half a step backwards. He peered closely at the glass case as if the jewels were somehow hiding. "There should be an earring and necklace set in here. This is very bad. These belong to Veronique. If she finds out…"

"If I find out what?"

Kat's heart sank as Veronique glided around the corner. She looked ten times more frightening down here than she did in the entrance hall. Kat shivered and moved slightly to put Maxwell and the display cabinet between her and the other woman. Veronique glanced at the empty case.

"Where are my jewels?" she hissed, her hands curling into talons, black nails looking wickedly sharp.

"We're just doing inventory. Perhaps they have been put away incorrectly."

"Or perhaps they have been stolen by a blood bag."

Kat flinched at the insult.

"I'll get to the bottom of it, Veronique. Give me the rest of the day."

"You will remove this human from our establishment immediately and we shall inform the agency that we no longer require our contract of employment."

Maxwell flicked a look at Kat.

"I will have to terminate the contract in person. There are requirements."

"Then I shall accompany you."

Kat's heart sank. Maxwell was trying to investigate nefarious goings on at the solicitor's firm, which was why she'd been employed. Now he was losing her as his cover, plus she would be out of a job.

Veronique tapped her foot on the floor impatiently.

"I'm waiting."

"After you," said Maxwell gallantly.

"No, no, I insist. Food first." Veronique eyed Kat hungrily, an almost red tinge to her eyes, and her fangs were certainly on display.

"Walk in front of me and do not run. Do you remember the way?" Maxwell asked Kat.

She nodded, barely daring to breathe. He inclined his head for her to take the first step and she moved cautiously around the two vampires, placing the clipboard and pen down on a bench and carefully walking for the exit to the storeroom. Thankfully, she had kept her coat on and her bag was slung across her body.

Chapter 13

As Kat exited the solicitors, there was a city car waiting with blacked-out windows. She hesitated. No way did she want to get into an enclosed space with two vampires. When Veronique left the building, a chauffeur leapt out and opened the passenger door. The woman seemed to slink into the car with effortless grace. Maxwell followed and peered up at her.

"Get in."

Kat clutched her bag and took a step back.

"It's not a request," said Maxwell darkly.

There was a loud revving, and a motorbike glided around the city car, coming to a stop just in front. A familiar leather-clad figure removed his helmet.

'Flynn!' Kat had never been more pleased to see another human.

'Get on,' he said to her.

'I insist that Miss Kritchley ride with us. We are going to talk to Mr Magus. She will be quite safe.' Maxwell's tone was even more clipped than usual.

'If you're headed to HQ, we can meet you there. No need to contaminate one of your cars with the stench of human.' Flynn winked at Kat as he unhooked a spare helmet from the side of his bike. 'No offense.'

'None taken,' she replied weakly, glad she was wearing trousers and a thick coat as she jammed the bike helmet over her head.

With a degree of trepidation, she clambered clumsily onto the back, not really knowing where to put her hands.

'You never ridden before? Don't worry. I'll keep you safe. Just wrap your arms around me and lean when

I do. You'll be fine.'

Flynn revved the bike loudly, making Kat yelp and grab onto him more tightly than she had meant to. He felt warm and up this close. She could smell his cologne. It was earthy and a little spicy. She liked it.

Maxwell slammed the door of the city car, but the chauffeur couldn't move until Flynn rode off, which he did with a jaunty wave. The bike soon lost the car, able to weave through stationary traffic more effectively, and they arrived at the agency first. Flynn parked at the rear of the building. It didn't look quite so illustrious from the back.

Kat stood with ever so slightly trembling legs and undid the helmet, proud of her hands for only shaking a little as she passed it over to Flynn.

'Don't worry. We're completely safe here.'

Flynn pressed his hand on the back door. It didn't open immediately, but the panel he was touching glimmered and the door finally swung out.

'What was that?'

'What was what?' Flynn grinned at her, clearly not planning to explain how he opened a door with no lock by pressing his hand on it.

'Kat? Is that you? I'll make some tea,' called out Amelia.

It was the last straw.

'No! I don't want tea. Maxwell and Veronique are on their way here because they think I stole some jewellery. I've been nearly eaten like three times. I just escaped another scary ass situation on the back of a motorbike and I reckon you owe me a bloody good explanation for... well, for everything.'

Kat was breathing heavily, flushing as she realised she'd been shouting and that Mr Magus had come out of his office and was regarding her with a wry smile on his lips.

'Yes, perhaps some explanations are in order,' he began, but was interrupted from saying anything further as the doorbell rang.

The vampires had arrived.

Chapter 14

"Amelia, activate the inner protective spell, if you please. Flynn, protect Miss Kritchley. Be on your guard. As Asmodeus was fond of saying, *Where there's one vampire, two more shall lurk in shadows dark*."

Kat had no idea who Asmodeus was but watched with a blend of annoyance and interest as Amelia closed her eyes, began glowing and flexed. It was the only way Kat could describe it. The woman grew larger as if she were breathing in with every fibre of her being. As she breathed out and returned to her normal size, Kat sensed a ripple of something pass through her. She craned her neck to try to see what it was, but nothing looked any different.

Flynn tugged gently on her arm, motioning that she needed to come and stand with him on the far side of the fireplace. That put Mr Magus front and centre, with Amelia just behind him. Kat frowned. She didn't like being tucked away in a corner. She shrugged Flynn's hand off and took a defiant step forward to stand next to Amelia. She wasn't an idiot. Vampires were about to enter the agency and Kat had only just come to grips with the fact that vampires exist, let alone how you protected yourself against them. Perhaps the movies had it right, perhaps not. Either way, she wasn't about to put herself in direct danger just to show everyone that she wasn't afraid, but she also wasn't going to cower in the corner. Flynn's huff of laughter behind her made her flush, but she stood her ground.

There was a loud knocking on the door.

"Everyone ready?" Mr Magus paused for quiet acknowledgments before calling loudly, "You may enter."

Maxwell and Veronique swept in so fast it was like they didn't even move. They just arrived. In the warm glow of the agency, they looked far less scary. More pointy and hard, but not as intimidating somehow. Kat put it down to the general sense of protection she always felt here.

'Magus,' Maxwell inclined his head elegantly in greeting.

'Thief!' hissed Veronique, staring daggers at Amelia, but she did not take a step towards her, which Kat thought was odd, given how much she liked to invade her personal space at Luciano's.

Mr Magus held up a finger as Amelia opened her mouth, glanced at him, and then closed it.

'Please, let us be seated and comfortable. Then you can explain the reason behind your accusation.'

Kat frowned. There had only been four chairs around the fireplace earlier. Now there were six. How had that happened? She touched the nearest one with her toe. It seemed solid enough. Maybe she just hadn't noticed the extra ones.

'Amelia, if you would.' Mr Magus gestured for her to go and make the tea.

'No. I'll do it.' Kat smiled sweetly and stalked in the general direction where she'd seen Amelia disappear to make tea in the past. She was taken aback at the look of surprise on Mr Magus's face. Maybe he wasn't used to people standing up to him.

'Use the gold cannister, dear. It makes the best brew,' called Amelia, her green eyes glinting.

Kat knew what she meant. That was the tea she'd been drugged with to be malleable and accepting of all the strangeness at Magus Employment Services. Well, tough. She wasn't going to make any special gold tea.

Swinging the door open to the kitchen, Kat paused in awe. It was a huge space that looked more like it should be part of a period drama series than the kitchen at a temping agency. There was little modern equipment. A giant range cooker almost filled one side of the room and there was a burnished copper kettle sat upon a gas ring. Kat looked around and saw a small pot with a bristle of matches in it. Turning on the gas, she lit the ring with a whomp and hefted the kettle over to the sink. It was one of those massive, deep, wide sinks with old-fashioned taps. It took the water a moment to chug through the pipes. Kat let it run for a short while, just in case, but it seemed clear. Realising that she was dithering and missing out on what was happening in the drawing room, she hurried to fill the kettle and put it on the hob. Assuming it was as old-fashioned as it looked, she guessed that it would whistle once it was done.

"Cups, cups, where are the cups?" she muttered to herself, opening cupboards that revealed various chinaware, glass bowls, champagne flutes, but no china.

"Top left," said a voice.

Startled, Kat spun around. A blonde man stood in the kitchen. She assumed it was another vampire.

"How did you get in here?" asked Kat, backing away.

"I was invited."

"Are you with Maxwell and Veronique? You didn't leave Luciano's when they did. I was there. Why are you here?" Kat was aware she was gabbling, but this guy was absolutely bloody gorgeous.

He didn't look sharp and angular like the others. His eyes were a dark brown, not black, and whilst his skin was pale, it glowed with an inner light. He made her think of smoked wood and cold November nights, crunchy leaves and fireworks.

'I came for you.' There was a highly suggestive quality to his voice that made Kat blush and she took a half step forwards without even meaning to.

"Stop it. You're doing something to me. That's not fair." Kat searched her memory of vampire lore from the various TV shows and books she'd read over the years. "Stop trying to glamour me. It won't work."

He smiled lazily at her, revealing a glint of fang.

"Worth a go. The cups are here." He pointed to the cupboard just above his head and then leant casually on the counter behind him. It was obvious he wasn't going to move.

The kettle on the hob started to whistle thinly. Kat braced herself for, well, for anything. Wondering what the hell she was doing, she strode to the cupboard, trying not to show any fear, and opened the door. True enough, there was a stack of delicate china cups and saucers. With semi-shaky hands, she took out six, allowing for this new guest.

As she reached into the cupboard, he shifted slightly closer to her.

"What are you doing?" Kat shrieked, the china chiming in her hands as she hurried backwards.

"They're right. You do smell good." And then he winked at her.

Thoroughly confused, Kat did her best to ignore him and clattered the cups and saucers down. She had to turn her back on him to take the kettle off the hob. It was whistling louder now. There was a teapot on the side and remembering what her mum always said about warming the pot, she hastily did so before casting about for any sign of tea bags.

"Here you go."

He was at her elbow, handing her a tea caddy. The scent of him made her tummy flip. She could feel his breath on her neck. *Wait, breath?* Kat spun around, but he had moved back to his spot on the other side of the kitchen. *If he had breath, then he can't be a vampire.*

She flipped open the tea caddy and smiled in relief at the familiar pyramid shape of the tea bags. Dumping several into the teapot, she filled it with hot water and grabbed a nearby tray. She banged the teapot, cups, and saucers on it. All she needed now were spoons, milk, and sugar.

"Drawer to the right, jugs in the cupboard next to the cups, milk in the fridge behind the door and sugar bowl next to the cookie jar."

Feeling utterly discombobulated and even more embarrassed, Kat retrieved everything, marvelling at the relatively swanky fridge hidden behind the cupboard door.

"How do you know where everything is?" she asked, but the mysterious man was gone. "What the…?"

Shaking her head, Kat resolved to add his sudden appearance and apparent familiarity to the long list of questions she had for Mr Magus, Amelia, and Flynn. But first, the vampires.

With the tray rattling in her hands, Kat backed out of the kitchen into the drawing room. Everyone was now seated, but no one was talking. The vampires were glaring, whilst the agency staff looked relaxed and at ease.

"I'll be mother," said Amelia, gracefully rising to take the tray from Kat and placing it on the low table in the middle of the chairs. Her eyebrows twitched at the less than perfect arrangement on the tray. She peeked beneath the teapot lid and her eyebrows raised even higher. "This will have to do, I suppose," she said quietly under her breath, but Kat heard her.

Nobody spoke as Amelia poured the tea out. Kat watched to see if the vampires would accept a cup. They allowed one to be put before them, but made no movement to drink from it. Did they even consume normal food? Another question for Kat's ever growing list.

Mr Magus took a large swallow of tea, his lips twitching in amusement. Kat figured he knew she hadn't used the gold tea caddy either.

"How may Magus Employment Services be of assistance?"

Kat sat down in the empty chair next to Flynn, who flashed a grin at her before turning his full attention to the vampires.

"Your... receptionist... has stolen from me. I want my jewels returned immediately." Veronique was practically gnashing her teeth and seemed oddly restrained in her chair.

"Amelia?" Mr Magus turned his attention to her, waiting for a response.

"I have absolutely no idea what you are talking about, dear." Amelia took a delicate sip of her tea, her eyes cast down in a picture of pure innocence.

"You are wearing them. My family heirlooms are literally sitting upon your flesh and you dare to say you have no idea what I'm talking about."

Veronique spat the words at Amelia. She was clearly being restrained in some manner, but Kat didn't know how. Then it dawned on her. The protection spell Mr Magus had mentioned was obviously doing something to the vampire.

"The angrier you get, the harder you will find it to speak or move. May I suggest you calm down a little?" Mr Magus radiated amusement, but his face was unsmiling.

Maxwell was sitting back in his chair, relaxed but alert. One knee draped artfully over the other. Veronique's shoulder rose and fell as if she were taking a calming breath, but no air was inhaled or expelled.

"The jewels I am wearing were a gift from a secret admirer. I have the note. One moment, please." Amelia rose with a lethal grace that Kat hadn't noticed before. At her desk, she removed a gilt-edged card from the in tray, bringing over to the hearth and passing it to Veronique.

Kat half expected the vampire to snatch Amelia's hand off, but instead she snaked her arm forward and plucked the card away. Veronique took a cursory glance at the card before flicking it towards Maxwell, who took longer to study the contents before handing it back to Amelia.

"The card reveals nothing of use," said Veronique in clipped tones.

"As I said, a secret admirer." Amelia sank back into her chair, stroking the diamond necklace that lay around her neck.

Kat could hardly breathe. You could cut the tension with a knife!

Veronique smiled, but there was no warmth in her face.

"It's a well-known fact that your... people are thieves and hoarders. I will accept that you had no knowledge of my ownership, provided you return my property immediately."

Amelia bristled at the open insult, but as Mr Magus

raised another finger in her direction, she returned Veronique's fake smile. She deftly removed the earrings and lifted her hands to undo the clasp on the back of her neck, flaunting it towards the vampires as she did so. Kat was surprised at their lack of reaction. If she had bared her neck like that at Luciano's, she would have been dinner for sure.

Leaning forward, Amelia tipped the jewellery onto Veronique's lap. The vampire whipped her hand out to catch it.

"I suggest you discover who your secret admirer is before I do." And with that, Veronique stood up, and in a quick blurred motion, left the building.

Maxwell sighed theatrically and stood, Mr Magus rising with him.

"An unfortunate wrinkle in our investigations, but thank you for the speedy capitulation, Amelia. An unusual turn of events that jewellery should be stolen at this precise time and discovered upon your premises, but I believe Veronique will allow Miss Kritchley to continue her work placement. After all, she was an innocent in this... show." He inclined his head at Mr Magus. "If indeed you do not know the identity of your secret admirer, I encourage you to find out fast, otherwise it is unlikely there will be anyone to discover. I cannot prevent Veronique from exacting retribution. A crime has been committed after all. Good evening."

Another rapid blur and Maxwell left. Mr Magus exhaled in relief and sat back down in his chair. Kat stared as she realised they were four again.

"How..?"

"The chairs are charmed. They'll expand and retract depending on need," explained Flynn. "Before you joined us, we only had three."

Huh, thought Kat. Charms and spells and vampires and god knows what else.

"I have questions," she said.

"I'm sure you do, but first…"

Kat interrupted Mr Magus.

"No. Sorry. I want my questions answered first. The secret admirer can wait. After all, I think I know who it is. The blonde guy? In the kitchen? Seemed to know his way around?"

Kat was startled by the reaction of the others. Amelia raised a hand to her mouth, trying to hide a smile. Flynn leapt up and dashed into the kitchen while Mr Magus tutted under his breath and leaned back in his chair.

Flynn shook his head as he returned.

"Tell me about the man in the kitchen, Miss Kritchley, please," asked Mr Magus.

Chapter 15

"Kat is right, we should've done more for her mum," said Amelia, clearing up the teacups and taking them out to the kitchen.

Mr Magus stayed in the drawing room. He was standing by the mantlepiece, staring into the fire. Flynn mirrored his father, gazing into the flames, but remained sitting.

"We tried. She wouldn't even let me cross the threshold. We respected her wishes." Mr Magus' voice was distant.

"You should have forced her to accept the help," commented Flynn.

Mr Magus shook his head, breaking his reverie.

"No, that would not have helped. Beside Dolores always was... resistant to my magics. And with all that grief and pain, it's likely to have back lashed anyway."

Flynn regarded his dad.

"You never talk about it. The accident I mean."

Mr Magus's face darkened, and he did not reply. Amelia returned, gathered her coat and bag, readying herself to leave for the day.

"At least Connor will keep her safe," she said.

Flynn's head whipped round to stare at her.

"What do you mean?"

"Well, I, ah... what I mean is..." Amelia looked helplessly at Mr Magus.

"She means that no doubt Connor has been drawn in to current situations."

Flynn scoffed at that.

"No, you mean that you hired him to protect Kat. Why didn't you tell me?" he demanded.

"We have not signed a contract. A comment may have been made in passing that Miss Kritchley had entered the agency but not yet manifested. We can only look upon Connor's attention as professionalism and diligence to the task ahead."

Flynn stood up, his face a mask of disgust.

"That or his own personal interest in her manifestation. He always was a power hungry cur." He stalked towards the front door.

"Where are you going?" asked Mr Magus.

But Flynn didn't reply. He let the door slam in his wake, leaving Amelia and Mr Magus to exchange worried glances.

"I'd better…" began Mr Magus.

"No, no. You stay here. I'll check in on Kat on my way home. I'll be able to tell who's lurking around and if necessary I can…" Amelia broke off and blushed.

Mr Magus smiled at her.

"You can strengthen the protective spells you laid around Dolores' house. It was very good of you to do that. It must have used a great deal of your energy."

Amelia swung her scarf gracefully around her neck.

"We were friends once upon a time. What happened to her wasn't fair. It could've happened to any one of us." She shrugged. "It seemed like the least I could do. She wouldn't accept my money either."

Smiling goodbye, Amelia left her boss brooding by the fire. It was colder outside than she had anticipated and within the first few steps, she felt the familiar zap of energy as her body dealt with the chill and lack of sunshine. She needed a good meal and to curl up with a decent book, but before that, she had enough stored energy to check on Kat.

It was pretty dark when she arrived on Kat's road

and the street lights were flickering, coming on for brief periods and then winking out again. Odd, but could be the result of a glitchy power supply and nothing at all to do with the supernatural. Amelia laughed softly to herself. As if. She cast out her senses and felt nothing unusual. That's not to say she didn't detect anything supernatural. Most mundanes would run a mile if they knew how close they lived to it on a daily basis, but there was no need to scare them needlessly.

She clocked Connor in the local Chinese takeaway. Interestingly, it was run by a family of Qilin who had learned over the centuries to shift into human form. Their regular dragonish slash unicorn appearance would have them hunted to extinction within months. It was good that they were nearby. They were natural protectors of the innocent.

Flynn was... ah, there he was. In the park. At the other end of the street to Connor, which was probably a deliberate ploy. Kat's house was located more or less in the middle of the two of them and, no doubt, if something were to happen, they would spring into action.

In casting out her senses, Amelia neglected to go above second-floor window height and completely missed the vampire following her along the rooftops, her mind too full of Kat's early reaction, Connor's appearance, and who might be her secret admirer.

As she lifted her hand to knock on Kat's door, it swung open and she was greeted with an equally startled Kat.

Then the vampire jumped her.

Chapter 16

Kat screamed in shock as Amelia was attacked from above by someone clad in black. Still holding the full and heavy rubbish bag from the kitchen bin, she swung it at the figure and managed to knock him marginally off centre. It was enough for Amelia to slither out from under her attacker, but they were undeterred and moved equally sinuously, shooting out a pale hand that grabbed Amelia by the neck and lifted her off the ground.

"No!" shouted Kat, flinging out her hand.

There was a blinding light and loud thunderclap and Amelia dropped to the doorstep, coughing and holding her neck with one hand.

The air fizzled and all of Kat's hair stood on end, like she'd experienced an electric shock. The rubbish bag she was still holding was now smouldering and smelt like burnt rubber. Mechanically, Kat stepped outside to put it in the outside bin.

"Are you alright? Who was that? Where did they go?" Kat extended a hand and helped a shaky Amelia up from the ground.

She coughed a little and pointed to the fine dust that lay along the path to Kat's front door.

"What?"

"That's what's left of the vampire. You killed it." Amelia rubbed her neck again, which had an angry welt across it. "I can't believe I let myself get jumped by one of those bloodsuckers. I bet they worked for Veronique. She's going to be so mad."

Amelia looked around, scanning the area for more menacing shapes, but there was nothing. Running footsteps could be heard coming towards them. Quickly,

Amelia clasped Kat's forearm and stared directly into her eyes.

"You saved my life. I owe you a blood debt and my loyalty is yours to command."

Kat watched as Amelia's eyes whirled green and gold, her breath feeling hot in Kat's face and her skin shimmering, revealing scales that sparkled in the streetlights that now glowed firmly.

"I, er… what..?"

Connor skidded to a stop outside the house.

"Everything alright? What happened?"

Flynn appeared from the other direction, and, completely ignoring Connor, asked his own questions.

"Are you okay? What happened?"

Dolores called from inside the house.

"Kat? Are you alright? What's going on out there?"

"I have absolutely no bloody idea!" she called back, holding open the door and gesturing for everyone to come inside and explain themselves.

Chapter 17

Kat had never seen her mother so flustered before. If she'd still had her legs, she would have been flitting in and out of her room like nobody's business. As it was, she made Kat go in and make tea – in the teapot, which Kat didn't even know they owned – open the posh biscuits and sent her back twice to exchange cups that weren't right.

Mikey wisely kept out of the way. He didn't like strangers anyway, but he miraculously appeared when Kat opened the chocolate biscuits – that was about as posh as it got at the Kritchley household.

"You alright Mikey?" Kat asked, letting him help himself to several biscuits before she put them on the plate.

"Be safe."

That was the second time Mikey had warned his sister to be safe. She turned around, but there was nobody else there.

"There's no one here, love," she said gently, reaching out to touch his arm but stopping herself in time. She didn't want to trigger a Mikey episode. "Everyone is in Mum's room. Do you want to say hi?"

She could tell that he was curious. His eyes kept flitting towards the stilted sounds of conversation they could both hear.

"You can stand behind me if you like. You don't have to go in. Just be nosy. What do you reckon?"

Mikey closed his eyes and cocked his head as if considering a huge dilemma.

"Okay, okay. Just a peek. Just a peek. Peek. Okay." He shuffled to the side to allow Kat through and out of the kitchen first, then followed in her footsteps.

"Everyone, Mikey wanted to say hi. Everyone, this is my brother." As Kat spoke, she lifted her chin a little, ready to defend her brother as she so often had in the past.

There was a chorus of greetings from Flynn and Connor, but Amelia stood up and gave a little bow. What was weirder was that Mikey returned it. Kat was left wondering what that was all about as Mikey escaped up the stairs to his room and Flynn nicked the plate of biscuits off her.

Everyone sat awkwardly, waiting for someone else to speak.

"Okay, I'll go first. What just happened?" asked Kat. She dipped a biscuit into her tea and nibbled the edge.

Connor and Flynn were doing an excellent job of not looking at each other. Amelia sighed in exasperation.

"Connor was keeping an eye on you. Flynn was keeping an eye on Connor. And I was popping by to make sure you were okay. After everything."

Both men opened their mouths to object, saw the other doing the same and obstinately closed them again.

"I'm not talking about them, I'd figured that much out for myself," said Kat. "Although you both did a rubbish job given that a vampire jumped Amelia right in front of me and tried to kill her."

Amelia was fidgeting like mad in her chair, which was very unlike the usual calm demeanour Kat had seen at the agency.

"A vampire?" Connor sat up straighter, as if he were about to leap up and do battle. "Are you sure?"

"Pale skin, superhuman strength, fangs? Yeah, pretty sure."

"Where did it go?" Flynn sounded relaxed, but Kat

could see his body was coiled, anticipating a fight.

"Um…" Kat glanced at Amelia for some help.

"Kat exploded it with light," she replied with a grin, and proceeded to contort her arm behind her back, trying to get a stubborn itch.

"You did what?" Dolores snapped. "Do you have any idea what you've done?"

"Actually no, not really. But my friend is safe, so surely that's the most important thing?" Kat flashed a small smile at Amelia, who looked like she was about to well up. Maybe the shock was beginning to set in. Kat felt shaky herself.

"No, what Dolores means is that you now owe the vampires," explained Flynn. "It's not a good idea to kill one of theirs without permission. I guess we find out how much protection Maxwell can really give you."

Kat sank back into her chair. She owed the vampires? That didn't sound good. She was pretty sure the only thing she had that they'd want was flowing through her veins, and she was rather attached to that.

"But we can go to them and explain, can't we? Amelia was attacked. She nearly died. Take a look at her neck and you'll see the bruises…" Kat trailed off as Amelia exposed her neck with a nervous laugh.

There wasn't a mark on it. In fact, if anything, it had a golden sheen to it. Amelia was still wiggling like mad in her seat.

"Ants in your pants, dear?" asked Dolores, not entirely kindly.

"No, it's my shoulder blades. It feels like…" Amelia broke off and looked up, wide-eyed. She sat stock still for a moment before abruptly standing and grabbing her bag and coat from the floor. "I have to go. Thank you Kat, I'll see you tomorrow. Thank you for the tea,

Dolores." Amelia gabbled as she hurried across the room and let herself out of the house.

"Well, that was weird," remarked Connor, who looked perfectly at home, lounging in an armchair, his mug of tea balanced on one knee.

Flynn opened his mouth to agree and seemed to realise who with and glowered at Connor instead.

"A vampire can't come in, can they?" asked Kat. "That's right, isn't it? According to TV lore and all that. They can't come in unless they're invited."

"Yeah, that's right," confirmed Flynn.

Kat stood.

"Okay then. Thanks for checking up on me. As you can see, I'm fine. So you can go. Home. Now."

Flynn rose reluctantly.

"What are you going to do about the vampires? We can set up a meeting with Veronique, have Xavier smooth everything out," he offered.

Connor snorted quietly. Clearly, he didn't approve of that plan.

"No. I don't think this was an attack on me. I think this was all to do with Amelia and her secret admirer, which we still know nothing about. So I'm going to go to work tomorrow as normal. Good night, gentlemen." Kat pointedly looked at Flynn and Connor.

Flynn huffed a little at that, but he thanked Dolores for her hospitality and glared at Connor as he walked out of the sitting room. Kat followed him to the door.

"Thanks. For earlier, I mean. I never got the chance to thank you for picking me up from Luciano's," she said. It seemed like it was a hundred years ago.

Flynn gave her a lopsided smile. He looked lost and vulnerable for a brief moment. Her heart ached a little, and she almost reached out to give him a hug.

"See you tomorrow?" asked Flynn.

Kat nodded and watched Flynn hunch his shoulders against the night as he walked away from her house. She nearly called out after him, but was distracted by the sound of her mum laughing. She turned and Connor was waving goodbye to Dolores as he left her chuckling.

"What was all that about?" Kat asked, smiling, wanting to be in on the joke.

Connor leaned in and kissed her on the cheek. She breathed in his unique scent, making her feel a little light-headed.

"Just saying goodnight. Goodnight Katerina."

And he was gone, loping off into the night. Kat pushed the door shut with a whirling head. That was twice he'd been up close and personal with her. She could feel the blush rising and tried to shake herself out of it. The last thing she needed right now was any kind of workplace feelings. Not that she was entirely sure Connor even worked for the agency at the moment.

Coming back into her mother's room, Kat plopped herself into a chair with a big sigh.

"I told you not to take that job," said Dolores. "Look at what's happening. A vampire attack right on our doorstep!"

Kat waved away her mum's concern.

"It wasn't anything to do with us. Amelia had some jewellery that belonged to Veronique. It was missing from the Luciano vault and Veronique thought Amelia had stolen it, but she hadn't. It was a secret admirer, only no one knows who the secret admirer is yet." She yawned. The day was beginning to take its toll on her.

"Yes, and look at what you did..." Dolores broke off.

"What do you mean, what I did?" Kat sat up, feeling

suddenly wide awake. "You mean, magic. I magically poofed the vampire away. Well, you know what? I'm glad I did. It was going to kill Amelia and I just, just reacted. Mr Magus says I'm manifesting. That he's glad I'm at the agency so they can help me with my... well, with my powers. Whatever that means." She glared at her mum. "Did you know this was going to happen?"

There was a long silence.

"I prayed it would not."

Kat stared at her. Dolores had the grace to turn away first.

"Well, that's bloody marvellous. I was a potential ticking magic bomb, and you *prayed* that nothing would happen." Kat pushed herself up. "I'm going to bed. Night." And she walked away from her mum, heading upstairs to her room, her mind a knotted tangle of confusion and wonder.

Chapter 18

"Mother. Please call me back at your earliest convenience. I've been attacked by a vampire." Amelia hesitated, not knowing whether to elaborate further. The problem was, she didn't know who might be listening. Amelia's mother, officially a Countess of a long forgotten realm, was important in certain circles and often had her minions screen calls and so forth. In fact, Amelia hadn't seen her mother for, well, for longer than she could remember.

Hanging up the phone, Amelia regarded her skin. It was scaly and not because it was dry in need of moisturiser. Actual scales were visible. Thankfully, not all over, but certainly noticeable on the backs of her hands. A closer look at her face in the mirror also showed tiny scales across the top of her cheekbones.

Her eyes were now fully golden with a vertical line iris instead of the usual human looking circle. At least she could explain that away with contacts or better yet, she could get some normal eye looking contacts to cover it up. And her shoulder blades. They were still itchy but not as bad as they had been. Perhaps she'd been allergic to… to the chair or something. They felt a bit knobbly, but she'd try to investigate properly later. There was a floor-length mirror in her bedroom. Right now, she needed something to eat.

Amelia was shocked to answer the door, about half an hour after she'd left the message, and have her mother sweep in, entourage-free for once.

"Mother! What a pleasant surprise. I didn't expect you to come in person. I appreciate how busy you are." Amelia took her mother's coat and hung it up, desperately hoping she still had some of the Da Hong Pao tea at the back of the cupboard. Her mother had expensive tastes.

"Amelia. Such a cute place. I got your message." She air kissed in the general direction of her daughter and settled herself atop one of the breakfast bar stools. She looked effortlessly glamorous. "Tell me everything."

After carefully setting the tea to brew just the way her mother liked, Amelia stood by the countertop, keeping the barrier between them as she spoke, describing the gift, the revelation and the attack. Then she poured the tea and waited.

The Countess took a sip and breathed in the aroma with a satisfied look on her face.

"And what did you say to the girl? Exactly," she asked.

"Um, I said," Amelia's brow furrowed as she tried to recall. "I said, *You saved my life. I owe you a blood debt and my loyalty is yours to command.*" She fussed with the edge of a tea towel. "I'm not really sure why. It just came over me. Before I knew it, I'd spoken the words but… but, it's alright, isn't it?"

Her mother delicately put her teacup back on its saucer and reached across the countertop to pat Amelia's hand.

"You've spoken words of oath. Your dragon is released. Exactly what will happen, I can't say. It's different for each of us. The fact that you spoke after being attacked is unfortunate. It may be somewhat more binding than we would expect, but there are ways around these things." She sat a little straighter atop her stool. "The easiest thing to do is to get rid of the girl. She dies, and the vow is broken. Your dragon will reabsorb and we can all move on with our lives."

Amelia stared at her mother in horror. She didn't know if she was more horrified that she'd suggested Kat be killed or that she had said it in such a calm voice. As if it were nothing.

"Judging from the expression on your face, I'm guessing that killing the girl isn't a workable solution." Her mother tutted. "We weren't so sentimental in my day."

"Your day was centuries ago!" exploded Amelia. "You can't just go around killing people. We'd be exposed for one thing and for another, Kat is my friend. I like her."

The Countess shuddered at that.

"But she's a human. What can she possibly have to offer you?"

"She's kind and thoughtful and caring. She bought me food, and she resisted the tea. Kat Kritchley is going to follow in the footsteps of her father. You mark my words, and I will be her dragonly protector."

The Countess snorted with laughter. The first time Amelia had ever seen her mother looking anything but sophisticated.

"Ha! She'll take one look at your scales and your wings and run for the hills. She'll want absolutely nothing to do with you. Take from me. I know what these humans are like."

Amelia shook her head stubbornly.

"Times have changed. You'll see. She'll accept me, scales and all. I'll be by her side when it matters."

The two women glared at each other, breathing heavily, one in disgust, the other in determination. Her mother gave in first.

"How far has the change gone?" she asked crisply.

Amelia waved a hand at her eyes and scaly skin.

"My back is itchy."

"Sounds like you're going to go through the full change. Watch out for the forked tongue. It takes a little while to get used to." Her own tongue flickered out of her mouth.

"But you don't, I mean, you haven't got wings. Have you?"

The Countess stood. The visit had come to its end. She swept towards the front door, turning back once to regard her daughter.

"I paid good money to have them removed. If you choose not to, you should be fully aware that will transform once a month and have little to no control over your inner monster. Let's see how well your *friend* supports you then." And with that, she left.

Amelia stood stock still for a moment, digesting what her mother had said, then she spun on her heels, found the box of expensive tea the Countess so enjoyed and tipped it away in the bin.

It was time to check out her wings.

Chapter 19

The sun shone brightly as if it were echoing Kat's happy mood. Kat wasn't quite sure why she was feeling so good. Even though she was manifesting amazing magical powers, she had absolutely no idea how they worked, and it hadn't fully sunk in that magic was real. Her mum was still angry at her, but she could cope with that. Dolores would calm down eventually. The idea that she might have to explain herself to the vampires was daunting, but even that didn't faze her. Instead, Kat walked with a spring in her step, sipping on a coffee that she'd treated herself to on the way to work. With a flourish, she popped the empty cup into a bin and jogged up the steps to the heavy doors of Luciano's. She rapped loudly, tapping her foot to the jaunty song playing in her head.

It took a while but the doors finally opened, half as much as usual. Kat squeezed through the gap, wriggling slightly to allow for her bag to fit through as well.

"Morning!" she chirped, turning to smile at Maxwell behind the door, only he wasn't there. Instead, a bungee cord extended into the gloom of the foyer. It was only once the door clicked fully shut that Maxwell came into view.

"Good morning Miss Kritchley."

He seemed paler than normal, if that was even possible. As Kat followed him through the deserted gloomy corridors, she wondered whether it was because of the lovely bright sunny day, or whether he was just tired. Did vampires get tired? Were they really nocturnal? Meaning that Maxwell being here with her meant he was effectively working nights. So absorbed in her thoughts, Kat paid no attention to where they were going and pulled up quickly when Maxwell held the door open for her to a boardroom.

Kat paused. There were people inside. Whilst the room was cloaked in gloom, she could hear their voices.

"What's going on?" she whispered.

"Performance review." Maxwell nodded for her to go through.

Instantly, Kat's hands felt clammy. Why was she having a performance review? She didn't work for Luciano's. She worked for the agency. If the solicitors didn't like her work, they should be having a meeting with Mr Magus, not talking to her directly.

There were two empty chairs available. One at the end of the boardroom table and another to one side. Kat took a step towards the chair at the table, but Maxwell hissed at her and she veered to the other chair. So it wasn't her performance review. And Maxwell probably couldn't leave her unprotected in the building. *Well, this isn't awkward at all,* thought Kat as she sat down as quietly as she could. Every head at the table swivelled to regard her, and she gulped. It was like having a pride of hungry lions mark you for dinner.

One of the ancient-looking vampires began talking, but it wasn't in English. Kat turned her head to hear better. It didn't sound like French or German either. Both of which she had studied at school, enough to recognise when someone else was speaking it. Feeling equally relieved and miffed at not knowing what they were saying, she watched the people sat around the table as her eyes adjusted to the gloom.

Everyone was paying attention to the conversation between the ancient one and Maxwell. Everyone except Veronique, who Kat hadn't initially noticed. She was staring at Kat, the kind of stare that bore right through your soul. Kat shifted a little, feeling uncomfortable. Veronique didn't move or even blink. Not even when the ancient one asked her a question. She just answered whilst glaring at Kat.

A niggle of worry began to grow in Kat's stomach. Maybe that vampire last night had been one of Veronique's men. She hadn't meant to explode him in light. If you asked her to do it again, she didn't think she'd have a clue how. If it hadn't been trying to kill Amelia right in front of her house, then she wouldn't have been involved at all.

That got Kat thinking. What if Amelia had gone straight home? Would she have been attacked there instead? Nobody would have come to her rescue then. That was sobering.

Kat's internal reverie broke when she realised the vampires had finished. Some were leaving the room, others were talking to Maxwell and shaking his hand.

That's got to be good, thought Kat, wondering if Maxwell was going to tell her what had happened.

'Where is Frederico?' hissed Veronique in Kat's ear, making her jump. She hadn't even noticed the vampire move from the other side of the room.

"Who?" Kat hoped she didn't sound too guilty. She was a rubbish liar, always had been.

"What did you do and your little friends do?" Veronique glanced over her shoulder, checking the room's attention was on Maxwell and not on her.

"Maybe you should tell your goons not to attack innocent women," Kat shot back and kinked out from under Veronique's imposing stance to go stand behind Maxwell's chair.

"I really need to talk to you," she whispered.

Maxwell inclined his head minutely but continued conversing with the other vampires. Out of the corner of her eye, Kat could see Veronique bristling with rage. It wasn't a good look, making her appear ugly for the first time. One of the ancient vampires noticed and elbowed the person next to him, leaning in to whisper. They both stared at Veronique. Finally realising she was under scrutiny, the woman whirled about angrily and stalked out of the boardroom. Her leaving was a catalyst for those left and soon the room was empty except for Kat and Maxwell. As the most ancient vampire had left, he had paused and patted Kat on the arm affectionately. Like you would pat a pet dog.

Maxwell looked better than before. Still pale and washed out, but more like normal.

"It went well?" asked Kat.

"What was it you wanted to tell me, Miss Kritchley?"

"I killed a vampire last night…"

Maxwell shot to the door, closing it with a thump, and dashed back to where she stood.

"Keep your voice down! What do you mean, you killed a vampire last night? Who?"

"I'm guessing Frederico, given Veronique's little chat with me just now, but honestly, I have no idea."

Maxwell pinched the bridge of his nose and took a deep breath, which surprised Kat. Vampires didn't breathe. She guessed it was a leftover human affectation.

"Tell me exactly what happened."

So she did. Kat explained the events, repeating things when Maxwell questioned her further and did her best to remember what the vampire had looked like before he went poof. By this point, they were both sat in chairs. Maxwell drummed his fingers on the boardroom table.

"It does sound like Frederico, but I don't think he was necessarily working on Veronique's orders. She's mad as hell about her jewellery having gone missing, but not at you or even Amelia. She's mad at the secret admirer. She is sure it's Giovanni, an on off paramour of hers. They're currently not together and are in the make each other mad stage of their relationship. I'm going to have to report this. A vampire death has to be logged anyway, and it's better for everyone that you came forward and owned up to what you did."

Kat bristled a little at that. It wasn't like she'd done it on purpose.

"Am I going to get into trouble?" she asked

Maxwell considered the question seriously.

"I don't think so. Magus Employment Services might not have the power they used to, but Xavier is well respected in the community and he has made it clear that you are one of his... employees. Perhaps you should return to the agency. Wait to hear from me whether we still require your services. You've been... a useful temp."

Kat guessed that was all the praise she was going to get and nodded, picking her bag up from the floor. It was with slightly less zip in her step that she followed Maxwell back to the building's foyer and left Luciano's, the bright sunshine making her eyes water.

Chapter 20

Kat pushed open the door of the agency, hoping to see Amelia's smiley face, but instead she was greeted with a grumpy-looking Flynn.

"What are you doing here?" they said in unison.

"I'm…" Both of them spoke again before each grinning at the other.

"You go," said Flynn.

Kat walked all the way into the drawing room and took the seat on the other side of Amelia's desk.

"Where's Amelia?" she asked instead of answering.

"Sick day, apparently. It's her first one ever, so must be something pretty serious," replied Flynn. "I'm covering the phones, but to be honest, it's been really quiet."

"Oh my god, is she alright?"

"I don't know, I haven't got any details."

"Maybe one of us should go round, make sure she's okay," mused Kat aloud.

"Consider yourself volunteered. Why are you here, anyway?" Flynn twirled a pen around his fingers, clearly riveted by his day so far.

"I told Maxwell about the vampire. He's got to report to the higher ups and will inform the agency if they still need me." Kat's insides squirmed a little. She wished she knew whether she was in trouble or not. Despite the fact that she killed a vampire, she didn't feel how she thought she ought to. There was no remorse. Her friend had been in danger and that was that. "He told me to come back here and wait for a phone call." For the first time, Kat considered the possibility that she might even lose her job. Her eyes pricked with tears.

Flynn cleared his throat and looked around. With obvious relief, he grabbed a box of tissues and handed them over.

"I'm, er… hey, everything will be all right. Xavier won't let anything happen to you. I'm sure." Flynn sounded about as convinced as he looked, but it made Kat smile a little.

He was obviously one of those blokes who panicked when a girl cried.

"Why do you call him Xavier?" she asked, blowing her nose as quietly as she could.

"It's a bit weird calling him Dad in the office." Flynn shrugged as if it were no big deal.

They sat in silence for a moment, Kat processing and drying her eyes while Flynn tried not to watch her. She decided to take advantage of the situation.

"Who's Mallory?"

Flynn stiffened, then let out a long, slow breath.

"She used to work here," he replied reluctantly.

"What happened to her?"

"You'll have to ask Xavier." Flynn's tone was curt. He clearly wasn't going to say anything else on the matter.

Kat sighed, packing the Mallory question away for now.

"Can you give me Amelia's address? If I don't have any work, I may as well go and see if she's alright." She frowned. "Does that mean I'm not getting paid right now?"

Flynn waved airily.

"You're on a retainer. We all are. Work ebbs and flows in our business, so Xavier likes to make sure we all get a base rate of pay to cover what he calls incidentals. Rent to you and me." And he chuckled.

Kat nodded, relieved. It would be a real kicker if she had to go home and tell her mum that she wasn't being paid for a little while.

"I'll take you to Amelia's if you like. On the bike. That way, at least I know you're not going to kill any more vampires. Too soon?"

Kat giggled. She couldn't help it. Nodding, she stood back up and waited for Flynn to grab his jacket. Leaving by the back door, Kat shivered, hoping it wasn't far to Amelia's place. The bright sunshine that had greeted her day had decided to hide behind some fast moving grey clouds. The last thing she needed today was to get soaking wet on the back of a motorbike.

Thankfully, it didn't take long. Waving goodbye to Flynn and laughing to herself as he revved the bike and shot off, Kat turned to look at the building Amelia lived in. It was a high-end complex with large luxurious flats. There was even a doorman. Impressed, Kat walked in and headed for the elevators. Predictably, Amelia's apartment was the penthouse, so she needed to travel all the way up.

The lighting was understated, the artwork on the walls was demure, and living plants were draped around the hallway tastefully. Being the penthouse, there was only one door. As Kat raised her hand to knock, she felt a little nervous, hoping Amelia wouldn't be cross that she'd just turned up. But Kat still didn't have Amelia's personal mobile number, only the one at the office. Kat knocked and waited.

She could hear a faint commotion and some banging from within before Amelia called out, *Just a minute!* The door opened and Kat gasped.

Chapter 21

A dragon stood in front of Kat.

She blinked.

No, it was Amelia. Of course, it wasn't a dragon. How would a dragon even fit in a doorway?

Amelia's form flicked before Kat's eyes. Wings and claws and scales winked in and out of existence.

"What is it? What do you see?" asked Amelia in a small voice.

"I see... um, I see... dragon?" Even as she said it, it sounded ridiculous, and Kat laughed nervously. "Can I come in?"

Amelia pulled the door open wider and Kat stepped through. The apartment looked amazing. It had colour and vibrancy and class. In fact, it looked exactly like a room you'd expect to find in a glossy magazine.

"Wow, this place is awesome," complimented Kat, as she spun around slowly to get a better look.

"Thank you. Do you want a drink? I've got tea, coffee, juice."

"Um, juice is fine. Thanks." Kat took a seat on one of the breakfast bar stools, not knowing it was the same one Amelia's mother had only recently sat on. "Hey, I came to check if you're alright. Flynn said you'd called in sick and you rushed off last night. And then..." She trailed off, not exactly sure how to mention the fact that Amelia was flicking between looking human and looking dragon. It was very disconcerting. A tail kept appearing.

But there was something fundamentally wrong with the dragon – it wasn't the right kind of dragon shape. It was way smaller. The wings looked ornamental rather than the type that you could fly with, and it was standing upright with perfectly proportioned arms and legs. All the images Kat had ever seen of a dragon did not look like that. Plus, it was a blurry overlay. The more it happened, the more Kat realised Amelia herself wasn't changing – it was Kat's perception. And when Amelia walked past a mirror whilst projecting dragon, she was all human.

Amelia perched on a chair on the opposite side of Kat, adopting the same defensive posture as earlier.

"Are you horrified?" she asked finally.

"No! Why would I be horrified?"

"Because I'm so scaly!" wailed Amelia, collapsing into a sobbing heap on the breakfast bar.

Kat dithered for a minute, not knowing exactly what to do. She spied a box of tissues, grabbed them and came around to Amelia's side. Putting the tissues down, she gently stroked Amelia's hair.

"Hey, you're not that scaly. And it's really pretty."

Amelia sniffed and lifted her tear-stained face.

"Do you really think so?"

"I really do," replied Kat, opening her arms for a hug. She wasn't usually a huggy person, but from the moment she'd met Amelia, she'd liked her. Kat didn't like seeing her friend upset.

Amelia squeezed Kat painfully, making her exhale with an oof.

"But what are you doing here?" Amelia asked, releasing her and pulling the stool out from under the table so they could sit side by side. "Shouldn't you be at Luciano's?"

"They sent me home."

"And you came to check on me." Amelia looked like she was going to burst into tears again, but instead, she squeezed Kat's hand.

"Why am I seeing… things?" Kat asked.

Amelia took a deep breath in and slumped a little as she breathed out. She chewed the side of her lip, clearly looking for the right words.

"Are you a dragon?" Kat tried to be helpful.

"I will be." Amelia smiled ruefully. "I come from an ancient lineage of dragons, but over the centuries, my kind has learned how to blend in with humanity and certain aspects of our dragoness have been lost. I appear human enough. Intense emotions can trigger occasional physical changes, but we're talking glowing eyes, that sort of thing. Not what you're seeing." She sighed.

"Hey, it's okay. I think being a sort of dragon is kind of cool."

"Well, good. Because I am your dragon."

There was a long pause as Kat digested this.

"What do you mean, *my* dragon?"

Amelia flushed and looked away, pursing her lips. Tears forming in her eyes.

"You don't have to be. I mean, I don't even know what we're talking about here, but you don't have to be anyone's dragon if you don't want to," said Kat.

Amelia pulled herself together.

"That's very sweet of you, but it's completely out of our hands now. Because you saved my life, my dragoness kicked in and I spoke the binding words. I am now your protector and I have unlocked my inner dragon." She took a deep, shuddering breath. "Once a month, I will fully transform. Into a real dragon. And the rest of the time I shall look like me but maybe a bit scalier."

Amelia looked so sad, Kat felt terrible.

"But what if I release you somehow? Would that

help? Then you can not turn into a dragon once a month."

Amelia was crying now, tears falling silently down her face.

"The only way to break the oath is for you to die."

Kat sat in stunned silence. Amelia reached out to hold her hand and the two women sat in joint misery. They were quiet for a long time.

"Will you always flicker for me?" Kat asked finally.

"No. It's just my dragon coming out for the first time. Only magical people will be able to see it. I've always been a magical being. The dragon magic was lurking beneath the surface and I could even use it a little, to strengthen wards that sort of thing, but now... now I'll be an actual dragon."

Kat sighed. A few weeks ago she'd been broke and jobless, now she'd turned her new friend into a dragon, destroyed a vampire with magic she didn't even know she had and all the things she thought lived in fairy tales were coming to life before her eyes.

"What are we going to do?" she asked Amelia.

"How do you mean?"

"Once a month we're going to have to look after you – protect you and keep you safe. I'm assuming we have a month to find the perfect place for you to change. Mr Magus must have some ideas. We should go and see him. Make a plan."

Once more Amelia's eyes filled with tears, but this time, they were happy ones.

"Oh, Katerina! You really are the best friend a dragon could ask for." And once more, Amelia nearly squeezed the life out of Kat in a huge dragon hug.

Chapter 22

Amelia and Kat had walked back to the agency. They'd both fancied a bit of fresh air and strolled arm in arm into town. They hadn't needed to speak, comfortable in their new relationship of human and dragon protector. Each processing what that might actually mean in the real world.

Pushing open the door to the agency, Flynn was nowhere to be seen, and the telephone was ringing. Instantly Amelia rushed to answer it, muttering about the inadequacy of leather-clad biker boys. Kat grinned to herself and took a seat.

"Good afternoon, Magus Employment Services. How may we help?" Amelia sat poised with pen and paper. "Maxwell, so nice to hear from you. Uhuh. Yes. Of course. I'll tell her. Thank you."

Kat's heart sank. It sounded as if she'd lost her position at Luciano's which was annoying because she still had one box of filing to finish; she hadn't entered all the financial information into the handwritten ledger and the stock take had been abruptly interrupted at the discovery of the theft of Veronique's jewels. Plus, there were the unpaid invoices for the blood, which was rather alarming when you considered the fact that supply might be cut. She didn't like leaving things unfinished. Even at a vampire filled solicitor's office.

"They want you to come back tomorrow as normal. Maxwell said you are a useful distraction." Amelia smiled.

Kat sat back in her chair, surprised.

"Wait, a useful distraction? What does that mean?"

"It means you need to be on your guard, but I think

you can take care of yourself," said Amelia.

"And if not, I've got my protector." Kat wondered what it would be like to have Amelia literally swoop into Luciano's and kick ass. "Hey, do you breathe fire?"

"I have no idea." Amelia's fingers tap tap tapped on the desk. "I guess we'd better add fire-proofing to the list." She looked at Mr Magus's closed door. "Are you ready?"

Kat nodded, hoping she appeared a good deal more confident than she felt. She really had no idea how Mr Magus was going to react. She barely knew the man, despite all the kindness he had shown her so far. She followed Amelia to the closed door and smiled encouragingly as her friend knocked.

"Come."

They pushed the door open and entered Mr Magus's office.

"Amelia, Katerina. What can I do for you?" Then he frowned and took his glasses off to peer more closely at Amelia. "Were you aware your, er... dragon is showing, my dear?"

Then he looked at Kat, and realisation dawned on his face.

"Ah. Flynn told me you saved Amelia's life last night. Well done. Saving someone is a wonderful way to help unlock your power. I understand Luciano's will be keeping the contract for now."

Amelia nodded and Kat wondered how Mr Magus knew that. Did he listen in on the phone calls or was it some kind of mystical power?

"And you spoke the blood oath." It wasn't a question. For a brief moment, Mr Magus looked sad.

It was so quick, Kat thought she'd imagined it as he clapped his hands together and rubbed them briskly.

"We need a plan," he announced.

"That's what I said." Kat was relieved. "We need somewhere Amelia can change safely once a month. Do you know anywhere nearby?"

"The catacombs in the Underbelly are the obvious choice, but we'll have to check with the undead that they don't mind."

The undead mouthed Kat with a shudder. She did not like the sound of that.

"I think it would be best coming from you direct, but with the full support of the agency, of course. I shall write a letter. Flynn will accompany you." Mr Magus bent to his desk, pulling forward a quill, ink, and parchment. Then he looked up again. "Perhaps Connor ought to come as well. Safety in numbers."

The room was quiet as he scratched a letter of introduction. He sprinkled some fine sand across the ink and leaned back to soften a block of wax in the fire. Rolling the letter up, he splodged the wax, pressing his signet ring into it to seal the letter. Satisfied with the outcome, he passed it over to Amelia.

"Tell the chaps to meet you around ten tonight. No need to go too early, but best to be out of there by midnight. Two hours should be ample time to state your case." Mr Magus smiled at them, but there was a finality to his tone that suggested they leave his office.

"Thank you, sir," said Amelia, clutching the letter and backing away from the desk.

Kat followed in her wake, desperate to ask about a million questions, but was forestalled by that at the appearance of Veronique at Amelia's desk.

What now? groaned Kat internally. She really, really needed to find out about the undead. The other undead.

"Hello Veronique. How may we help you?" asked

Amelia in a soft, polite voice.

Kat blinked in surprise. This was the creature that had set an assassin on Amelia and triggered her dragon. Why wasn't she being more aggressive? Kat sure felt angry. She went and stood behind Amelia at her desk, hoping that she was projecting protective vibes and not looking like she was trying to put as much distance between herself and Veronique.

"I had a visit from your mother," said Veronique in clipped tones. "I came to accept your apology for the unintended possession of my jewels."

Kat snorted. Surely Veronique should have been apologising for trying to kill Amelia.

"Thank you. That's very gracious of you," replied Amelia, cocking her head slightly to one side, allowing Veronique the opportunity to say more.

"Should the secret nature of your admirer be revealed, I trust you will inform me immediately?"

Amelia inclined her head.

"I will not stop my investigations. But words have been said."

Kat guessed that was the best apology they were going to get from the bloodsucker.

"I appreciate that. May Magus Employment Services assist you in any further capacity?"

Veronique sneered at Amelia's words and, in response, turned and glided quickly out of the building. As always, Kat was surprised at the turn of speed.

"That was weird," she said.

"Agreed. I can't imagine why Mother would go speak to the vampires on my behalf. But at least that is all behind us now."

"Hmm." Kat wasn't so sure. "Don't you want to know who your secret admirer was?"

"Not anymore. I suspect my involvement was all part of a vampire plot. They are always jockeying for position and status. The ancient ones encourage them. They take performance reviews very seriously."

Kat nodded. She'd witnessed that for herself.

"Right, about these other undead. What do I need to know?"

Chapter 23

Amelia had made Kat wait for her to brew some tea, promising it wasn't the mood altering one. Once she was satisfied and they both had cups, she began to explain.

"So, as you can imagine, the undead are something a little bit different in our world. When ordinary humans die, that's it. Unless necromancy is involved, but we won't cover that one today. It's rare, anyway." Amelia took a sip of tea, oblivious to the look of horror on Kat's face.

"We have the vampires but they are in a league of their own and they certainly don't live in the catacombs or the Underbelly, that's what it's called. Except for the banished ones. Those vampires do live in the Underbelly. But they keep to themselves. Mostly." Amelia sighed. "There's going to be a lot of exceptions in the explanation."

"That's fine. Life is messy, I get that. If we all fit into neat little boxes, it would be super boring. Just tell me the gist. What can I expect?"

"Zombies, mummies, lurches, fades, ghosts, liches, animated skeletons, wights, banshees, ghouls, revenants, golem, wraiths, the banished. Oh, and Death."

The way Amelia said it, there was definitely a capital letter.

"Death?"

"Yes. Human belief is a powerful thing. It sustains so many monsters, and it also sustains an anthropomorphic version of Death. It's sad because it wants to reap but cannot. Death Death deals with it. You'd think they could job share, but it's best not to get involved with the undead. Unless you qualify, of course.

There's a complicated hierarchical system, and no one seems to have written it down. Plus, we try not to spend too much time in the Underbelly, if we can help it."

Kat's head was reeling. She'd expected to be greeted with the unexpected now that the veil had been lifted between the normal world and the magical, but... this was a lot. She wasn't even sure she knew what all the creatures Amelia had listed were.

"We don't have to worry too much. The undead don't like visitors, so there's usually someone on guard at the entrance. We should be able to put in our request and have it taken to the appropriate authority." Amelia seemed utterly unruffled at the thought of begging for a place to shapeshift once a month amongst the undead.

Kat tried to emulate her calmness.

"Who is in charge, anyway? And how big are the catacombs?"

Amelia made a dismissive gesture.

"No one really knows. How big it is, I mean. They've never been mapped, but they are ancient. Creatures of the night have always needed a safe space. Bless them, the humans get so excited when they stumble upon a section. It absolutely blows their mind. Imagine if they knew that what they'd found was a mere scratch on the surface." Amelia laughed, but Kat could only half smile. She hadn't quite got used to being a magical human yet. "As for who is in charge... I'm not sure. Depends. As I said, it's a complicated hierarchy."

Kat sipped her rapidly cooling tea, trying to marshal her thoughts. Amelia handed her a piece of paper.

"Here, I'm so sorry you didn't get given this before. It's everyone's mobile phone numbers."

Kat looked and saw numbers for Amelia, Flynn and Connor. There wasn't one for Mr Magus, but that was to be expected. Based on what she'd noticed so far, it was highly unlikely that he even owned a mobile phone. Not even a basic brick phone. She entered them into her phone, feeling a little better that she had another method of getting hold of Amelia and feeling a small tickle at putting Connor in her phone. She actually already had Flynn's from their first meeting at the Chinese takeaway. She supposed everyone must have hers now as well.

"Yes. Ten pm at the North Street entrance. It's the easiest one to access."

"Sorry?" Kat looked up, but Amelia wasn't talking to her. She was on the phone. There was a pause.

"Yes, weapons might be a good idea. Okay darling, see you later!"

She must have been talking to Flynn, thought Kat, wondering if the two of them had ever... hung out.

"That's Connor all sorted. Can you call Flynn? He's screening calls from the office, but he'll answer you."

Flustered, Kat looked up Flynn's number and pressed the call button. He answered almost immediately.

"Hi. It's Kat," she said at the exact time Flynn said *Hi Kat*. There was nervous laughter on both sides.

What can I do for you?

"Um, we're going to the catacombs? Tonight. At ten pm and your dad, I mean Mr Magus, wanted you to come with us. Me and Amelia. Safety in numbers and everything. Um, we're going to see if they'll give her some space because..." Kat trailed off, realising that Flynn didn't know Amelia had turned into a dragon yet.

Are you asking me out, Miss Kritchley?

"No! I mean, this is a work thing." Kat could feel herself blushing. "Connor's coming," she blurted, and the line went quiet.

Which entrance?

All the humour had gone out of Flynn's voice, making Kat's inside squirm.

"Um…" she looked up at Amelia, having completely forgotten where they were going and was relieved when she mouthed the answer. "North Street. The North Street entrance. Ten pm."

OK.

And he clicked off. Kat stared at her phone. She hadn't meant to upset Flynn deliberately by saying Connor's name. She'd been flustered at the date comment and how quickly he'd answered the phone.

"They really don't get on, do they?"

"Who?" asked Amelia.

"Flynn and Connor. What's the deal?" Kat leaned forward, hoping Amelia would dish the dirt.

"It's a bit sad, really. They were best friends. Grew up together, in each other's pockets, really. Mr Magus sort of took him in as a ward. The boys attended the same school, all that. It was when Connor turned fifteen that things began to change." Amelia looked sad. "It's not really my story to tell, but I guess the dynamic changed. Things were said. The kind of things that are silly now when you look back at it, but at the time, they were said with anger and pain. Both boys are stubborn. Neither one will give in and take the blame or extend an apology and now it seems every little thing they do becomes intensely annoying to the other."

Kat knew what that was like. That was exactly how she and her mum always fought. Blowing up over the smallest thing and then being stupid mad at each other for no reason for ages. They always forgave each other in the end, though. Maybe Connor and Flynn could do the same.

"You can go home if you like. Get some rest before tonight. Wear something warm. It can get chilly in the catacombs," said Amelia.

"Do I need to bring any weapons?" joked Kat.

"Oooh, what have you got? Anything good?" Amelia cocked her head on one side and Kat began to stammer a reply before she saw the amused twinkle in her eye.

"I guess I'll just bring myself," she smiled.

"See you later," called Amelia as Kat let herself out of the agency, heading home, wondering what she was going to tell her mum this time.

Chapter 24

Kat made her mum a cup of hot chocolate. She knew, and her mum would know, that she was trying to make amends.

"Thanks, love," said Dolores, eyebrows rising at the contents of the mug.

"Sorry about snapping at you."

"Likewise."

They sat quietly, each one slowly unbending and forgiving each other.

"How's work?" asked Dolores, offering the ultimate olive branch.

"Er… I left early today. Maxwell said he'd have to report the um… the…" Kat couldn't think of the right word.

"Vanquishment."

"Er… yeah, that. But then they called back and told me I could return as normal tomorrow, so I guess everything is alright." Kat squirmed a little. "Is it okay that I don't feel bad? I thought I would. Feel bad, I mean. But I don't."

Dolores nodded, showing her understanding of Kat's predicament.

"I think what you have to say to yourself is they are not human. You are not deliberately taking a life. You were protecting your friend. A vampire would not hesitate to end you and believe there was absolutely nothing wrong with their actions. You must remember, they are not human."

"Did you know about Amelia?" asked Kat, changing tack but grateful for her mum's support and agreement.

"What about her?"

"Well... she's a dragon and my protector."

Dolores's mouth actually fell open in surprise.

"A dragon! Oh, that explains so much. She was always such a magpie, attracted to anything and everything glittery. But why is she only a dragon now?"

"When I rescued her the other night, she spoke a blood vow? Apparently that unlocked her dragoness and know she's going to change once a month into a huge winged beast!" Kat wailed a little on that last part, tears escaping, finally allowing her emotions to catch up to her and letting it all go.

Dolores wheeled her chair as close to Kat as she could get and gave her the best hug she could manage. It wasn't perfect, but it was enough and Kat cried out her fear and worry and guilt over what she'd done to Amelia.

"Hey, hey, don't cry. Come on. Amelia's a tough cookie. She can cope with this. I'm sure Xavier has a plan."

Kat blew her nose loudly and wiped her face dry.

"He does. We're going to the catacombs tonight. Me, Amelia, Flynn and Connor. We're going to go speak to the undead about renting some space."

She waited with bated breath to see what her mum's reaction would be.

Dolores pushed herself away from her daughter, her hands fluttering a little.

"Oh Kat. It's not safe down in the Underbelly. The undead are... well, they're a league of their own. Do you have to go? Can't the others deal with it? I'd much rather you stayed here."

Kat was touched, and a little relieved. Her mum hadn't flown off the handle screaming and shouting at her. In fact, even though she was questioning whether or not Kat had to go, she wasn't saying she couldn't, and that was practically giving her permission.

"There's something you should have. It belonged to your father. It will protect you."

"Oh, I have this…" Kat pulled out the amulet Amelia had given her, showing it to her mum.

"Pfft. That is as much use as a chocolate teapot. This has real power." Dolores wheeled over to the locked cabinet in the far corner of her room. The one Kat and Mikey weren't allowed anywhere near. She pulled on the necklace around her neck, lifting a key from beneath her top. Kat stared. She'd never noticed that before.

Kat craned her neck to get a better look, but her mum effectively blocked her view, secretively opening the cabinet and retrieving one thing. It looked like a black gift box but without any ribbons or bows.

"One day you're going to show me what else is in there," said Kat softly.

"One day."

Dolores held out the box for Kat to take it. She looked at her mum for confirmation. Dolores gestured, a little reluctantly, for Kat to open the box. Inside nestled a ring. It looked like the cheap mood rings you got at the fair. Kat's heart sank. That wasn't exactly what she'd been expecting.

"Don't be deceived. Yes, it looks like a cheap mood ring, but I promise you, it's the most powerful piece of protective jewellery you'll ever come across."

Kat looked sceptical. Unwilling fingers took the ring out the box and turned it over. There was nothing about it to suggest it was a ring of power in any way, shape or form, but it was pleasant in her hands and she had a sudden urge to put it on.

A whoosh of heat and light ran through her. She felt

like she'd run a marathon, climbed a mountain and won the lottery all at once. It was so fast, she half thought she'd dreamed it and looked down at the ring in wonder.

"You felt something?" asked her mum.

"You didn't see it?"

Dolores shook her head.

"I'm completely unmagical," she said ruefully. "What time are you meeting the others?"

Kat was still regarding the ring in wonder.

"Katerina! What time are you meeting the others?" repeated her mother.

"Oh, er, ten pm," she replied distractedly.

"Help me do some dinner, then. We can eat together." Dolores shushed her daughter out of her room and into the kitchen. It was too small for them both to be in there at the same time, but Dolores did a great job of directing Kat and very soon, steaming bowls of veggie noodles were ready to eat.

"Mikey! Come and get it!" called Kat as she pulled the small dining table out in the front room. It was a foldaway one that clipped to the wall and ideal for their needs. Two small stools were stacked in one corner.

"Chop chop!" exclaimed Mikey when he saw the dinner and disappeared into the kitchen to get chopsticks. He loved eating with them.

When they were all seated, Mikey kept lifting his hand up and pinching things out of the air near Kat. He wasn't looking at her while he was doing it. It was almost as if he wasn't aware of what he was doing.

"Mikey! Stop it!"

Every time he pinched the air, he made Kat flinch, and she was beginning to get annoyed.

"Chop chop," he replied quietly, his whole focus on his noodles utterly unaware of what he was doing.

Dolores watched him with a worried frown, but smiled brightly at Kat when she looked at her in exasperation.

"It's just Mikey. Ignore him."

Kat grumbled to herself and shifted her stool closer to her mum. Mikey stopped pinching the air immediately. *Maybe I was too close to his personal space,* thought Kat, putting his strange behaviour out of her mind. After all, it was nothing new for Mikey to be a little odd.

Chapter 25

Kat tapped her foot on the pavement, waiting impatiently for Amelia. She wasn't even late. But Kat was equal part nervous, scared and excited about going to meet the undead. She had a million questions, but didn't really know where to start in asking them.

After what seemed like ages, a BMW drew up to the curb. Amelia opened the rear passenger door. This was the second time she'd arrived with a driver. Kat wondered if she knew how to drive.

"Sorry! Had a dragon thing. Get in, get in. The boys are going to meet us there."

Kat wanted to ask what the dragon thing was, but before she had the chance, Amelia launched into her explanation.

"Some things you should be aware of now that I'm your protector. Working at the agency was deeply frowned upon by my family. Mother did not approve. It was Mr Magus's interference in the end that kept me in my position. No one disagrees with Mother. As far as she is concerned, a dragon does not work. Ever. I know, I know, you're thinking, how do we live if we don't work? Well, we're rich. Like stupidly. Centuries ago, that's what we dragons did. We hoarded gold and jewels and we were very, very good at it."

Kat tried to imagine Amelia hoarding gold. It wasn't actually that much of a leap.

"Now, lots of people say we're thieves because we stole the gold from people, but it wasn't our fault that people collected it for us and then reneged on their word. It was a whole other life back then. Not like it is now. Now there are investments and stock markets. We can hoard more than gold."

Amelia's eyes were glinting and Kat thought back on what she'd just said.

"I'm sorry, you said we and our. You mean like, the family, like some kind of dragon mafia lineage that stretches through time, right?"

"Ooooh, dragon mafia. I like that. And yeah, sort of."

Her avoidance of the topic made Kat even more suspicious.

"How old are you, Amelia?"

"Bit of a personal question."

"Not really. We are friends. And I did save your life…"

Amelia huffed a little, checking the rear-view mirror as she drove along the deserted street.

"Fine. I'm three-hundred and twelve, but it's hardly any age at all."

Kat was stunned into silence. Three hundred and twelve!

Amelia regarded her.

"Aren't you going to say something?"

"Um… you look great for your age?"

The two girls stared at each other before both breaking out into slightly hysterical laughter.

"Oh my days. Stop it, you'll make me smudge my mascara," wheezed Amelia, laughing so much she was nearly crying. "We're here."

They were both still giggling when they got out of the car by North Street Cemetery and were met by Flynn and Connor, standing on opposite sides of the cemetery gates.

"What's so funny?" asked Connor with a grin of his own.

132

"Nothing," chimed both girls, which set them off again, and it took a moment for them both to collect themselves.

"When you've quite finished, we've got an appointment to keep." Flynn sounded as clipped as his dad in a bad mood, which made the corners of Kat's mouth twitch, but she managed to keep her mirth in.

Pushing open the heavy gates, Flynn led the way to the midpoint of the cemetery. Kat looked around in apprehension and interest. The last time she'd been around death, she'd been too young to understand what was going on. Her over active imagination and watching too many supernatural TV shows more than made up for it. She was a bit disappointed when Flynn stopped walking.

"There's nothing here," she said. "All the crypts are over there, aren't they?"

"Yes, but we don't want human remains. This is where we need to be. Who's doing the sacrifice?" asked Flynn.

Kat blanched. No one had said anything about a sacrifice.

"It's my request, so I'll do it," offered Amelia, and she held her hand out.

Flynn slashed at her hand, making Kat gasp in horror.

"What are you doing?"

"Relax, she's already healing."

Tears in her eyes, Kat looked, and it was true. The slash across the palm of Amelia's hand had bled on the ground, but already her injury was beginning to heal itself.

"Are you alright?" whispered Kat, feeling massively out of her depth.

"Of course I am. Look."

Kat turned her attention back to the ground where Amelia had bled. It had started to cave in on itself, forming a series of muddy steps that led down into the earth.

"We're going down there." Kat had deep misgivings.

"Yep." Flynn took the lead once more, with Amelia not far behind him.

"Come on, it's not as bad as you think it's going to be. Promise." Connor stood close to Kat. She could sense the heat of his body through her clothes.

With a partially suppressed squeak, Kat began walking down the mud steps. They were actually a lot more solid than she thought they would be, given that they'd just appeared. The air was dry and her eyes adjusted quickly to the gloom. There was some kind of luminescence on the walls which gave everything an eerie glow. The steps had become a hallway of sorts. They were definitely underground, but instead of dirt, there was stone. This was the catacombs.

Chapter 26

Kat looked around with a touch of morbid curiosity. She had imagined she would see bones littered about the place or hear the gut wrenching groan of a zombie. Adrenalin had been coursing through her at the thought of having to fight the undead, but now there was no one here. She stifled an unexpected yawn, wondering if the evening was going to be a bust.

"How will they know we're here?" she asked.

"Oh, they know we're here. Fresh meat." Flynn grinned evilly at her.

"Don't be a meanie. Only magical people can get access to the catacombs, and when one of us enters, it sets off a sort of pulse. Someone will no doubt be along to see us shortly." Amelia sounded completely at ease and was looking around calmly.

Connor was fiddling with a random pen lid he must have had in his pocket. The only outward sign that he was nervous. It made Kat feel a little better. She walked closer to him.

"Have you been here before?"

"Cute pickup line," he replied.

"No! I wasn't, I mean, I didn't…" Kat trailed off, realising Connor was laughing at her. "Ha ha. Very funny. I just meant, have you been down to the catacombs before?"

Connor bumped shoulders with her to show he didn't mean it.

"Yeah, once or twice. Lots of strange folk down here. It'll be interesting to see who they send to speak to us. There's a hierarchy…"

Kat interrupted.

"Yeah, Amelia said. It's complicated. Apparently."

"You got that right. With so many different types of undead creature, they all have some kind of leader or at least a representative and they all need a voice at the Council."

"The Council?"

"Oh right, right. You don't know about that, do you? Being all new to this. Well…" But before Connor could launch into any kind of explanation, there were half a dozen vampires arranged around them.

These weren't the slick, fashionable vampires Kat had met at Luciano's. These looked starved. Their eyes glowed red, fangs down, claws out, ready to feast on the fresh blood that had walked into their den. She moved slightly closer to Connor.

"Don't move!" he hissed.

All six vampires cocked their head at Kat, staring at her like she was their next meal.

Amelia clapped her hands loudly, making Kat jump, but it took the hungry attention off her for now.

"Now, now. The Exiled are not allowed to hunt visitors. We seek an audience and we will defend ourselves if necessary. Can you run along and tell whomsoever is in charge that we are here, please."

Her voice was laced with saccharine and Kat felt sure the vampires would ignore her politeness and descend upon the lot of them, ripping them all limb from limb. Instead, they inclined their head as one and as fast as they had appeared, they went.

Flynn let out a breath.

"I thought we were goners for a minute, then." He exchanged relieved grins with Connor before the pair of them realised what they were doing. They were soon replaced by their usual frowns.

"I think we should form up in a protective stance, Kat in the middle. Where there are six Exiles, there are likely to be more," ordered Amelia.

She put herself front and centre, which Kat guessed made sense. She was, after all, a dragon. The lads flanked her, and Kat felt a bit foolish following them. What if someone snatched her from behind? The thought brought prickles to her neck, and she had to force herself to turn around and make sure there was nobody there. There wasn't, but the shadows looked deep and dark.

Then came the noises. Hoots and hollers. Wails and excited yips. The sound of many feet travelling towards them at speed. The team braced themselves as a motley group of things poured out of several tunnel openings and fanned out around them, encircling them completely.

There were the exiled vampires plus others, Kat could recognise the zombies. They looked exactly as they did in the movies, only more intelligence shone out of their eyes. Which was probably why they hadn't immediately rushed at them trying to eat their brains. She couldn't put names to much else. There were huge men made of stone and pure white women with red mouths and black hair, people dressed in dark robes that completely covered everything and what looked like a group of beings who had drowned but not died. She could still hear shuffling coming from down the corridor. Finally, they appeared. The mummies. And they were carrying some kind of throne. Atop it sat Cleopatra. Or at least what the history books said Cleopatra looked like.

"Ooooh, this isn't good," whispered Connor in Kat's direction. "The mummies are in charge. They are buggers to deal with."

But before Kat had a chance to whisper back and ask why, Amelia genuflected gracefully at the current leader of the undead. Flynn and Connor dropped to one knee, fist to shoulder, leaving Kat exposed and embarrassed. No idea what she should do. She settled for a quick bob. The kind she'd seen servants do on those upstairs, downstairs period drama programmes on TV. It seemed to be enough for now. At a gesture from the Egyptian Queen, the others rose.

"Why are you here?"

The Queen did not speak. It was one of her mummy attendants.

"We come seeking use of a refuge. I have a letter from Mr Magus," explained Amelia, holding out the scroll.

It fitted in much more now than it had in the agency office earlier that day. A frisson of excited energy ran around the room at the mention of Mr Magus. Clearly, he was well known among the undead.

At the tiniest flick of Cleo's pinkie finger, one of the mummies shuffled forwards to take the scroll from Amelia. She bowed deeply, offering it up to the mummy as if it were an important historical artefact. Kat had to fight to not smile.

The mummy passed the scroll to Cleo who unrolled it, a bored expression on her face. She scanned the contents and dropped the scroll to the floor.

"You ask a lot for someone who is not undead. For someone who owes the undead a great deal."

Kat watched as Amelia stiffened. It seemed the ancestral hoarding was still a bit of an issue.

"But we don't hold grudges. You can have your safe space here in the Underbelly if you get rid of a vampire problem for us." Cleo cocked her index finger this time and the six Exiles who'd rushed them before reappeared. "They don't belong here. They have been exiled for forbidden drinking, but their supply was cut off at the source. This is not justice working. This is a power play. Pieces are being moved, and the game rewritten. Uncover the culprit and have the exiles reinstated. Then you may have your lair."

Kat gulped. That didn't give them much time to figure out what was going on, but if Cleo was talking about a cut off blood supply that might have something to do with the unpaid invoices Kat had uncovered.

"I accept your terms and thank you for your audience. We will leave last, as is the custom." The way Amelia spoke the words, they had a small challenge to them.

Kat didn't think them leaving last was a real custom, but Cleo seemed to accept the reasoning. It wouldn't do to have any undead crawling out after them. The very thought made Kat shiver.

In no time at all, they were alone once more. By mutual consent, they were all quiet as they quickly left the way they'd come in. No one spoke as they exited the cemetery as fast as they could, all of them bundling into Amelia's car.

"Well, I don't know about you lot, but I need a bloody drink," said Amelia.

Chapter 27

Flynn had dropped Amelia's driver off and now parked the car in the dark foreboding carpark of a pub Kat had never seen before. She got out and peered around. There were no working lights and only one or two other cars. Trees lined three sides of the car park, closing them in.

"Is this a magic pub?" Kat asked.

"No," Amelia giggled. "Not everything is magical. This is just a pub where no one asks any questions." She regarded Flynn and Connor. "And probably the only one where these two reprobates are allowed in. Come on. Come and meet Daisy. She owns The WigWam."

WigWam? mouthed Kat. What an odd name for a pub.

They entered via a side door and walked immediately through an eighties beaded curtain. A shiver passed through Kat as the beads clacked over her. A thick set man gave Amelia a nod and jotted something down in a small notebook he had. The beads clacked again as Flynn and Connor pushed through, each one trying hard not to let the other go first but also not seem like they were doing so deliberately. The bouncer, or at least that's what Kat assumed he was, held up a hand and pointed to a wicker basket on the floor.

Flynn muttered something under his breath and dropped a couple of knives into the basket. He took a step, but the bouncer eased himself off his stool to standing and raised an eyebrow. A smile twitched Flynn's lips, and he added a set of knuckle dusters and another knife from his boot. Connor strolled on past. Disbelief flashed across Flynn's face as the bouncer sat back on his stool, making no effort to stop Connor. Kat was surprised. Surely, Connor must have some weapons on him as well. From her brief experience in the catacombs, she didn't think fists would have got them very far.

"Kat, Daisy. Daisy, this is our newest recruit. Kat Kritchley."

A tall, willowy woman stood behind the bar. She had long silvery braids that were caught up in a loose ponytail, threatening to escape at any moment. Something about her didn't seem real and, for a brief instant, pointy ears peeped through the braids. Kat stared.

At the mention of her surname, Daisy's eyebrows rose, and she regarded Kat. Then she extended one hand over the bar. They shook. Her hand felt cool and smooth to Kat.

"Welcome to The WigWam, love. Nice to finally meet Kieron's daughter. You've the look of him."

Kat was flustered. It used to be that she rarely met anyone who knew her dad. These days, it seemed that everyone did.

"Why is it called The WigWam?" she blurted, wanting to say something, but her mind veering away from the obvious question of how Daisy knew her dad.

"Ah, an excellent question. This is a place of meeting and peace." She smiled as she said it, and Kat could feel her tensions drain away. "Go find a booth. I'll bring you some drinks."

Amelia half dragged Kat away from the bar and over to a cosy booth near the fire, Connor and Flynn following.

"I thought you said this wasn't a magic pub!" hissed Kat.

"It's not," replied Amelia blithely. "It's a regular,

normal building. The people who run the pub, well, that's a whole other kettle of fish."

Kat glared at her, feeling put out at being the butt of the joke.

"You knew what I meant," she muttered, pouting a little.

"Oh, don't be cross. I was only teasing. I wanted you to get the full experience. Isn't it just darling?"

Kat nodded begrudgingly. There was certainly something about The WigWam that made you feel completely at ease.

"So, this is a supernatural pub then," she tried again.

"Normals can come in and they usually have a great time, but then they forget where exactly they had that great night out. It becomes a beautiful memory," explained Connor. "This is a safe place for people like us. We can be ourselves." His voice grew serious. "More or less."

"Yeah, absolutely. Feel free to lie by the fire if that's what you want," joked Flynn, only there was a harsh edge to his tone.

Connor's face darkened, and he dropped his gaze.

"Boys, enough!" snapped Amelia just as Daisy came over with the drinks.

She put the tray down smoothly and then smacked both Flynn and Connor lightly round the ear.

"The WigWam is no place for your spat. Keep it up and you'll be outside for the foreseeable." Daisy looked from Flynn to Connor, making sure they understood she meant it. Satisfied, she nodded. "Enjoy your drinks."

Daisy had brought them all some warm spiced cider. It smelled amazing and Kat cupped her hands eagerly around her glass, savouring the first sip. They were all quiet as everyone enjoyed the drink.

"Would she really bar you? And how come she knew exactly what kind of drink we needed?"

"Yes, Xavier's barred from The WigWam and Daisy will not relent and let him back in," said Flynn.

"No way!" breathed Kat. "What did he do?"

"No idea," shrugged Flynn but clearly enjoying Kat's amazement. "He won't tell me. But at least I can have a drink here without the old man busting in."

"And Daisy knows what to serve you because she's an elf," said Connor.

Kat's mouth dropped open, and she darted a glance to the bar where Daisy was busy talking to another customer.

"An actual elf? Like from fairy tales?"

There was a sharp intake of breath from everyone else in the booth.

"Never mention the fairies to Daisy," warned Amelia.

Kat's brow furrowed, and she took another sip of her spiced cider.

"You know, since I came to work for you guys, my life has got ridiculously confusing. I feel like I need to go to a special magic school just to learn about all the different people that now live in my world. How do you guys keep on top of it all?"

"Um, we've never known anything different?" replied Flynn, sounding confused.

"Right, you've never been normal," said Kat, not thinking.

Connor barked a laugh.

"You've got that right!"

Flynn couldn't help but grin and the two of them thawed slightly at each other, their usual animosity quelled for the time being.

Kat was mortified.

"Oh no! I didn't mean it like that. I meant this world has always been here for you."

"It's fine. I knew what you meant." And he bumped shoulders with her, sending a tingle down into her tummy. "And there is a book that might be useful. Your dad was working on a field guide for people not inherently magical, like your mum. To dispel the myths and give you the facts. There should be a copy in Xavier's library."

Kat nodded. Having something like that would be great and not only for learning about her newly expanded existence. She had very little of her dads.

"That's a beautiful ring, Kat. Where did you get it?" asked Amelia, changing the subject.

Kat flexed her hand out to admire the ring, having completely forgotten until that moment she wore it.

"It was my Dad's. Mum gave it to me for protection."

"You told her we were going to the catacombs and she let you go?" Flynn sounded shocked.

"Of course I told her. I don't keep secrets. And why wouldn't she let me go?"

Amelia shook her head minutely at Flynn, but Kat caught the motion.

"What? What are you not telling me?"

There was an awkward silence, as no one was willing to talk about it. Finally, Connor spoke.

"Your dad's accident… it was down in the catacombs."

Kat sat stunned for a moment.

"What? No, it wasn't. It was a road traffic accident. That's how mum lost her legs. It was… it was…" Realisation came crashing down on her. Of course, it

144

had been a magical accident. Of course it was. Knowing what she knew now, there was no way her dad had died in a run-of-the-mill traffic accident. Her mum had lied to her for years. Years!

Blind anger rose through her and she abruptly stood.

"I've got to…" But she didn't finish the sentence. She stalked out of the pub, leaving the others dumbfounded.

"Way to go, Connor," said Flynn.

"No, it wasn't his fault. She would've found out sooner or later," said Amelia softly.

"Should one of us go after her?" asked Connor, just as Daisy hurried over to them.

"Vampire pack, just landed in the carpark. Where's Kat?" She scanned the guilty faces. "You let her leave? It's not safe. Get out there!"

Everyone froze for a moment before there was a mad scramble to leave the booth and run out of the pub. Flynn was the slowest having to stop and gather his weapons, but the scene that greeted them outside was one of pure devastation.

Chapter 28

Kat blazed with light. Some of the vampires had scarpered, a couple were cringing on the edge of the carpark in the shadowy treeline while the rest were piles of dust around Kat.

"Why are we the muscle again?" asked Connor, before wincing when Amelia elbowed him.

"Kat?" she called. "Are you okay? Can you hear me? It's Amelia."

There was no response.

"I'm going to come to you now, okay?"

Again, nothing.

"Do you really think that's a good idea?" hissed Flynn. "What if she melts your face off?"

Amelia waved away the concern. She was, after all, a dragon. But still, even for a dragon, the heat rolling off Kat was intense and she couldn't make it all the way to her. Scowling, Amelia returned.

"You'd better call your dad," said Connor.

"But he's barred..." began Flynn, pulling his phone out.

"We're not in the pub right now and I don't know what else to do," snapped Amelia. "Connor, go back inside and tell Daisy we might need, we might need... well, I don't know! Just tell her."

Both of them jumped to it. Connor dashing into the pub and Flynn dialling.

"Dad? Yeah, um. No, that was okay. Well, mostly. But listen... Kat's sort of on fire. We think. She's blazing in the carpark of The WigWam and we can't get to her. You need to hurry. Okay."

Before Flynn had time to put his phone back in his

pocket, Mr Magus was strolling through a portal into the carpark. It was impressive magic and Flynn felt relieved to have him there.

"Xavier! What do we do?" wailed Amelia.

That made Flynn's eyebrows arch in surprise. He'd never heard Amelia call his dad anything other than Mr Magus.

Mr Magus didn't reply. Instead, he walked around Kat, as close as he could get without singeing his eyebrows. He peered at her face. He stirred his foot in the ashes on the floor. He looked at the vampires who were still at the edge of the carpark. It was only when Daisy came out of the pub that he returned to the others and spoke.

"Miss Everglade." He gave her a small bow, ever the perfect gentleman. "It seems Miss Kritchley is stuck. May I ask, was she angry when she entered the carpark?"

The red faces before him confirmed just that.

"Very well. I need you to link with me, please. Everyone. Chop chop." Mr Magus turned his back on them, facing Kat once more, and stuck his arms out on either side.

For a brief moment, nobody moved, then Amelia held one hand, Flynn the other. Connor moved quickly so he could hold Amelia's, leaving Daisy to take Flynn's. Mr Magus closed his eyes and took a deep breath.

As he breathed in, he delved for power. Daisy pulled away marginally before inclining her head in submission. Flynn leaned towards Xavier, used to pooling his power. Amelia began to glow, her scales shining through, and Connor growled. It was a low sound that vibrated throughout his body.

"I can't…" he gasped.

"Give in to the change," ordered Mr Magus, not even looking at him.

A whimper escaped from Connor as he dropped to his hands and knees, Amelia maintaining her hold on him. With a snarl, he transformed into a huge russet coloured wolf. Amelia twirled her fingers in his fur, shuddering as his animal magic joined her own.

"Focus!" snapped Mr Magus sharply and as one, they all took a step towards Kat. Then another. And another. With each step they took, her brightness dimmed, and the heat began to ebb away. By the time they reached her, the light went out, and she collapsed. Flynn barely caught her before she hit the floor. Kat's eyes were closed, her breathing shallow.

Sensing an opportunity, the vampires lunged forward faster than light. Mr Magus barely had time to react before Connor leaped bodily over Flynn and Kat, baring his teeth and growling loudly.

"If I were you, I'd leave," said Mr Magus, calmly brushing an invisible speck off his jacket sleeve. "It wouldn't do to start a fight you can't finish. Again."

The vampires snarled back at them but as one, darted to the left, giving them all a wide berth and vanishing into the night.

"You might consider strengthening the wards you have in place out here in the carpark, Miss Everglade. I would be happy to offer the agency services, if required."

It seemed like something unsaid passed between Mr Magus and Daisy. She touched his arm lightly. He clicked his heels together and gave her another bow.

"What about Kat? Should we take her to the hospital?" asked Amelia, hovering anxiously.

Mr Magus shook his head.

"She's had a massive expenditure of energy that she barely knows how to control. What she needs now is rest."

As he was speaking, Kat began to stir, blinking her eyes open. It took her a moment to realise she was lying half on the floor, half in Flynn's lap. Blushing a little, she pushed herself up on shaky arms. Now she was eye level with the wolf. Kat gulped.

"Connor?" she whispered.

The wolf whined and lowered its massive head. Unthinking, Kat scratched behind one of its ears.

"Um… what happened?" she asked, as Connor used his huge frame to help nudge Kat to her feet. She stood a little unsteadily between Flynn and Connor-wolf, both of them ready to catch her should she fall again.

"You don't remember?" asked Mr Magus.

"Mr Magus? When did you get here? I thought you were barred?" Kat's voice was faint and her legs buckled.

"You should all come inside. Everyone. You need some food and a shot of ambrosia for Kat should perk her right up." Daisy took charge and began shushing everyone towards the pub.

Only Mr Magus held back, looking unsure.

"You too, Magus," said Daisy with a small smile. "One hundred years is long enough. I think you've learnt your lesson by now." She neglected to add that even she couldn't remember what she'd banned him for in the first place.

Chapter 29

Back in the pub, by the fire, and snugged into a booth with Amelia on one side and Connor's wolfy bulk propping her up at the other, warmth and safety surrounded Kat. Tears sprung to her eyes at the enormity of what had just happened and while she had no memory of the vampire attack, she was horrified at the destruction.

Daisy bought over hot chocolates for everyone, even Mr Magus, plus a tiny cup of gold liquid for Kat.

"What's that?" she asked nervously.

"Ambrosia. Liquid of the gods. Should make you feel better." Daisy smiled encouragingly and waited for Kat to drink the cup.

Self conscious at everyone watching her, Kat picked the tiny cup up with trembling fingers and brought it to her lips. It smelled amazing. Forgetting everything else, she tipped it up and felt the warm honey-like liquid pour silkily down her throat. She was instantly revived, energetic, loved, powerful, and very, very hungry. Licking her lips, she looked inside the cup, disappointed to see there was nothing left. Not even a single drop.

Daisy held her hand out, and Kat reluctantly handed it over.

"How do you feel now?" she asked.

"Amazing. And starving."

Everyone chuckled, and there was more than one relieved face at the table.

"I'll bring some food over."

As Daisy left, Kat looked around.

"Don't we get to choose? Isn't there a menu or something?"

Flynn shook his head.

"The WigWam doesn't work like that. Daisy will make what she thinks you need. Obviously, she has an enhanced kitchen out there." He craned his neck, but there was nothing to see. "Won't let anyone back there, not even the muscle. I think she's got pixies. Or brownies."

Kat wasn't going to go there. An elf running a pub was one thing. The help she hired wasn't something Kat wanted to get into. Not now.

Amelia took both of Kat's hands gently in her own.

"Katerina, I am so sorry. I must apologise to you for failing to protect you." She sounded utterly devastated.

"What do you mean? I stormed out of here. You didn't know the carpark was going to be infested with vampires."

"Yes, but I am your sworn protector. I made a blood oath." Amelia looked wretched.

"Well... the next time I get jumped by a bloodsucker, I'll make sure you're around to protect me."

"Really! Oh, thank you so much!" Amelia squealed and hugged Kat, who managed to cock an eyebrow at Flynn. He hid his smile behind his mug of hot chocolate.

There was no time to say anything else as Daisy began bringing food over to the table. There were ribs for Amelia, a pile of sweet chilli noodles for Kat, a burger for Flynn and fish and chips for Mr Magus.

"What about Connor?" asked Kat.

Daisy knelt down to eye level with the wolf.

"I have a sanctum where you should be able to reverse the change. If you want to."

Connor regarded her, looked at Kat, and leaned into her a little, whining.

"I'm fine. Nothing's going to happen here. Go, do what you've got to do," she urged, concerned that Connor was stuck in his wolf form because of her.

The wolf stood and padded gracefully after Daisy to the far corner of the pub. She opened a door, and they disappeared within.

After a bit of noodle slurping, Kat had to ask.

"Why didn't any of you tell me about Connor?"

Mr Magus spoke for the first time since entering The WigWam.

"It is not my place to share another's story. Anyone is welcome to work for the agency, in anonymity or fully open about their lineage."

Kat nodded.

"So what are you two, then?"

Flynn and Mr Magus shared an amused glance, but it was Flynn who answered.

"We're as human as you are. Just with access to our magical powers."

Mr Magus snorted at that and Flynn scowled.

"Some of us have more access than others. A little more application to your studies would unlock a great deal more potential." Mr Magus sounded like he had said much the same to his son many times before.

"I've been busy," muttered Flynn, his focus now on the plate of food in front of him.

The door at the back of the pub swished open and Connor appeared, dressed in purple parachute pants and an oversized tie die t-shirt.

"Don't laugh, it's all Daisy had."

Kat could see he was super embarrassed, so she just held out a hand, indicating he should come and squeeze in next to her. Amelia shuffled around a bit and there was almost enough space. Kat could feel the heat of

Connor sitting next to her, and she leaned a little into him. He returned the lean. It was an unspoken *thank you, you're welcome*.

Daisy placed a large steak in front of Connor, who whistled his appreciation before attacking it with gusto. Kat was relieved to see that the steak was at least medium rare and not blue.

They chatted about this and that, avoiding the topic of what had happened in the car park until everyone had finished eating.

"Now, Miss Kritchley, we really ought to discuss tonight's incident."

"Well, first we need to tell you what happened down in the catacombs," interrupted Amelia. "A faction of exiled vampires asked us to clear their names so they could return. They've been falsely accused of blood stealing and feeding on humans. If we find out who's behind that, then Cleo will grant me a cavern to shift in."

Mr Magus steepled his fingers, his gaze inward.

"Hmm. It appears young Maxwell has stumbled upon something greater than he first thought. We have a few ends of a bigger tangle to figure out." He looked at Amelia. "We know someone gave you Veronique's jewellery." His eyes shifted to Kat. "You discovered the unpaid invoices for the vampire blood supply." He opened his arms to include everyone. "You were approached by exiles demanding retribution. That in itself is unusual. A banishing is never questioned. The fact that they had the nerve to do so suggests nefarious motives."

"What about the piles of dust out there?" asked Flynn, flashing Kat an apologetic look at his bluntness.

"Yes, that does rather add a wrinkle to things," mused Mr Magus. "We will have to report it to the vampire senior partners. Perhaps I should accompany you to work tomorrow morning, Miss Kritchley."

There was an instant hubbub.

"You can't be serious about sending her back in there!"

"It's not safe. She'll be eaten alive!"

"Why does she even need to return? We should call for a formal hearing."

That last comment was Flynn. Mr Magus regarded him with a measure of respect.

"A formal hearing will most likely be our unavoidable course of action, but we must be seen to play the game. We must go and make nice, see what we can find out, and keep Kat at Luciano's for as long as possible. Having someone on the inside is a big advantage."

"But at what cost to her safety?" Amelia was scowling.

"I think Miss Kritchley has proved beyond reasonable doubt that she is perfectly capable of looking after herself." Mr Magus pointed at Kat's hand. "I see you have your father's ring. I'm glad Dolores held onto it. It's an excellent magnifier when used correctly."

As soon as he said that, Kat had a hundred questions, but she sensed now was not the right time to ask them. Instead, she gave a small nod. She might well have defended herself against however many vampires had attacked her in the carpark but she had absolutely no idea how she'd managed it and no clue whether she could do it again.

A huge yawn cracked her jaw, and she suddenly found herself incredibly tired. She wanted to ask about her powers, but she could barely keep her eyes open.

"Time to go home. Connor, would you escort Miss

Kritchley, please? Flynn, Amelia, I'd like a moment."

It was a clear dismissal from Mr Magus and whilst Kat wanted to know what he had to say to them; she was too exhausted to argue. She linked arms with Connor, grateful for his comforting bulk, and walked with him out of the pub, calling out their goodbyes to Daisy. She completely missed Flynn's sorrowful face as he watched them leave.

Chapter 30

"So…"

"So…"

They both laughed, neither one sure whether to ask questions or explain as they slowly walked along.

"How did…"

"When did.."

More embarrassed laughter.

"Okay, I'll go first," said Kat, but as soon as she spoke, she realised she didn't know how to ask.

"I was born a werewolf," Connor bit the bullet. "An ancient lineage, yada yada yada. I came to town, scrapping and changing and getting into trouble. Not following the rules."

"Why haven't I heard about you, then? I mean, in the papers? If you weren't hiding or whatever."

"Ah, the Council kept it out of the media. And in exchange for not being sent into exile, I work for the agency, maintaining the balance."

The Council had been mentioned before, but Kat didn't really understand what it was. Some kind of governing body, she guessed. No doubt she'd be hauled up in front of it sooner or later if she didn't get a handle on her powers.

"I don't really know what happened. I was so angry when I left the pub. I could sense it seething inside of me. I was going to go home and confront Mum, get some answers once and for all, when suddenly all these vampires were surrounding me. I didn't think, I just reacted. All that anger boiled over and then, and then…"

Kat's voice shook as the enormity of what had happened hit her.

"I killed them. How many did I kill?"

Connor put an arm around her.

"Hey, you can't think like that. You protected yourself. If you'd done nothing, you'd be the dead one and that would've been a much bigger loss than some vamps. They were warned not to come after you again."

"No, they weren't."

"I'm sorry?" Connor sounded confused. "The other attack? Outside your house?"

"That wasn't an attack on me. He tried to kill Amelia, remember? I just saved her." Kat dug her hands deeper into her coat pockets, feeling the cold. "I reported it to Maxwell. He said he would speak to the Senior Partners but when they rang the agency, they wanted me back. Veronique turned up and made some kind of weird apology, saying that she wouldn't be retaliating on Amelia, but I'm not even sure she sent that first guy at all. She seemed as surprised as the rest of us."

"If he was one of hers, she had to take responsibility for his actions. It's how it works," explained Connor.

"Because she... sired him? Is that the right word?"

Connor nodded.

"But Veronique might not have sired him directly. It could've been done by one of her progeny. She's pretty old and older vampires don't sire that much. It takes it out of them. They are linked to their progeny's progeny's progeny and so on. Like a weird ass family tree, although they call them nests."

"There's so much I don't know," sighed Kat, feeling a little defeated.

"Ah, you'll get there. It's like joining a new school. Nothing makes sense at first, but then you sit with the cool kids at lunch and it's plain sailing after that."

Kat giggled at the mental image of Mr Magus being

one of the cool kids at school.

"I am surprised that Veronique came and apologised, though. That's not like her at all."

"Oh, apparently Amelia's mum had a word," said Kat.

Connor hooted with laughter.

"Now that makes sense!"

"Why? Is she uber powerful or something?" asked Kat, once again feeling like she should already know.

"Ah well, Amelia's mother is… well, she's… she's one of the Ancients. A ruling member of the Council. And at least a thousand years old – that she will admit to. She's been here for as long as anyone can remember."

Kat took a moment to digest this.

"A thousand years? Really?" She peered up at Connor's face, trying to figure out if he was pulling her leg or not.

"That she will admit to."

"So she's a dragon."

"Yes, and no. She apparently never activated, like Amelia has. Although rumour has it, she was originally in dragon form and it was her and her brother that created the spell to make them look human."

"Amelia has an uncle?"

Connor kicked a loose stone.

"Not anymore."

They fell into a reflective silence. Kat noticed they were almost at her street.

"You were very protective back there," she said shyly, thinking about the gentle kiss Connor had given her previously.

"Ah, natural wolf reaction to a pretty maid in peril," Connor replied lightly, but Kat thought she could see a faint blush.

"And you stayed right by me the whole time after, as well."

"Well, I didn't want you to embarrass yourself and fall flat on your face or anything," Connor said before coughing to clear his throat.

Kat's hopes dashed a little.

"So if it had been Amelia…"

"I would've protected her, yeah, of course."

"Okay. Well, this is me. I'll see you later." Kat gave a breezy goodbye as she hurried off down the street to her front door, not wanting to deal with an awkward farewell. She looked over her shoulder before she let herself in, but there was nobody there.

Chapter 31

Kat had never been so nervous before in her life. She took a shaky breath and raised her fist to knock on the front door, but as always, it swung open before she even touched it.

Kat squared her shoulders. Apparently, she could protect herself against vampires without thinking about it or being able to remember how. She would be fine. It's what she had been telling herself the entire journey into work.

The door snicked close behind her and Maxwell loomed out of the dark.

"Miss Kritchley."

"Maxwell."

"I heard about the incident."

There was a pause. Kat didn't want to reference The WigWam carpark in case the incident he was referring to was something else entirely.

Maxwell lifted his head from side to side as if scenting the air.

"In the catacombs," he clarified softly.

"Oh right, yeah." With everything that had happened since, the catacomb visit seemed like a million years ago. "They asked us to…"

But Maxwell had put a cold finger over her mouth, his eyes narrowed at her. When he felt sure she wasn't going to continue speaking, he removed his digit and pointed to his ears.

Enhanced hearing, thought Kat. And probably best not to talk about it out in the open like this. Who knew what lurked in the shadows. That made her shudder.

"Come. You are to finish the filing you were

originally tasked. It has been questioned as to why that job was left undone." Maxwell smiled. "I reminded them of the short attention span of a human."

Kat couldn't tell if it was all an act for whomever could be listening or whether Maxwell really did think humans had a short attention span. She supposed that if she were immortal, someone who only lived seventy-odd years and packed in as much life as possible, changing their minds all the time, might very well be seen as having a short attention span. Realising that she was getting distracted, she increased her pace to keep up with Maxwell.

Remembering that the filing room was the one with the windows and the natural light, Kat smiled. But when they got there, heavy drapes covered the windows and an unappealing florescent strip illuminated the room.

Maxwell followed her inside and locked them both in.

"This room is soundproof, but anyone walking by can see what we are doing. Go and file while I talk to you about what happened at The WigWam."

A chill ran down Kat's back and she woodenly did as she was told.

"Um… what did you hear?" she asked, hoping not to give more away than she needed to.

Maxwell reclined in a chair and affixed a bored as hell expression upon his face, inspecting his fingernails.

"I heard the banished approached you at the catacombs, requesting you investigate the unusual circumstances surrounding their exile. Accusations of blood theft and human attack were their crimes. I did not sit on the hearing, but the evidence spoke for itself. A little too neatly, but if there is one thing vampires like, it is neatness."

Kat filed that nugget away for later. *Really? Vampires were neat freaks? Huh.*

"They asked us to investigate, claiming the evidence was falsified. They said if we did that for them, then Amelia could have a lair for…"

"For her dragon change. Another life that you have completely turned on its head." Maxwell regarded Kat with a bland look, but she swore she caught a glimpse of humour in his expression.

She guessed if you thought about it, she was making waves, intentional or not.

"Do not stand there doing nothing. Tongues will wag if anyone thinks we are actually having a conversation." Maxwell said it in such a withering tone that Kat flushed and immediately bent her head to the pile of paperwork in front of her.

"You know this system makes no sense. It's why it takes such a long time to put the paperwork away."

Maxwell made a dismissive gesture.

"We get a human in once a year to file for us. You always seem to manage." He yawned, exposing sharp white fangs, and adopted an even more bored, sprawled position than before. "Their claims of being framed for blood theft could be linked to those missed payments of blood."

"How do you mean?" asked Kat, careful not to look in his direction and keep her focus on her work.

"If someone authorised finance to stop paying for the blood supply but didn't inform anyone there would be a smaller delivery, then when there wasn't enough to go around, the lack could be blamed on a likely scapegoat. Someone low on the food chain who didn't have much influence. Someone expendable."

It was odd hearing Maxwell talk about vampires

being expendable. He'd always spoken as if humans were the second-rate beings, but Kat guessed that there must be some kind of hierarchy within the vampire society as well.

"Wouldn't the sire of the banished be affected by their... exile?" she asked.

Maxwell narrowed his eyes, considering her question.

"Yes... but not in the way you're thinking. Any loss from a sire line opens up the possibility for permission to rebuild. It's not like the old days when anyone could sire anyone. We have to be much more discreet now. Technology is too advanced for us to be utterly invisible. Efforts have been made to blend."

"Who's sire line got exiled?" asked Kat.

"Veronique's."

"But that doesn't make any sense," argued Kat. "If she's lost some of her line, why would she send another to attack Amelia and then more still to attack me again? Surely that puts her in a position of weakness if re-siring isn't something she can do easily."

"No, it does not make sense. Veronique would never put her line in danger like that. Siring is dangerous. It's not like they portray it in the movies. Nine times out of ten, the human never survives."

Kat digested this fact.

"Vampires exist in clans. The Luciano's are one of the biggest here in the UK. They travelled over with the Romans, liked what they saw and stayed. The exact size of the clan has ebbed and flowed throughout the centuries. And Veronique's contribution to the family has been sizable."

Looking at Maxwell's face, Kat wondered if he had been a Roman soldier once upon a time. Or perhaps an ancient Briton. Did he remember what life was like in those days? She tried to pull her thoughts back.

"So… if Veronique's part of the… family is being destroyed, then someone clearly wants to discredit her and maybe takeover her… position?"

"And by destroying her sire line, discrediting her actions and causing a real blood crisis, they are hoping to slip through the cracks of the chaos that will inevitably ensue, re-emerging as the hero when the time is right."

"You know," said Kat, not thinking as she spoke. "You are in an excellent position to be that hero. Running the investigation would be a really good double fake." Then her brain caught up with what she just said and she looked at Maxwell who was sitting stock still in his chair, every fibre of his being on super alert, his eyes hooded, pining her to the spot.

Then he fluidly relaxed and winked at her. Kat's seized heart began to beat loudly again.

"If I were the mastermind, and I thank you for your consideration, you would be long dead by now, Miss Kritchley."

Kat stammered her thanks and bent over the filing, intent on keeping her shaky hands busy and try to clear her mind a bit. Maxwell was content to sit in silence while she gathered her thoughts.

"If that's the case – someone is trying to wipe out Veronique's line and destabilise the blood supply – they've obviously hoping to what – take over her position? Overthrow the ancients? And why keep attacking me?"

Maxwell snorted.

"The answer to that last question is obvious. You're highly skilled at destroying us."

The matter-of-fact way he said it made Kat blanch a little. She didn't mean to be really good at destroying vampires. It had happened by accident.

"As for the other question, I'm not sure. With Veronique weakened, there are several opportunities for a power-hungry vampire to expand their own empire. Especially someone more in tune with current human society, but there aren't many who fit that mould here at the firm."

Now it was Maxwell's turn to look worried.

"Would it even be a vampire?" wondered Kat aloud, but Maxwell had no answer for her.

Chapter 32

Kat hurried to the agency to catch Amelia and hand in her time sheet before she left for the day. She had a lot to tell her. And Amelia might have some ideas about who would want to cause so much trouble for the vampires.

"Hiya, you alright?" she called out as she entered the building, but her voice echoed in the hallway. Nobody was there. Mr Magus's door stood shut and the whole place had a real abandoned air about it. As Kat got closer to the reception desk, she saw an envelope with her name on the front. Putting down her time sheet, she picked it up, turning it over in her hands.

DO NOT OPEN ME was written on the back.

"What?" Kat frowned. Why leave her an envelope if she couldn't open it? Feeling thoroughly unsettled, she quickly left the building. As soon as she did, she felt better, like a weight had been lifted. The lettering on the back of the envelope had changed as well. In fact, it had disappeared.

"I suppose that means I can open you now," said Kat and then looked around quickly, realising she had spoken aloud to herself. Luckily, nobody had noticed.

She began strolling towards home as she opened the letter, but there was only a single note inside. It read:

Come to The WigWam.

With no signature, the note could've been from anyone, but figuring that Daisy at least didn't mean Kat any harm, she thought it would be alright to go to the pub. But first she rang her mum to keep her in the loop.

"Hiya, it's me. I'm just going to The WigWam for some after-work drinks. Are you okay? Do you need anything? Is Mikey back?"

Kat listened as her mum confirmed her brother had come home and that she was fine. True, her clipped tone suggested annoyance, but Kat had grown used to that. Her mum often wished she could go out and about at will, but felt trapped by her wheelchair and was incredibly self-conscious on the rare occasions she did venture into the world. That's all. Her snippiness wasn't down to anything else.

A little guilty about not going home but wanting to visit Daisy again–and maybe get a second hit of ambrosia–Kat angled away from her house and set off with a skip in her step. She might even have another delicious meal from the mysterious kitchen.

When she entered The WigWam, the pub seemed completely different from the last time she'd been. True, the dated beaded curtain was still there, as was the bouncer, but everything else had changed. No fireplace, no booths. Instead, a pool table took centre stage with a couple of fruit machines on one side and some stools against the bar. It didn't feel like the kind of pub you came to for food.

Everyone there looked at Kat as she walked in. She did not fit in with this crowd. Her smart office wear stuck out like a sore thumb amidst the popular bike leather and punk look.

Worst of all, Daisy was not behind the bar.

The bouncer came to her rescue when she looked at him in desperation. He raised his eyebrows and gave the vaguest of nods up towards a staircase that led to another room. Relief coursed through Kat's body and she hurried over to them. Aware that she her heels clopped up the stairs loudly, she didn't care, pushing herself to go as fast as possible so that when she got to the top, she was breathing a little heavily. Pushing open the door, she found Mr Magus' library-like office.

"What?"

"Ah, Miss Kritchley. Forgive the subterfuge. It became apparent we needed to add an additional layer of security to things, and Daisy was kind enough to supply her conference facilities. I trust you didn't have any problems getting here?"

Kat shook her head mutely, not really understanding, but hoping all would be made clear.

"I want to talk to you about your ring and what happened last night. Please, take a seat."

As if summoned to the principal's office, Kat reluctantly sat down. With no sign of Amelia or Flynn or even Daisy, she felt a little ambushed and her stomach squirmed as she prayed she wasn't in any trouble.

"Tea?" asked Mr Magus.

Kat shook her head, wanting to get things over and done with.

"When exactly did you obtain the ring, Miss Krichley?"

"Mum gave it to me. She said the ring belonged to Dad and that it would protect me." Kat hoped Mr Magus wasn't going to ask any more questions because she really didn't know anything more.

He made a note on some paper in front of him.

"And how did the ring make you feel when you first wore it?"

"Um…"

Thinking back to when she'd tried the ring on in her front room, Kat tried to recall. Yes, she'd experienced heat and light, a sense of massive achievement and strength, but that had been in her house. How had it felt after that? She frowned.

"There was something when I first put it on. Like a

whoosh of energy, but that faded and to be honest, I forgot I was wearing a ring." She lifted her hand out in front of her. "Like now, really. Don't even feel it."

"It's a part of you already," said Mr Magus thoughtfully, jotting something else down on his piece of paper. "And what about last night? In the car park?"

"I don't... I don't remember. I was angry, and I felt hot. I wanted some air and to get away... from everyone."

Mr Magus looked at Kat with a soft expression on his face, which made her feel worse because she couldn't remember anything.

"Why did you want to get away from everyone, Miss Kritchley? What were they doing?"

Kat frowned. She ought to feel cross. She should have some residual memory from what made her so angry. Her brow creased as she tried desperately to remember something, anything.

"I don't... I don't know. I can't remember..."

"Hmm."

Mr Magus' tone suggested she was deliberately keeping something from him. He began writing.

"Can't remember how she slaughtered a dozen or more vampires..."

He spoke softly as he wrote, but loud enough for Kat to hear him. She winced.

"No, it's not like that. They were attacking me..." She trailed off. She didn't actually know that.

"Are you certain? Do you have any proof?" Mr Magus was deliberately pressing on all of Kat's insecurities about last night. "All we have is that you got incredibly angry but you can't remember about what and that you destroyed a group of vampires but you can't remember how or why so for all we know they could've been innocent patrons of The WigWam and you are just hell bent on starting an interspecies war."

He steepled his fingers and regarded Kat over them.

"Is there anything you'd like to say in your defence?"

"Am I on trial? Maxwell said it was alright. He said it wasn't my fault, and that there were other factors at play." Kat's hackles rose. She didn't think it was completely fair that she was going to be judged for something she couldn't remember doing or have a clue about how to do again. "You put me in danger in the first place. Sending me to a vampire solicitors when I didn't even know vampires were real." She felt her fury rising and unconsciously clenched her fists. "In fact, if it weren't for you and Amelia's drug tea, I probably wouldn't have accepted that job. You admitted you lured me in. No one will tell me what happened to Mallory, my predecessor. You... you blindsided me, kept facts from me, and put me in deliberate danger to *see what would happen*. I think I have the right to be angry–at you!"

She took a deep breath, ready to do some more shouting, when she became aware of Mr Magus sitting back in his chair, smiling up at her. Why was he looking up at her like that?

"Why are you smiling?" she asked peevishly.

"Why are you floating?" he replied.

She glanced down and noticed two things. One, she was about half a foot off the floor and two, her ring was glowing. Once she'd realised both things, the ring stopped glowing, and she dropped back to the floor with a thump.

"What is going on?" Kat pleaded. She needed some answers.

"Anger is a trigger for your power. We need to overcome that, but congratulations. An excellent start."

Kat became more confused.

"What are you talking about?"

"This marks your first magic lesson. You did well. Much better than Flynn in his first session. Let's go have some supper, shall we?" Mr Magus stood and indicated that Kat should open the door and return downstairs.

"What about my questions?" Kat was less confident pushing for answers now that her anger had faded away, but this might be her only chance.

"All in good time, Miss Kritchley. All in good time." Realising that Kat wasn't going to give in and go downstairs dutifully, Mr Magus tutted softly under his breath and answered one of Kat's questions. "Mallory decided to go in another direction. She left the Agency in good faith and I wish her well in her endeavours. Let us return downstairs, shall we?"

Kat didn't entirely believe Mr Magus about Mallory, but for now, she decided to accept his explanation. At least she wasn't dead. Still unsettled by the whole magic thing, Kat reluctantly led the way down.

"It's not the same in there. I don't think Daisy is working or that the kitchens are even open," she began to explain but stopped talking when she opened the door and saw the pub returned to normal.

"A little glamour. Part of the lesson," explained Mr Magus with a smile.

Kat felt both relieved and irritated. This wasn't how she'd expected her second visit to The WigWam to play out.

Chapter 33

The WigWam was indeed back to its former cosiness. Kat grew annoyed. Sure, she'd only recently discovered this whole other world of magic and mystery, but it seemed things were being kept from her all the time and that the other members of the agency were getting a kick out of keeping her in the dark. She didn't like it.

Grumpily, she slung herself into a booth, bumping into Amelia and not saying sorry.

"We need to talk," whispered Amelia, but she said nothing else as Mr Magus joined them, instead flashing him one of her brilliant smiles.

Flynn looked broody, nursing a glass of what appeared to be coke, but could've been anything to be honest, and Connor was nowhere to be seen.

Daisy slid a cappuccino in front of Kat. It had a cute dragon foam motif, but Kat scowled. She didn't want a stupid cappuccino with a stupid foam design on it. Daisy's hand fluttered back and forth as if she couldn't decide whether she should take the drink away. Kat defiantly wrapped her hands around the cup. No matter that she didn't want it in the first place, it was hers now.

"Right, now that we're all here, shall we debrief?" asked Mr Magus cheerfully. "How was your day, Miss Kritchley?"

"Shouldn't we wait for Connor?" Kat didn't care that she sounded rude, despite the warning look Amelia shot her for her tone.

"He's away. On assignment," Mr Magus replied with a definite tone of his own. One of finality.

"Someone's trying to destabilise Veronique. At Luciano's. But Maxwell doesn't think it's one of their vampires, so it's either one from somewhere else or something different entirely." Kat slurped at her cappuccino. It tasted really good.

"Why would anyone want to meddle in vampire politics if they weren't already a bloodsucker?" Flynn had perked up a little when Mr Magus had explained that Connor wouldn't be there.

"Vampire politics in itself is a fine art, but I tend to agree with Maxwell. The British vampires are too well established to rock the boat. Everyone knows their place in the family." Mr Magus drummed his fingers on the table as he thought.

"Just because you've put everyone in a neat little box doesn't mean they're going to stay there." Kat was spoiling for an argument.

"Oh, I didn't put them in the boxes, but if they know what's good for them, they will stay there. It wouldn't do for the Council to get involved." Mr Magus twitched his lips in distaste. "It took decades to settle things down again last time."

Once more there was a story, a lore that Kat knew nothing about, but Amelia and Flynn were nodding in agreement.

"You know, this is all a bit much. You come along, changing my life forever. Dumping all this stuff on me and expecting me to roll with everything. Accept everything. And to not question a goddamn thing. Well, I am questioning. I'm questioning a lot. Why has this happened? Why me? Why have you turned me into a vampire killing machine? I'm not some stupid little girl you can point at the bad guys and wait for me to blow them up. I deserve some answers. I deserve to know what's going on. I deserve… I deserve…" Kat ran out of steam. The anger that had been building and building and building inside of her seemed to ebb away.

Realising that she'd unintentionally leapt to her feet, she plopped back down again, instantly weary and drained.

"Feeling better?" asked Mr Magus.

Kat nodded as Daisy reappeared to clear the now empty coffee mug and replace it with a lemonade and plenty of ice.

"What was in it?" asked Kat as the cup got cleared.

"How do you mean?" Mr Magus looked genuinely puzzled.

"Well, the tea at the agency was drugged to keep me compliant and stop me from asking too many questions. So was the coffee laced with something to help me get rid of my anger?"

"You know, you're a very suspicious young lady– with a rather overactive imagination."

"That's not an answer," Kat retorted, crossing her arms, feeling a residual flare of annoyance flicker.

Amelia laughed nervously.

"The tea wasn't drugged. It just helped you to accept things without asking too many questions. I never expected it to work quite so well. It was a new blend..." She trailed off as Kat looked daggers at her.

"It's because she's magical," said Flynn, locking eyes with Kat and them both flushing a little. "I mean, she's one of us. The tea hit harder because her powers were ready."

"Yes, it's fortuitous that you came to us when you did, Miss Kritchley. I'm sure there were lots of unexplained events occurring that at least you can now understand." Mr Magus was smiling indulgently at Kat.

A flicker of annoyance ran through her.

"There was absolutely nothing happening in my life

that I couldn't explain, thank you very much. Everything that's been weird and inexplicable has been since I met you lot."

"Ah."

It was all Mr Magus said, but for some reason it really tickled Kat and she began laughing. A giggle at first, which grew louder at the bemused expression on everyone's face. Flynn joined in with a chuckle that became a more contagious belly laugh and soon everyone at the table was stuck in one of those gasping, tummy hurting, laughter attacks with tears running down their faces.

"Is everything alright?" asked a very worried Daisy, but no one had the breath to answer her.

It took a while for them to all gain control and for a good five minutes, small ripples of uncontrollable laughter kept escaping, setting them all off again. Even Mr Magus had to extract an exquisite handkerchief to wipe his eyes.

"Are we all alright?" he was the first to recover enough to speak.

Everyone else nodded, and Kat was relieved to discover she did feel better.

"I think that ring you are wearing is enhancing not only your magic, but also your mood. Ergo, if you feel a little miffed, it will expand on that, making you feel rather ticked off."

A giggle escaped Kat, but she tried to absorb what was being said seriously. She pulled the ring off her finger and experienced an instant sag in energy.

"Oh, I am not suggesting you stop wearing it, Miss Kritchley. Some training and control would come in handy." Mr Magus' eyes gleamed at the fingerless ring.

Not liking everything that gleam hinted at, Kat

quickly put it back on her finger.

"Can I get some warning next time there is going to be a magic lesson, please?" she asked.

"Of course. Flynn will be handling the early stages of your training. I merely wanted to confirm any blocks and triggers." Once more, Mr Magus sounded like he knew a lot more than he was letting on, but Kat knew he wasn't going to expand.

"So what do I do now? Go to magic school? Where am I supposed to find the time for that?"

"No, not to school, just magic lessons, and I'm sure you will find a way." Mr Magus stood. "Come Flynn, there are some books and other important resources I want you to have before you start Miss Kritchley's training. Ladies." He gave Amelia and Kat a small bow before he left the pub, Flynn close on his heels.

Kat watched them go with a slight frown on her face.

"I hope that's not going to be too awkward," said Amelia. "What with Flynn having a huge crush on you and everything."

"I'm sorry, what?" Kat was instantly pulled back into the here and now. "What do you mean, crush?"

"Well, just between a dragon protector and her damsel, he was gutted when you left with Connor last night. Oh, and I'm going to need some details there, please. Got them both wrapped around your finger, haven't you?" Amelia's tone was light and teasing.

Kat blushed bright red.

"Nothing happened with anyone. Connor walked me home. There's definitely nothing going on there. And anyway, what about you? You're the one with the secret admirer."

"Yes, and look where that got me. Nearly strangled

176

to death and jump started into dragon mode, still with no idea who the actual admirer is." Amelia pouted. "It's beginning to look a lot like I don't even have one, anyway. I was just a prawn in the big game."

It took Kat a moment to realise what she meant.

"A pawn. You were a pawn." She tapped the table. "But I don't think they meant for you to manifest, and now the two of us together will be unstoppable. No one is going to want to mess with us. Especially hoity-toity Veronique." Kat eyed the lemonade, wondering briefly if that's where her bravado was coming from, and decided to just go with it.

"Do you really mean it?"

"Mean what?"

"The two of us, together I mean." Amelia sounded very nervous.

"Yeah, why not?" Kat grinned. "Who else is going to be my bestie?"

And whilst she meant it semi-seriously, there was literally nobody else she could talk to about the current level of madness her life had become. She also really liked Amelia and was hoping she'd be someone to hang out with.

"Bestie!" Amelia's eyes filled with happy tears and she squeezed Kat's hand tight. A portion of cheesy fries were delivered to their table and the two women tucked in with gusto, all their problems for the moment put to one side.

"What did Mr Magus want with you and Connor, anyway?"

Amelia instantly looked guilty.

"Come on, you can tell me. Please? No secrets between besties."

"That's not fair!" squealed Amelia in mock horror.

177

"He spoke to me first. Was just asking about the whole dragon thing and how it was going to work. And then I left so I don't know what he said to Connor, honestly I don't."

Kat believed her. She just hoped Mr Magus hadn't sent Connor anywhere too dangerous.

Chapter 34

For the following week and a half, Kat settled into routine. She went to work at Luciano's, undertaking the menial tasks the vampires deemed themselves too good to do, but she didn't mind. Completing the filing felt like a battle won and when Kat realised she was halfway through entering the last of the accounting information into the ledger, she had a small pang at the job being finished soon. Sure, she would be happy not to walk into a vampire solicitor firm each morning putting her life on the line, but also, what on earth would be her next temping role?

Every evening after work, Kat spent a couple of hours at the agency to train with Flynn. So far she'd managed to make her hands glow but had been unable to directionalise the energy. There were a few singed corners in the dusty training room.

"Why is it so dusty in here?" Kat asked after another wonky and lazy energy ball floated into a particularly neglected corner, causing plumes to rise and she and Flynn to sneeze.

"We haven't had a full staff for a while and we've not had a new magical to train for ages. You're the first that I'm aware of."

"What about you?"

"I attended magic school and had Xavier as a dad. I've been training every day my entire life." With practised ease, Flynn shot a few energy balls at the floating targets Kat was supposed to be hitting. He hit them all.

"No one likes a showoff."

Kat lowered her hands, turning off the glow. That

much, at least, she could do.

"Hey, you've only been doing this a week. You're doing fine."

Kat came to perch on the desk next to Flynn.

"Tell me about magic school. Where is it? What are the lessons like? Do they do night classes?" The last question was more wistful than the rest.

"Magic school is… It's… You see, the thing about magic school is…" Flynn was getting flustered.

"You can't talk about it, can you?"

Relieved, he shook his head.

"Sorry."

"No, it's fine. I should've known. I mean, I didn't know anything, before stumbling into here that day and turning my whole life on its head." Kat picked at her fingernails. "Can you tell me about the accident?" she asked hesitantly. It was the first time she'd brought it up since losing her temper.

"Have you spoken to your mum about it?" Flynn looked at Kat sideways, trying to gauge her reaction.

"No. To be honest, I've hardly seen her. Or Mikey. I've been so busy with work and whatever this is, I've not been home much."

"Family is important."

Kat sighed and pushed herself to standing.

"You're not going to tell me, are you?"

Flynn stood too. They were so close, they were almost touching. Kat could feel Flynn's breath on her neck. She tilted her head to look at him.

"I… I want to but…" Flynn physically drew back. "You should talk to your mum first."

Disappointed and feeling rejected, Kat grabbed her stuff and left. With Connor off doing god knows what, she hadn't been able to talk to him or figure out if anything was going on. Flynn had been fun to hang out while she tried to learn how to do magic, but she didn't know how she felt about him, either. Amelia said he liked her, but… was it all just a competition between the two of them? She needed to sort her own feelings out first.

Feeling decidedly grumpy, Kat came home noisily, banging the door and stomping upstairs to dump her stuff. Mikey's music was blaring from his room. She stuck her head in and he was busy playing some racing game.

Kat gave him a thumbs up and got a miniscule nod back, but no eye contact, which was normal. Wishing an interaction with her mum would go so smoothly, she headed downstairs.

"Do you want a cuppa?" she called from the kitchen, not bothering to listen for a reply she wouldn't be able to hear over the kettle, anyway. The rule was if you were making tea, you made one for everyone, regardless.

Kat took a moment before heading into her mum's domain. Be calm.

"Hey, brought you a cuppa. Have you eaten?" Kat smiled brightly, knowing full well that her mum wasn't going to be fooled.

"Thanks, love, and no. Mikey had that microwave meal he likes, but I thought I'd wait for you. Feels like we haven't spoken in days."

There was an awkward silence.

"I've been busy," Kat said finally.

"Hmm. Work keeping you on your toes." It wasn't a question.

"I've been… I've been having magic lessons. Look!" Kat focused on her hands and lifted them both. A very faint energy ball surrounded the left hand, and the

181

right did nothing.

"Put those down!" snarled Dolores, wheeling rapidly over to the window and fiercely pulling the curtains together. "Someone could see you."

Kat, already disappointed at how feeble her attempts had been, was taken aback at her mum's reaction.

"No one is watching. And even if they were-which they're not–they didn't see anything."

Dolores sighed.

"Magic is not just waving your hands around, a pretty light show. It's drawing upon energies you know nothing about, opening a portal to things you cannot trust and putting yourself in danger. Anything could be watching, waiting, ready to pounce. To destroy you from the inside out." She wheeled herself directly in front of Kat. "Have you learnt how to cast a protection circle? Do you know how to close down an energy portal? Have you got a quick release spell to end magics?"

Kat shook her head at all three questions, barely understanding what her mum was asking her.

"Flynn is teaching me…"

"Flynn! Flynn! What use is a child teaching a child?" she snapped.

Kat snapped back.

"Maybe if you'd told me I was a magical being when I was younger, I could have gone to magic school and learnt how to harness my power like a normal person."

Dolores and Kat stared at each other.

"Ah, there is nothing normal about you, love," said Dolores. "You are one of a kind. My Katerina." She caught Kat's hand and gave it a squeeze. Kat hugged her back.

"Mum, how come you know so much about magic?"

Kat finally sat down in the armchair, putting herself at the same height, something she knew her mum appreciated.

"Well, I was married to your father, and I did work at the Agency." Dolores drew herself up, sitting proudly in her wheelchair. "I know many things."

Kat couldn't help but smile. For the first time, her mum looked and sounded a little like she used to, how Kat remembered from before the accident. Full of life and vigour.

"Is there anything you can tell me? I feel like I'm in a tiny boat in a whirlwind with no life jacket, no paddle, no idea. And everyone is expecting so much from me because of who I am."

"Kieron's daughter," said Dolores softly.

"Yeah."

Dolores nodded and patted Kat on the knee. She turned her wheelchair and wheeled over to the cabinet where she'd taken the ring from.

"I suppose it does no good being locked away in here. You might as well have it." Dolores hefted a huge book out of the cabinet, laying it on her stumps. "But be careful. There is so much in here. So much more than you'll ever need to know." She wheeled slowly back over to Kat, placing the heavy book on her lap. "Promise me something?"

Kat nodded, eager to start looking through the book.

"No. Please listen, this is important. Promise me you won't let yourself become consumed with the magic. Don't let it be all you can think about, all you dream about it, all you want. It's no life being consumed by magic. You need friends and lovers and to make mistakes and get it wrong. Live. Promise me you'll live."

The urgency in her mum's tone threw Kat. She looked directly at her.

"I promise. I won't let the magic consume me."

Even as she said it, Kat's fingers were tingling at being so close to answers and not being able to throw the book open and delve inside. With huge effort, she put it down to one side and reluctantly removed her hands.

"What shall we have for dinner?"

Chapter 35

All Kat could think of as she walked down the road to the Chinese takeaway was the book. She'd been this close to finally getting some answers. It had taken everything she'd had to put it down to one side and offer to go get the takeaway. At least physically going to collect would be quicker than delivery. She'd nearly cried when they'd said it would be around forty-five minutes. Hopefully, if she could distract her mum with noodles and the TV, then Kat would be able to disappear upstairs with the book.

Not paying any attention, she walked right into the person coming out of the Chinese. It was Connor.

"Oh! What are you doing here?"

"Kat! Are you okay? Did I hurt you?"

Connor's arms held onto Kat tightly, as if to keep her safe and out of trouble. She shook her head and shimmed her arms free.

"I'm fine, I'm fine. Why are you here? I thought you were on assignment?" Kat watched as Connor opened and closed his mouth. Nothing forthcoming. "Look, I get it. You can't tell me. Don't lie to me."

She was disappointed. It was one thing that Mr Magus had secretly asked Connor to do something and nobody had told her what it was, but why couldn't he spill the beans?

"But you're okay? No more…"

"No more vampire attacks? No. I've managed not to vanquish anything for a good week and a half." She looked around. "Shouldn't we be a little more circumspect?"

Connor chuckled and held the door open for her,

following her back inside.

"This is a supernaturally run Chinese. Mai and Lee are Qilin. Their family originates from Ancient China, but they've been here a long time."

"Living up to the stereotype," muttered Kat, looking around at all the typical things you'd expect to see in a high street Chinese takeaway—lanterns, lots of red everywhere and plenty of waving gold cats.

"What can I say? Humans like their little boxes." It was Mai, smiling and handing over Kat's order.

Flushing, Kat paid and gave Mai a warm smile. She'd always liked coming here, and that wasn't going to change now that she'd found out the people running the takeaway were Qilin. The food was still the best around.

Connor followed her out again.

"Aren't you eating?" Kat asked.

"Ah, no. I was just checking up on something."

"Not me, I hope."

There was a long pause. Kat peeked sideways at Connor, who grabbed the back of his neck in embarrassment, trying to think of an answer.

"I don't believe it. Did Mr Magus put you up to this? Is this your secret mission that no one knows about? Checking in at my local Chinese to see if I've ordered ribs with my rice or not. Seriously?"

She quickened her step, feeling mad and just wanting to get away from Connor.

"No! Wait up, Kat! Listen to me." Connor jogged forwards and snagged Kat's arm, spinning her back around to face him.

He was met with a glowing energy ball inches away from his nose. He froze. Kat froze.

"Oh my god. I'm so sorry. Hang on."

Kat quickly lowered her arms, but the energy ball didn't dissipate. She shook her hand a little, but still nothing. She shook it a little harder. If anything, the energy ball grew brighter, joined by a second ball in her other hand.

"What do I do? What do I do?" Kat's voice was shrill with panic. The takeaway bag floated of its own violation next to her.

Connor stepped forward, slid his hands on either side of her face, and kissed her. A liquid fireball went off in Kat's stomach. Butterflies and fireworks all rolled into one. Her eyes had closed, fingers hanging limply down, as she froze in surprise. The takeaway bag dropped to the floor. Connor pulled away and looked down at her hands.

"That seemed to do the trick," he said softly.

Kat touched a finger to her lips.

"Yeah. I guess it would."

Connor picked up the takeaway bag and handed it to her. She took it wordlessly but didn't seem to know how to move or what to do next.

"That way?" suggested Connor, pointing in the direction of Kat's house.

"Right."

They began walking, Kat's mind racing. Her body acutely aware of Connor beside her.

"That was…"

"I'm sorry I…"

"No, you go," said Kat, wanting to marshal her thoughts some more.

"No, please," said Connor at the same time.

Kat chewed on her lower lip, desperate to say something but not wanting to ruin whatever was going on. She liked Connor. A lot.

"Um…" Great. Now she felt too embarrassed to speak. "You, er… you felt that, right?"

"The kiss? Yeah." Connor wasn't giving anything away.

"No, I mean. You felt that. There was definitely a connection." Kat held her breath, wondering if Connor had indeed experienced the same burst of something.

"Er, yeah. I mean, I guess."

Oh my god, thought Kat. *He so didn't.*

They arrived at her door once again.

"Okay, I've got it from here. Sorry for trying to blow you up or whatever," Kat said in a rush.

"Yeah, of course. Sorry for kissing you." Connor half smiled at Kat, and she wished her butterflies would shut up.

"Are you though?" Kat surprised herself by asking.

"Am I what?"

"Sorry for kissing me." She decided to just be brave and go for it. "It felt like, like it meant something."

Connor stepped closer to her and, once more, Kat was aware of the butterflies and fireworks going mad. She thought she might even be trembling.

"I…" Connor's voice was hoarse. "Kat, I…" With a huge physical wrench, he pulled himself away from her. "I have to go. Be safe." And he left.

Kat felt like she'd been punched in the stomach. Tears pricked her eyes. She should have known better that someone like Connor would never be interested in someone like her. He was an Alpha Male literally, and she was only half magical, with no idea on how to control her power. The food was beginning to cool as she let herself in, appetite completely gone, and even the lure of the book had lost some of its appeal.

Chapter 36

Kat sensed her mum looking at her, but she pretended not to notice, handing her a plate of food and settling herself back into a chair. Her father's book perched on the arm. Kat looked at it with a mixture of fear and longing.

"Are you okay? I mean, really okay?" Dolores asked in a soft voice.

Tears began welling up in Kat's eyes.

"I'm just… I'm just so all over the place. I'm scared every time I go to work–I could literally die, but now I know I could also probably destroy them all, like I did in the carpark and that frightens me even more. Six months ago, there was nothing special about me at all. Now I'm this, this… killer and…" Kat's bottom lip quivered and her words trailed off as the tears fell.

Dolores reached over and held her daughter's hand. It was really hard to comfort someone when one of you sat in a wheelchair and the other had grown too big to sit on your lap.

"You never told me about the carpark," Dolores said.

Kat closed her eyes and winced. She'd even forgotten to do that.

"There's a lot I need to tell you." Kat pulled her legs up and crossed them in the chair. Her food ignored on her lap. She began to explain to her mum everything that had occurred. It took a while and when she'd finished, they both sat in silence for a long time.

"Why didn't you tell me what really happened to Dad?" Kat finally asked.

Dolores flicked her hand.

"You were so small. How could I explain to you that your father had died in the Underbelly Catacombs? It was another world that you knew nothing about. Kieron kept you babies away from the magic. He said…" Dolores faltered a little, tears springing to her eyes. "He said your gifts would manifest when the time was right and he didn't want to force it." She put out a hand to cup Kat's face gently. "He said you would bloom into it."

"Is that why we didn't go to magic school?" asked Kat.

"Who told you about that? Let me guess, Flynn." Dolores did not sound impressed. "Magic school is for pure bloods only. You would never have been allowed in and why should you feel rejected for something that isn't your fault."

Kat digested this. Having never known about magic until a few weeks ago and having had a good time at school with a great bunch of friends, on reflection, she realised she wasn't that bothered at missing out.

"Promise me it's nothing like Hogwarts," she said with a grin.

"I promise. Your father always said it was a load of stuffy old professors teaching archaic magic the way it's always been done, with no consideration for how the world has changed." Dolores smiled faintly. "He was working on modernising the craft when he… when he passed."

Kat realised her mum still hadn't answered her question.

"But what happened down there, Mum?" she pressed.

Dolores shifted in her wheelchair.

"I don't know. Xavier took my memory."

Kat gaped.

"He did what? He had no right!" Hot anger rushed through her.

"No, no. I asked him to." There was a long pause. "I am so sorry, my Katerina. I was injured and alone with two small children to bring up. It seemed like the best thing to do at the time."

"But, but... we can get them back, right? We can find out what happened?"

Dolores shook her head sharply.

"No! I do not want them returned. Your father died. That is the end." She shot a piercing look at Kat. "How many vampires have you killed now?"

It was like a body blow and Kat actually winced.

"Mum!"

"Sorry, that might have been a little harsh. But... how many?"

Kat looked down at the now congealed food on her plate.

"I don't know," she whispered. "I was so angry when I found out you'd lied to me and Dad hadn't died in a car accident that I was boiling with rage. They surrounded me in the carpark, said something about tying up loose ends and I just..." Kat shrugged. "I exploded. Light shot out and then there were piles of dust everywhere. I didn't think, I just... reacted."

Dolores stared at her daughter, faint awe on her face.

"Well, Xavier had better get his act together and teach you how to control your powers. Before the Council gets called in to deal with it."

Kat frowned.

"Yeah, the Council has been mentioned a few times. Who are they?"

Dolores chose not to answer and instead collected Kat's unwanted plate and wheeled through to the kitchen. Clattering about in the sink. Kat followed and stood in the doorway. They couldn't both fit in the small kitchen.

"Mum? Who are the Council?"

Dolores clattered loudly in the kitchen, washing the dishes up with angry energy.

"They are a collection of fools. Meant to protect the magical community from the humans and vice versa. They are in charge of making sure the two worlds don't meet and the balance remains." She pointed a soapy finger at Kat. "Your precious agency works for the Council to smooth those edges."

Kat pondered this for a moment.

"But Flynn said they hadn't been that busy lately. Does that mean things are good or bad?"

Dolores spun her chair around to face her.

"I guess we're about to find out."

"Why do you say that?" asked Kat.

"It's November. The Council usually sends a representative to the Agency around November to discuss the year's work and lay plans for any problem areas. A bunch of robes in a room with no real fingers on the pulse of life. They live by archaic rules and still believe themselves separate from humans. In this world, you cannot think like that. Old magics resurface in unusual ways."

Kat wanted to ask more about that, but their conversation was interrupted with Mikey pushing into the kitchen and clamouring for chocolate.

Kat wandered back into the front room and picked up her father's book. It felt warm in her hands, as if it belonged there. She stroked the cover thoughtfully.

"Goodnight!" she called out to her mum and brother before heading upstairs for a little light bedtime reading.

Chapter 37

Almost too hot to drink, the coffee burned a little as she swallowed, but Kat didn't care. She was so tired; she needed the caffeine. She'd fallen asleep reading her dad's book and her brain had been so full of the weird and wonderful that her dreams reflected that verging on nightmares at times and Kat spent most of the night tossing and turning. She'd barely begun to scratch the surface of all the information. Each page was filled with cramped handwriting detailing different people, monsters, magics and events. Far too much to take in at once. Reading the book also reminded Kat that Flynn had mentioned a similar volume on Mr Magus' bookcase that she should check out. Perhaps she could compare the two and see what her dad had been working on.

Kat almost called in sick so she could get to grips with the book again, but her common sense told her it wasn't worth risking her job. Plus, her mum had made her promise not to get obsessed with the magical world. That was going to be a hard promise to keep, thought Kat as she waited for the door at Luciano's to swing open. She greeted Maxwell with a nod, content to not speak, and dutifully followed him to the room where they were filling in the ledgers.

Since the incident in the car park, Kat had not seen that many vampires lurking in the corridors of the solicitor's office. She guessed she made them nervous. She was still surprised that there hadn't been any significant repercussions, but like Amelia said–if those vampires who attacked her were doing so of their own volition, then the Senior Partners couldn't condone that behaviour by investigating it. It was best, for them, that the whole thing got brushed under the mat and Kat herself avoided at all costs.

Working on entering the numbers was soothing. She had to focus on it in order to not make a mistake, so there was no opportunity for idle thoughts. The day flew by and before she knew it; it was time to go home.

"Miss Kritchley, a word if I may?"

Maxwell had not unlocked the door, so Kat didn't really have a choice.

"It has been decided that no further action will be taken." Maxwell's tone was stiff and exceedingly formal.

Kat waited, but nothing else was said. But Maxwell remained standing still, barring the door. Clearly, he was waiting for her to say something.

"Um, okay. Thank you for letting me know."

It seemed absurd. She'd obliterated at least half a dozen vampires and nobody was going to do anything about it.

"Whilst the partners are grateful for your swift completion of the menial tasks assigned, it was deemed prudent not to add fuel to any flames. Therefore, your employment services are no longer required."

Kat's heart fell. She had sort of expected this to happen, but it was still a blow. Her first job for the agency and she'd been let go.

"What about… the investigation?" Kat wasn't sure if there were extra ears listening. She thought there might be, given the way Maxwell was talking to her. Sure, he didn't usually talk that much, but he also wasn't this wooden.

Maxwell put a finger to his lips and darted his eyes upwards. So there was someone listening. Kat gave a small nod of understanding.

"Allow me to escort you out of the building." And with that, Maxwell turned smartly and unlocked the door.

This time, vampires lined the corridor. Some Kat had seen before, but most were new scary faces. They didn't move, just watched her as she walked away from the relative safety of the little office. Every eye regarded her coldly. Kat could feel her power flickering deep inside her.

Keep it together! she thought to herself desperately. This was not the time or place to lose control.

When they made it to the front door, Kat let out a breath she hadn't realised she'd been holding on to. Veronique glided out of the gloom.

"This isn't over, human. You and your dragon pet have destroyed part of my lineage. My advice? Stay out of my way." Veronique's eyes glittered with malice. "Accidents happen all the time. Even with the best will in the world."

Kat swallowed. So, although the Senior Partners had called a truce, Veronique still wanted revenge. She couldn't blame her.

"When you find out who has targeted my sire line, you will report to Maxwell immediately." Veronique swept away, leaving Kat slightly stunned.

She opened her mouth to ask Maxwell a question, but he shook her head and nodded towards the door. She let him open it for her and looked back in surprise when he followed her. It turned out to be a gloomy afternoon; the sun hidden behind grey clouds. Maxwell hid his eyes in a pair of thick shades.

"Allow me to escort you to the Agency, Miss Kritchley." He clicked his heels together and bowed smartly at her.

With no real choice but to nod her assent, they began walking. Once they left the imposing solicitor's building, Maxwell relaxed a little.

"I am sorry that you won't be employed at Luciano's anymore. I have enjoyed working with Kieron Kritchley's daughter."

Kat blinked back sudden tears at the unexpected warmth in Maxwell's words.

"Thank you. It's been an interesting experience."

"Obviously, Veronique let the cat out of the bag. That woman always has to stick her fangs in," Maxwell tutted. "The Senior Partners and I would like you, and the Agency, to get to the bottom of who has framed the exiles and why they tried to start a fight between the dragons and the vampires. Someone is making a play, but it's unclear at the moment as to who or why."

"Does Mr Magus know you want us to keep investigating?" asked Kat.

Maxwell nodded.

"Well, how am I supposed to do that if I'm not working at Luciano's anymore?"

"I think we have gleaned everything we can from the firm. The people involved are aware of your power. They will not try anything too open for fear of saving their own skin. You shall have to follow other leads and see where they go."

Maxwell walked with a long stride, and they were at the Agency already.

"Good luck Miss Kritchley. I bid you adieu." He picked up one of Kat's hands and brushed cold lips against it. It was the most old-fashioned and gentlemanly thing that had ever happened to her, making her feel giddy.

Before she could react properly, he disappeared. Kat

pushed open the door to the Agency in a bit of a daze. She had some investigating to do.

Chapter 38

There was nobody at the reception desk and Mr Magus' door was closed. Kat wasn't confident enough to knock and enter, not without Amelia to back her up, so she wandered into the kitchen.

"Ooh hi! You're early. Everything alright?" Amelia guiltily shut the fridge with a bang.

"Um, you've got…" Kat pointed her finger to the side of her lips, indicating that Amelia had a blob of cream on her face. It was the first time she'd ever seen Amelia less than perfectly composed.

Amelia flushed and groaned.

"Oh my gods. It's these cream donuts. I just love them so much. I couldn't resist. I know they're meant to be for everyone, but they are so, so good!" She opened the fridge and took out a pink delicatessen box. "Look."

Opening the lid, she displayed the donuts to Kat. They did look amazing. One of them had a huge bite out of it.

"I think you should probably eat the rest of that one," said Kat, grinning. "I'll put the kettle on."

"Oh my gods, they're so good!" mumbled Amelia around a mouthful of donut. She proffered the box to Kat, who helped herself and took a bite.

"Wow, these are good. Where are they from?"

"I don't know. They were left on my desk. Probably a gift from someone who really, really, really, really, really loves us so much." Amelia's cheeks were pink with excitement.

Kat felt a little lightheaded herself. She put the donut down on a nearby plate.

"How many have you had?" she asked Amelia.

"Two! I've had two. This is my third. But it's okay because dragon metabolism is really good at working fast, so I'll burn the calories off like that." Amelia snapped her fingers and let out a tiny burp that was accompanied by a flicker of flame. "Oops!" She clapped her hands over her mouth.

"Come on, I think we should ask Mr Magus to have a look at these." Kat popped her donut back in the box and picked it up before encouraging Amelia out of the kitchen.

She was all over the place, like she'd been drinking. Bumping into things and laughing, her sense of balance was completely off. Kat managed to manoeuvre her out the kitchen door and down the corridor, but then Amelia had a fit of the giggles and slumped down the hallway wall she had been leaning on.

"What's so funny?" asked Kat.

But Amelia couldn't speak. She was laughing too much. Kat stepped over her outstretched legs and, taking a deep breath, knocked on Mr Magus' door.

"Come!"

She pushed the heavy door open and peered inside, nervous about going in by herself.

"Miss Kritchley. How can I help?"

"Um, there's something wrong with Amelia. I think she's been drugged." Kat held up the donut box. "By these."

Mr Magus leapt into action, leading the way to where Amelia still lay giggling on the hallway floor. He scooped her up easily and brought her back into his office, laying her down on a red chaise longue that sat beneath the window. Kneeling down at her level, he pressed the back of his hand on her forehead.

"Hmm. No temperature." Mr Magus peered into her

eyes. "Pupils are dilated, and she's clearly leaning towards hysteria."

"She burped in the kitchen, and a flame escaped." Kat was feeling a little woozy herself.

"Loss of control over her dragoness. Now that is not good. We need to purge her, get whatever it was she ate out of her system."

"She had three whole donuts. I had a mouthful. Just one. Tasted really nice." A giggle escaped from Kat as she staggered one way, then the other.

Mr Magus stood up and caught her arm, stopping her from weaving.

"Let's have you sitting down as well. I'll mix up some salt water. Should do the trick. Back in jiffy. Don't try to do anything, okay?"

Kat nodded, but once she started, her head kept going and she had to catch herself to stop it from bobbing. Amelia was talking to herself quietly, her hands in front of her face, picking something invisible out of the air.

Mr Magus returned with two glasses of swirling water. He kicked over his office bin, balled up pieces of paper tipping out to the floor.

"Here, take this." He gave one of the glasses to Kat and picked up the bin. "Take a mouthful and be ready."

Kat didn't even think about it. She gulped the salt water and instantly gagged, heaved and threw up into the bin. Her whole mouth twisted in disgust and she shuddered.

"Ugh!"

"Well done." Mr Magus didn't seem bothered in the slightest that he was holding a bin full of vomit. "Your turn, Amelia. Sit up for me, darling."

Kat blinked. *Darling*?

Amelia looked up lovingly at his face and tried to put out a hand to pat his cheek, but she kept missing. He grabbed her hand and gently pulled her up into a seated position.

"Xavier! You're here."

"Yes, I am. Now take this glass and have a drink, okay?"

"Anything for you," replied Amelia, doing exactly what he asked. She had the same reaction as Kat, but was sick for rather longer.

When she finally lifted her head, there were tears running down her face.

"Oh Xavier! What happened?"

He quickly tied up the rubbish bag in his bin and moved it to the doorway.

"Let me get you both some normal water and we'll discuss." He bustled out, taking the bin bag with him.

Amelia ran one hand through her hair, fanning herself with the other. Kat came to sit next to her.

"Are you okay?" she asked.

Amelia nodded, but still had tears in her eyes.

"Don't cry." Kat leaned over to where a small box of tissues sat on a side table, grabbing a couple. "Here."

Amelia leaned in for comfort and dried her eyes.

"Thank you. I'm so embarrassed. Donuts are a bit of a weakness of mine, but I should've been more aware that they could have been tampered with. I mean, a box of my favourite thing turning up on my desk out of the blue with no note."

Kat patted her shoulder, but before she could say anything, Mr Magus was back with fresh glasses.

"Just regular water this time, I promise," he said, handing them over and pulling a chair towards him so he could sit with them. "When did the parcel arrive?"

"It was on my desk when I got in. I was a little late this morning, as you know." Amelia's brow wrinkled as she thought back. "There was no note, but it was such a lovely box, done up with a bow and it smelled divine. I knew what was inside the moment I saw it, the aroma was so…" She closed her eyes in appreciation. "I decided I would just have the one. And it was so delicious—you have no idea. I managed to put them in the kitchen, but I couldn't stop thinking about them. I went back for a second and then Kat caught me eating a third and…" She shrugged. "Here we are."

"New office policy," said Mr Magus. "Anything that arrives unexpectedly needs to be magically cleared before opening and using. Agreed?"

Both women nodded. A fresh tear rolled down Amelia's face.

"I'm so sorry. I should know better."

Mr Magus gently wiped the tear away.

"It's okay. You're safe now. Let's see if we can figure out where this box came from. Where's Flynn?" he asked.

"I haven't seen him yet today," replied Amelia.

"And I'm not due to see him until later. Maxwell said the Senior Partners are letting me go, but he still wants me to investigate why those vampires we saw in the Catacombs were exiled and why the blood hasn't been paid for and why Veronique is being targeted." Kat spoke in a rush, wanting to say everything before she forgot something.

"We'd better get to work," replied Mr Magus. "Amelia, message Flynn and ask him to come in. Connor too. We're going to need the whole team."

That sent a warm tickle down Kat's tummy. She was part of the team now.

Chapter 39

Flynn clattered in through the door.

"I'm here! I'm here. Sorry, came as quickly as I could. Is Kat alright? What happened?" He blushed when he realised everyone else was sitting waiting for him, including Connor.

Adjusting his jacket, he tried to stroll more nonchalantly into the room and took the remaining chair.

"Yes, quite. Both Miss Kritchley and Amelia are well. Nothing a little purge couldn't handle, but it seems our mystery groweth. I trust you all received my update?" Mr Magus looked around, waiting for nods from everyone. "Good. So, ideas, thoughts. What do you suspect?"

It was like being back at school. There was no way Kat was going to say something first, especially as she had a greater chance of getting it wrong given her brief baptism into this magical world.

Connor stood up and paced around the offending box of donuts. It took Kat a moment to realise he was scenting the box and its contents. She surreptitiously pulled her t-shirt over her nose for a quick sniff. God, she hoped she didn't have body odour. Connor's cheeks twitched.

Damn it! thought Kat. He'd seen her do it. Well, it was done now, and as far as she could tell, she smelt just fine.

"Nothing I'm afraid, Boss. Smells like a box of sweet, fresh cream donuts."

Amelia gave a little moan. They really had been delicious. Connor chuckled.

"If there's no scent on the box and no clue as to who

delivered it or where it came from, then we're completely in the dark," said Amelia. "Obviously they knew I'd be here and that I like donuts so they used a drug strong enough to affect me."

Mr Magus nodded his agreement.

"Whoever it was that is targeting the agency obviously knows our strengths and weaknesses. They knew enough about Amelia to tempt her with her favourite cake and enough about Connor to make sure the box couldn't be traced."

"What about a magical signature?" asked Flynn and before Mr Magus had a chance to reply, he weaved a spell and shot it at the box.

Mr Magus held up a finger and opened his mouth, but he was too late to stop him. The spell bounced off an invisible shield with a fair amount of force and slammed back into Flynn so hard it knocked him backwards off his chair.

"Oh my god, Flynn! Are you okay?" asked Kat, rushing over to help him up.

Flynn's nose was bleeding slightly, but he looked more embarrassed than hurt. He shrugged off her support and picked his chair up, grabbing a tissue for his nose.

Kat returned to her own chair, a little miffed. She had only wanted to check he was alright.

"As I was about to say, the box appears to be magically warded, and any attempts to pierce that ward result in a rather impressive rebound." Mr Magus rubbed the back of his head. He had made a similar mistake to Flynn earlier, while they had been waiting for him and Connor to arrive.

"Have you thought about checking the security footage?" asked Kat, flushing a little when everyone turned their gaze on her.

"Sweetie, we don't have security cameras in here," replied Amelia, reminding Kat of the lack of modern technology in the building, but she quickly rallied.

"No, I don't mean in here. I know we don't. I mean the ones on the street, outside. There are CCTV cameras all over the place, plus you've got the shops on either side. Maybe one of them captured the culprit. Can't hurt to check it out, right?"

Mr Magus looked thoughtful.

"You might be on to something there, Miss Kritchley. Flynn, Connor, go next door and speak to the establishments. Ask them if we can view their footage. Tell them we've had a break in. Amelia, I'm afraid you and I will have to go to the police station and speak to our contact there. Bring some tea. What they serve in that place isn't legal."

Kat was disappointed at being so utterly left out.

"What about me? What can I do?" She really didn't want to be told to stay here and man the desk.

"Ah well, in the spirit of joining the next century and expanding our horizons, I had Amelia order you a device to assist in our investigations. Given that so much can now be found on the line, we are going to join up."

It was a little bit adorable hearing Mr Magus try to explain a laptop and the Internet. Kat stammered her thanks at the top of the range equipment that was revealed.

"I trust you can get this all set up and working?" Mr Magus waited for Kat's assent. "Excellent. Then you start researching local blood suppliers. We know the vampires stopped paying for their usual one, but they must be getting their blood from somewhere. We need to find out where and who put the order in."

Kat felt a tingle of excitement. She was going to do some real investigating using equipment she actually understood and was comfortable with.

"Don't worry, Mr Magus. I'll have a list by the time you return," she said.

"Wonderful." Mr Magus smiled at the others and made a little shushing motion. "Shall we?"

There was a flurry of activity as people got coats and bags and then called out their goodbyes to Kat, leaving her on her own with a router and a laptop and most of an idea on how to get online.

"Shoot! I should have asked who we have our phone line with–are we even hooked up to the Internet?" she said, talking to herself, looking around the main reception area for any sign of a telephone wire and connector box. Surprisingly, she found one in the corner. It was labelled BT. "Great!"

Unpacking the router and following the instructions within, Kat spent the next ten minutes getting everything set up. Despite never having used it before, the Agency clearly paid for the Internet as it connected almost immediately. In fact, there were none of the usual teething headaches Kat had experienced in the past, setting up these things. She patted the wall of the building. "You're helping out, aren't you?"

She'd spoken without expecting any kind of reaction and yet the wall pulsed under her hand. There seemed to be a happy glow in the room, and it wasn't just coming from the fireplace.

"Huh!" said Kat, then jumped a foot in the air when Connor spoke behind her.

"Talking to yourself?" he asked.

"No! Jesus, you scared the life out of me." She breathed heavily. "Did you know this place was alive?"

Connor shrugged.

"You can't expect the building that has housed a magical agency for several centuries not to pick up a trick or two."

Centuries mouthed Kat in surprise, wondering if that was how long Mr Magus had been here, but before she had the chance to ask more questions, Connor started talking again.

"The shop next door won't show me their footage. Said I needed a warrant."

"Oh, that sucks. Maybe we can get one after Mr Magus has spoken to his contact at the police station."

"Or…" Connor pulled a tape from his pocket. "I slipped around the back and let myself in." At the shocked look on Kat's face, he held his hands up in surrender. "I'll return it once we've watched it."

Kat plucked the tape out of his fingers and waggled it under his nose.

"What are we going to watch it on, genius?"

But before Connor could reply, Flynn returned.

Chapter 40

Flynn held out an identical tape.

"They let you have it?" he asked in surprise.

"No. Connor *borrowed* it, so it has to go back once we've seen what's on it. What about you?" Kat nodded towards the tape in his hands.

"Borrowed." Flynn and Connor grinned at each other while Kat tutted at them.

"Now that we have these videos, how exactly are we going to watch them?" she asked.

"Ah, um, you'll have to come up to my room. I should have something that will do the trick." Flynn headed for the stairs in the hallway and the others followed.

Kat was surprised. She hadn't known that Flynn actually lived here, and she hadn't been upstairs in the Agency yet either. All her magic training had been done downstairs, but thinking about it, it made sense. It was his father's agency. It was a large building. Why wouldn't they live here?

"I'm all the way up," said Flynn.

He kept his head down as they walked along an immaculate hallway with an intricately patterned carpet runner that felt super thick under Kat's feet. The walls were wood panelled, like out of an old-fashioned haunted house. As soon as she had that thought, Kat got goosebumps and couldn't help herself from looking over her shoulder to double check there was nothing there. There wasn't.

A family portrait hung on one of the empty walls, but instead of a photo or printed canvas, it looked to Kat like it had been painted. She slowed to have a good look and saw Mr Magus, a younger looking Flynn and a woman who must be Flynn's mother. The odd thing was that they were wearing period clothing. Kat was no expert, but it appeared Victorian? It definitely wasn't modern.

Realising that she'd fallen behind the others, she hurried to catch up and tugged on Connor's arm, stopping him.

"Is that Flynn's mum?" She nodded backwards, indicating the family portrait on the wall.

"Yeah."

"It's some kind of period thing, right? Something rich people dress up and do." Kat kept her voice down, not wanting Flynn to overhear.

"I don't think so." Connor sounded bemused.

Kat snorted.

"So Flynn's one hundred and fifty years old then," she said.

"Er, no. More like two hundred," Connor replied, then caught the amazement on Kat's face. "You didn't know?"

"Know what? That he's immortal?" she hissed.

"No, he's not immortal. Just long lived. Being a full blood will do that to you. Especially when both your parents are full blood too, and lifetime practitioners." He cast a quick look at Flynn, who was climbing the next staircase and not paying attention to them. "Using magic, having access to the Source, lengthens a human lifespan."

Kat took a moment to digest this.

"Are you telling me that I'm going to age slower than everyone I know?"

Connor shrugged.

"Depends how much you touch the Source."

Kat scowled. Yet again something else she hadn't been told. A side effect of being exposed to magic. What other things would happen to her?

"What about his mum?" asked Kat.

"What about her?"

Kat gestured around.

"Oh, she's not here." Seeing the concern on Kat's face, Connor quickly carried on. "She's not dead. They split up. Years ago. Differences in the craft or something. Best not to mention it to Flynn. He's a bit touchy about it. Come on."

They both hurried after Flynn.

The room was a full conversion to a bedroom with a proper staircase up to the doorway and only the sloping ceilings giving away the fact it was the attic. The ceilings were still high and light came in from a circular window at each end with more windows set into the roof.

It was the first time Kat had been in a man's room— other than her brothers. She looked around with curiosity. Flynn had a bookcase stuffed with paperbacks that Kat itched to go and poke through. A large bed, unmade and a pile of clothes next to the wash basket. As Kat glanced to the right, she stopped short. It was a wall of technology.

Multiple screens, laptops, various games console and a huge TV screen.

"Woah! Cool set up."

Connor sounded just as impressed as Kat felt.

"Does your dad know about this?" she asked as Flynn watched them both in amusement.

"Nah. This is not his area of expertise, but it fascinates me. I reckon I've got something that will play these CCTV tapes. Grab a seat." He pointed to a pile of bean bags.

Connor and Kat made themselves comfortable, watching as Flynn tinkered with this, that, and the other. Finally, the large TV screen flickered into life and a grainy video began to play.

"Which one is this?" asked Kat.

"Er, this is the shoe shop. The one Connor got."

Flynn came and joined them on the floor and began to fast forward through the footage. There were a lot of grainy blobs coming in and out, in and out. To Kat's eyes, they all looked exactly the same.

"Why are you fast forwarding so much? Shouldn't we be watching it in real time? Looking for anything suspicious?" She leaned forward, trying to make sense of the blobs.

Flynn didn't reply, and she was about to ask again when he let out a *ha!* Pausing the video, he turned to Connor.

"What do you think?"

"Well, it's definitely one of ours."

Kat looked from Flynn to Connor in exasperation.

"What are you talking about?" she asked crossly.

Flynn stood and pointed to the TV screen.

"That is a supernatural being."

Kat peered at the recording. This particular grainy blob was glowing.

"Do we glow? Does that mean I'm going to glow on video? How come this isn't all over TikTok or in the news? Weird glowey people walk among us or whatever."

Connor laughed.

"Where do you think alien sightings come from?" he said.

"And reports of angels," added Flynn.

Kat wasn't entirely sure they were being completely truthful with her, but it did make a sort of sense. She slumped back in her beanbag.

"Okay, so there's a person glowing on the footage. It doesn't get us any closer to knowing who it is, does it?"

Flynn went over to the tape player and fiddled some more, getting the other video to play. The TV screen split into two, one half paused on the glow person and the other half playing the CCTV footage from the shop on the other side of the Agency. This time, the video quality was much better.

"They've obviously upgraded their system," remarked Connor.

"It is a jeweller, isn't it? They ought to have a good security system," said Kat, trying to keep up with Flynn's fast forwarding. "Wait! Stop. Go back. There. Look. Walking past the window. A glowey person."

Flynn rewound and, sure enough, a man surrounded by a glow walked past the window. He paused the footage, and they looked at the two images side by side.

"Is it even the same person?" asked Kat, tilting her head to one side.

"I think so. There's a white stripe down the sleeve of the jacket, clearly visible on both. And chunky white trainers. It's not much, but it certainly links both images," replied Flynn.

"Time stamp works as well," said Connor, pointing to the screen. "You've got a grainy glow blob showing up at nine am carrying a box. Obviously we can't see the colour, but from the size and shape, I'd say it's the same one as the donut box downstairs." He then jabbed a finger at the other, better quality image. "Here he is, quarter past nine, with no box at all. Delivery job complete. This is definitely our guy."

"Just because he dropped the box off, doesn't mean he was behind the poisoning though," said Kat. "And we don't have a lot to go on. White trainers and a black top with a white stripe down the arm–have you walked around town lately? You've just described nearly the entire youth population."

Flynn was still staring at the images.

"I reckon he's about six feet tall, you know. Look at where that lamp post is in relation to his shoulder when he walks by. And that's a pretty long stride. I think his trainers seem so chunky because his feet are massive."

They all peered more closely. It was hard to see his face at all because he had pulled his hoodie up over his hair and all his features were cloaked in shadow.

"He's got a big nose though, hasn't he?" said Kat. "Look at how it's poking out despite trying to hide his face with his hoodie. Is it enough to try to find him? Do you have some kind of magical database?"

Aware that she was probably going to get laughed at again, she braced herself for having the mick taken out of her.

"Do you know what? We don't, but the school does. And if this guy is aware that he's a super, then he will have gone to school," replied Flynn.

"Unless he's like me," Kat retorted.

"There's no one quite like you," replied Connor with a wink that made Kat blush a little.

Flynn busied himself taking a photo of the two images from the CCTV on his phone and then sending them over to Connor and Kat.

"I'll go to the school. You guys have a mooch around town. See if you recognise a tall super with a giant nose. You never know."

Kat was a little disappointed. She desperately

wanted to see the magic school for herself, but Flynn's tone had been firm and she didn't think she would be able to change his mind.

"Meet back here at..." Flynn checked his watch, prompted Kat to check the time on her phone as well. "At six? Give us a couple of hours to canvas."

Kat winced a little. She'd be late for dinner again, but this was important–they had to find out who had tried to drug Amelia. This was twice now that her friend had been in serious danger.

Chapter 41

"Where do you think we should go first?" asked Connor as they stood outside the Agency.

Kat shivered. It was pretty miserable with a dingy light rain attacking anyone brave enough to be out and about.

"I dunno," she replied.

"I thought you'd know all the cool places to hang out." Connor bumped her shoulder, making her smile a little.

"Well, Maccy D's obviously and afterwards we could try the roller rink?"

"Sounds like a plan. Lead on!" Connor bowed grandly at Kat, who rolled her eyes at him as they walked across the square to where the ever popular fast-food restaurant sat.

Pushing open the doors was like walking back into Kat's teenage days when she and her mates had nothing better to do than hang about town and get a strawberry milkshake for lunch. Nowadays, the smell of the food wasn't as great as it used to be, but she could still be convinced to eat a chicken nugget from time to time.

They scanned the crowd downstairs, but nobody stood out, so they headed up. This was the true domain of the teenager. Large groups sprawled in various booths and sections of the restaurant, staking their territorial claim, all of them looking up with hostility at the newcomers daring to enter.

Kat made a beeline for the toilets, hoping this would make them less conspicuous and doubly hoping that Connor would catch on to her lead. Thankfully, he did, and slowly the teenage conversations bubbled back up, ignoring the two adults that had wandered into their midst.

"Won't be long," said Kat as she pushed the door open to the Ladies toilets, thinking she might as well have a pee while she was here. Her tummy still felt a bit swirly after the effects of the poisoned donut and the saltwater purge.

Emerging a few minutes later, she saw Connor leaning against the wall, his attention on the groups of youths, and Kat took a moment to watch him. He was a hell of a good-looking guy.

"Ready?" she said softly, her heart skipping as he greeted her with a huge smile.

"Yep, come on. He's not here. Let's try the roller rink."

They trotted downstairs and walked all the way through the shopping precinct, not saying much but keeping an eye out for their lanky target.

The roller rink had been attached to the side of the shopping centre for ever. It was a little dilapidated, but practically everyone had been there either as a child, a teenager, or a harassed parent. Kat had fond memories of going skating with her dad and even taking Mikey there. He liked the music and the sound of the wheels whooshing around. She felt a small pang of guilt at not having taken him roller skating for ages and made a promise to herself to rectify that soon.

It would be too suspicious to go into the rink and not skate, so they lined up to pay and get their wheels.

"Have you skated before?" Kat asked.

"Er, no actually. First time." He flushed, admitting it.

"Oh, I'm sure you'll be fine. We'll do a few laps, see who's there and find out if anyone has seen our guy."

Kat couldn't suppress bubbles of excitement. She loved skating.

Pulling on the skates, wiggling her toes at the tightness, she pulled the laces and wrapped them around the top of her boot. Connor watched her quizzically.

"You don't want them to come undone, or be too long. If they get caught in a wheel…" She puffed out her cheeks. She'd seen it happen. Crashing on the rink never looked good, but a fall due to poorly tied laces was beyond embarrassing.

Connor copied her method, and she gave him a hand to stand.

"The front plugs are your brakes. Well, one way to brake. They'll also help you keep your balance if you need to get up after falling." She grinned.

Together, they walked awkwardly over the carpet to the rink entrance. It wasn't that busy, with a few ushers casually skating backwards in big loopy glides, chatting to each other. Kat looked up at the small café upstairs and saw a gaggle of teenagers. It was too difficult to tell from here if their guy was amongst them, so she decided to just enjoy a few laps.

A small push and she was on the rink, the ground feeling smooth beneath her wheels.

"So you sort of push off and glide, one foot after the other. Bend your knees a little. Go on, give it a go."

Connor stood uncertainly on his skates and made a sawing motion with his feet, but stayed where he was.

"Like this." Kat demonstrated a short push and glide, turning gracefully and coming back to where Connor stood. "You can put your stopper down and use that as a static push if you want."

Nodding, Connor did as she said, and on wobbly legs, set off. His strides were short and his arms pinwheeled as he fought to stay upright, but in no time at all, he mastered the motion. It was a bit galling that he picked it up so easily, but Kat guessed that his supernatural abilities probably helped with his spatial awareness and balance.

She couldn't help but watch how graceful he looked. Pushing with her legs to go faster, she glided past him and extended one leg out to execute a perfect turn. Connor's was more choppy, but by the time they got to the other end of the rink, he copied her motion exactly.

Feeling as if the gauntlet had been laid, Kat sped up, crossing her skates like a speed skater and whipping around the rink. It took Connor longer to get the hang of that, but sure enough, he matched her skill. Despite not having been skating for a while, it was all coming back to Kat, so she flipped around and began copying the lazy motion of the ushers skating backwards. She checked over her shoulder for other skaters, but the rink was still pretty clear.

Connor watched her for a moment and then, with a little shrug, attempted to turn and copy her. The only problem was he clanged wheels, stuttered with his skates, trying to gain his balance before one foot slid out in the opposite direction of his body and he landed with a jolt on the floor.

"Oooooh!" came a collective cry from the teenagers who had come down from the café and were now lounging at the entrance to the rink.

Kat wheeled over to Connor and helped him up.

"Do you see what I see?" she whispered as he gratefully took her hand.

"Big nose? Yeah. What's the plan?" he whispered back, surreptitiously rubbing his backside with one hand.

"Let's see if they come on the rink. We can try to

isolate him, but no more backwards skating, yeah?" Kat grinned as Connor nodded and they set off more slowly this time, moving together, not trying to outdo each other.

The teenagers poured onto the rink, about ten of them in total.

"Why do they always hang out in packs?" muttered Kat, then flushed as she realised who she was talking to.

Connor just grinned. They let the teenagers clump up in front of them, slowing their skating, trying not to make it too obvious that they were watching one in particular.

The lad was six feet tall at the very least and the skates on his feet looked huge. His nose was prominent, but somehow it still fit his face. He wasn't one of those skinny, lanky looking teenagers. He had some bulk about him. And he was still wearing the black jacket with the white stripe.

In order to not appear too suspicious skating behind the group, Kat grabbed Connor's hand, so they were moving together. He started at first, then gave her a crooked smile and a little squeeze. They slowed their rhythm, skating in unison, listening in to the teenagers talk.

"We all going to Macs after?" asked one of the girls.

"Nah, I ain't eating there no more. It's nasty. They got rats and the servers spit in your food. I've seen them do it." Her friend replied, flicking a long lock of hair over one shoulder and sending a waft of strong, cheap perfume towards Kat and Connor. It was so powerful it made Connor double over and cough.

"You okay?" asked Kat as she clenched her muscles in order to keep her balance as Connor inadvertently pulled on her.

"Yeah," he wheezed. "Perfume's a bit strong."

There was a bit of a gap between them and the teenagers now, so Kat angled herself and Connor over to one side so they could allow them to pass, picking up speed to slot in behind them again.

"Let's crash at Piper's. Get some pizza–my shout." It was their mark talking.

"You sure?" The teenage collective perked up at the prospect of someone else paying for food.

"How come you got money? You've never got any." One of the other lads poked big nose in the ribs, causing the mob to ebb out and in as they deftly avoided each other.

"I did that job, didn't I? Got paid, so yeah, pizza on me."

Kat glanced at Connor in excitement. He had to be talking about delivering the donuts. If only he would tell them who paid him.

"You did a job? As if." The other began teasing big nose who clearly had a reputation for being lazy.

"Nah, nah, nah. It were Big Al. You don't say no to Big Al. And anyways, it were easy work, just deliver a box."

It was like a dream confession. Kat had no idea who Big Al was, but they literally had proof that this lad had delivered the donut box. But the reaction from the other teenagers and from Connor was different. Connor squeezed Kat's hand so tightly it hurt. The pack of skaters collectively gasped and made negative noises.

The lad who had poked big nose in jest, hit him on the shoulder.

"What are you doing getting involved with Big Al? He's bad news, Alex. You shouldn't have done it."

"Pft whatever, you're just jealous he didn't ask you."

Alex lengthened his skating stride, pulling away from the others and heading for an exit from the rink. About half the teenagers followed him.

Kat pulled Connor wide so she could talk to him without being overheard.

"What's going on? Who's Big Al?" she asked, keeping one eye on Alex, who was now leaning on the wall of the roller rink watching the rest of his mates.

"This is not good. Big Al is..." Connor fell silent as a group of people skated close by. He watched them to make sure no one was listening. "Big Al is Pack Leader."

Tension filled Connor's whole body, like he was ready to fight right now. Kat knew that this was a huge deal, but she wasn't sure exactly why.

"Do we need to talk to Alex?" she whispered, guiding Connor over to a different rink exit.

"No. He was literally just the messenger and if he won't listen to his friends about not working for Big Al, then he's not going to give us the time of day."

"What do we do now?" asked Kat, finding a chair to sit down, feeling the effects of skating already in the backs of her legs. It had been a long time.

"Now, you go home, be with your family. I've got to go see mine." Connor did not sound happy about the prospect.

"But I might be able to help, act as a buffer at the very least." She reached out and touched his arm gently. "I don't want you to be alone." Kat didn't know exactly how she felt about Connor, but she knew that she didn't want to see a friend suffer.

"It'll be a hostile experience. Are you sure you're ready? They might not even let you in." Connor sounded like he really wanted Kat to come with him.

"We're a team, right?" She beamed at him, but he was only able to return a half smile, which didn't fill her with much confidence. What on earth was she letting herself in for now?

They took off their skates and handed them back in. It felt weird walking without the weight of them on their feet.

"What kind of super do you think he is, then?" asked Kat as they put their normal shoes back on.

"What?" Connor sounded distracted.

"Alex. What is he?" Kat glanced around to see if anyone was eavesdropping, but all the teenagers were on the other side of the rink.

"Oh, I don't know. He's not powerful. You would've probably smelled him if he was. He's probably a sprite of some kind or maybe a mixling. They're pretty common."

Kat's nose wrinkled. *Smell him?* All she could smell were roller skates and a tinge of body odour, which she fervently hoped wasn't her.

"Do magical people smell differently?" She was learning all sorts of weird stuff today.

"Yeah, although it takes a little while to notice if you don't have a sensitive nose like me."

"What's a mixling?" Kat asked as they walked out.

"You know, a bit of this, a bit of that." Connor looked at Kat to see if she understood. "Um, I guess, magical creature lineage isn't as pure as it used to be. There are less fae than there used to be and so more intermingling happens. A mixling is a fae creature with lots of different heritage, so it might be part elf, part pixie, part brownie—that sort of thing. It's rare to meet pure fae these days."

Kat mulled that over.

"But Daisy at The WigWam is pure elf, isn't she?"

"Absolutely."

"Does Alex know he's a mixling?"

Connor scratched his head.

"Huh. That's a good question. Possibly not. All his skater friends were normal. Just because he glowed on the CCTV doesn't mean he even knows he's a super. And if his parents are half and half, there's a strong chance he doesn't have any powers, anyway. But, on the other hand, he did do a job for Big Al, so…"

They walked back through the shopping centre in silence, Kat's head swirling with a million questions, trying to decide which one to ask first.

"Is it usual for someone with a normal parent and a magical parent to not have any powers?" Kat watched Connor closely as he answered her question.

"Actually, it is. Which is why you are so special," he replied with a smile. "And so surprisingly strong."

Kat could feel herself glowing a little, inordinately pleased to be called special by Connor.

"Look, are you sure you want to come with? It might be dangerous."

"I'll be with you," Kat replied, this time making Connor blush. "You'll look after me. Besides, I can hold my own." And although she sounded confident, she had no idea if her powers would work against werewolves.

Chapter 42

As they exited the shopping centre, Kat's phone rang. It was Flynn.

"Hello?"

"No luck at the school. They wouldn't even entertain the possibility that one of their students could have done something wrong. I mean, you'd think anyone and everyone that goes there is a perfect angel, well, you know what? I could tell you some stories that would make your toes curl..."

Flynn continued ranting for a few minutes. Kat covered the mouthpiece of her phone and told Connor who it was. She made the appropriate noises in all the right places until he finally ran out of breath and she was able to talk.

"Good news. We found him," she said.

There was a long pause on the other end of the line.

"Turns out that he was doing a job for Big Al, so we're headed over there now."

"No! Wait. You can't go. It's not safe, for either of you," Flynn nearly yelled down the phone at her.

"We'll be fine..." Kat tried to say, but Flynn talked over her.

"Did Connor even explain what will happen to him if he returns to the pack? He's an outcast. He'll be skinned alive. Literally. It's way too dangerous for him to go anywhere near Big Al and his followers. Look, just wait. Where are you? I'll come to you."

But before Kat could tell Flynn where they were, he appeared outside the door of the Agency, across the square from where they were. One minute nobody was there, the next moment he was. Kat hung up and waved.

"How does he do that?" she marvelled.

"Huh?" Connor looked up as Flynn hurried over to them. "Oh, the popping up thing? Yeah, it's one of his little magic tricks."

"Flynn said it's dangerous for you to go back to the pack," said Kat, waiting for Connor to give her some kind of explanation.

He stood there, looking at her, a thoughtful expression on his face, as if he were deciding whether to tell her the truth or not.

"Connor!" shouted Flynn. "Wait!"

Connor looked away, the moment broken, and Kat felt like she missed out on learning something really important.

Flynn wheezed slightly as he reached them, out of breath for having hurried so much.

"Don't go to Big Al's. It's not worth the risk. I'll go," he said.

"But they won't listen to you, you're not pack. At least if I go..." Connor trailed off.

"Yeah, if you go, they'll probably kill you, or worse."

What could be worse than being killed? Wondered Kat as Flynn and Connor stared at each other aggressively.

"Oi," she said, inserting herself between the two of them. "Pack it in. I'll go with Flynn. I'm an unknown quantity. That should keep them off balance, especially if they heard about the car park incident."

"Everyone's heard about the car park incident," muttered Flynn as Kat glared at him.

She put an arm out to Connor.

"This is not worth risking your life for. We only want to ask a few questions."

"And what if they don't want to answer them?" Connor did not sound impressed.

"Then we'll say thank you very much and walk away," Kat tried to smile confidently, feeling anything but.

"Look, I get that you don't want me to put myself deliberately at risk, but you walking into Big Al's territory is exactly the same. I can't ask you to do that. I have another idea."

Kat was relieved. The thought of going to see a bunch of werewolves without Connor had made her nauseous. She was only just coming into her powers and had no clue if they even worked on werewolves.

"Go on then, what's your great idea?" Flynn asked.

"Invite him for a drink. At the WigWam. That way, he'll be unarmed and Daisy can prevent them from shifting. I mean, he's a big guy, so if he decides to punch you, it'll be lights out, but at least you won't get eaten alive."

Kat hoped that Connor was speaking more to Flynn about being knocked out than her.

"Will he go for it?" she asked. It seemed unlikely to her that the leader of the pack would want to meet her for a drink. She was nobody.

"Yeah, just to satisfy curiosity, if nothing else. You're the great Kieron Kritchley's daughter, recently come into her amazing and terrifying powers and responsible for wasting a carpark full of our mortal enemy. What's not to like?"

There was a little twinkle in Connor's eye that made Kat think he was teasing her.

"Mortal enemy?" she asked, deciding to focus on that part.

"He means centuries old. Werewolves versus

vampires was a thing, like a million years ago," replied Flynn.

"Ancient enemies die hard."

Kat thought about it. The WigWam was a public place. Maybe Mr Magus would come with them as well. And the bouncer at the pub had seemed perfectly capable of dealing with any trouble that might come his way.

"Okay, let's do it. We can wait for Mr Magus to come back from the police station and then we can all go for a drink. With werewolves."

"I'll send the invite," said Flynn, whipping out his phone while Connor looked on bleakly.

"You can't come, can you?" asked Kat.

"It's probably not a good idea. If I'm there, it's likely to put everyone's hackles up and there's no point in putting you all in needless danger." Connor twisted his lips, clearly hating the fact that he couldn't be with her.

"Hey, it's okay." Kat smiled at him. "Do you think he'll tell us why he sent a box of poisoned donuts to try to incapacitate Amelia?"

They began slowly walking back to the Agency now that they had a plan.

"Actually, it's weird. It's not like werewolves to be underhand like that. If they want to pick a fight, they usually come right out and pick one." Flynn's words sounded challenging, but Connor just nodded.

"So, maybe Big Al is still a middle man. Someone told him to use a kid to deliver the donuts," suggested Kat.

"Possibly. But who is powerful enough to tell an Alpha what to do?"

Connor's question stumped them all, and they let themselves into the Agency in silence.

Chapter 43

Amelia and Mr Magus swept into the Agency so dramatically, Kat couldn't help but smile.

"I'm guessing it didn't go so well at the police station?" she asked.

"You are correct in your assessment, Miss Kritchley. In fact, the whole lot of them are about as much use as a chocolate teapot. Speaking of which…" Mr Magus arched an eyebrow at Flynn, who huffed a little as he left to make the tea.

"Could your contact not help?" Kat patted Amelia on the shoulder in sympathy as she leant in for a support hug.

"He had retired and passed on. I really did not think it had been that long since I had impressed upon the police force to help me in an investigation." Mr Magus sighed, pressing a hand to his head. "Time has a habit of sneaking up on you."

Kat didn't know what to say to that. They fell into silence waiting for the tea and she wondered exactly how old Mr Magus was. And would the same thing happen to her now that she was tapping into her powers? Was there a ratio of how much you used them to how many years you added to your life? And what about ageing? Did it occur at all? Or was it like a last minute all at once dramatic event where you suddenly shrivelled into an ancient husk? She was so lost in thought she jumped out of her skin when Flynn tapped her on the shoulder, offering her a mug of hot chocolate. Kat took it gratefully and looked around, a little sheepishly.

However, it seemed that nobody had noticed, as they were all absorbed in their own thought clouds. Mr

Magus did frown initially at having a mug shoved in his hands, but nodded faintly when he saw the contents.

"Hot chocolate. A good choice, son. We need fortification."

Kat had no idea what that meant, but as she sipped the drink, warmth spread through her body and she began to feel like they could conquer whatever lay before them.

"Did you have much luck?" asked Amelia.

Connor quickly filled them in, finishing with their plan to lure out Big Al at the WigWam.

"And you've already sent this message?"

Kat couldn't tell if Mr Magus was pleased or not. He was sitting ramrod straight in a chair, as if ready to leap into action at a moment's notice. His face was devoid of expression.

"Er, yes." Flynn answered without looking at his father, his eyes firmly glued to the drink in front of him.

Mr Magus stood, placed his mug on the edge of Amelia's desk, and began pacing. Kat opened her mouth to speak but Amelia grabbed her arm and shook her head, making wait motions with her hand. Clearly, this was something Mr Magus did regularly, as everyone else sat quietly and waited.

After a couple of torturous minutes of silent pacing, Mr Magus spun on his heels to face the group.

"It's a good plan. Dangerous, but I believe you're right Flynn, this will capture their attention at the very least. Big Al will come. It's neutral ground and he will need to see for himself what the vampire killer is like. We should forewarn Daisy, so she is prepared."

Both Kat and Flynn flushed a little whilst he also bobbed his head in acceptance of the praise.

"And Connor, you have made the right choice. You

cannot go to the meeting." Mr Magus paused. "But I see no reason why you cannot lurk in the carpark."

Connor grinned fiercely.

"Amelia, you will, of course, accompany Miss Kritchley. Perhaps you ought to dress for the occasion, mmm?"

Amelia let out a little squeal and clapped her hands.

"How long have we got?" She checked her watch and gasped. "Oh, we don't have a moment to lose. Come on, Kat, let's get ready."

Amelia dragged Kat by the hand, out of the reception area and up the staircase. This time Kat went in the opposite direction to where Flynn's room was and was surprised to be thrust into a large space with row upon row of racks of clothing.

"How did I not know about this?" she asked, looking around in awe.

"Oh, there is so much I haven't told you. I forget what you do and don't know," said Amelia as she began sorting through the racks. "Sometimes it feels like I've known you forever." She flashed a giant smile at her.

Kat grinned back.

"What are we looking for, exactly?" she asked.

"I'm thinking modern day Xena Warrior Princess? Something that makes you look totally bad ass basically," replied Amelia.

Kat's grin grew. This was the best job.

After rejecting some of Amelia's more out there clothing suggestions. Kat decided on a pair of skinny fit black jeans, a white tank top and a leather jacket. It was a classic choice, but she felt good about it. She didn't want to be super uncomfortable as well as being worried about how the meeting would go. A chunky pair of biker style boots completed the look, or at least she thought it did until Amelia opened a cabinet stuffed full of jewellery.

Kat was more than a little nervous coming down the stairs. She had never had her outfit scrutinised before, especially not by her boss and work colleagues. But she needn't have worried. A sharp nod from Mr Magus was all that she got besides a surreptitious thumbs up from Flynn and a wink from Connor. The wink made her go all gooey inside, but she did her best to squash those kinds of thoughts. Now really wasn't the time.

Chapter 44

It was different entering The WigWam, knowing they might be walking into danger. Kat's eyes darted around, examining the different patrons dotted throughout the pub, trying to remember if they had been there last time or whether they looked particularly wolfish. To be fair, she hadn't known Connor was a wolf just by looking at him.

Daisy greeted them from behind the bar.

"Hiya, find some seats and we'll bring your drinks over."

Kat nodded tightly, not even sure what drink she wanted. The booths were bigger than she remembered. Mr Magus, Flynn, Amelia and Kat could all fit comfortably along one side of the booth, leaving plenty of space for Big Al and whoever he brought with him.

"Relax, Miss Kritchley. Nothing can happen here in the WigWam." Mr Magus looked ever so slightly pained as he spoke. "Daisy has tightened the wards. I feel like I'm in a straight jacket."

Kat was going to shake her head, but then she realised her skin did feel tight. It wasn't massively uncomfortable, though. She mentally flexed and her magic reacted beneath her skin. If Mr Magus hadn't told her about the wards, she would've assumed her power was still within reach.

Amelia looked flushed.

"I can't dragon. I can feel it, coiled and ready to pounce, but I can't aspect at all. This is amazing!"

Kat wasn't sure she would agree. Her powerful protector was not completely scaleless, but she guessed that for Amelia, who hadn't wanted to dragon-out in the first place, it must feel pretty good.

"You okay?" she asked Flynn.

He answered by flicking a knife out of a sleeve, rapidly twirling it about his fingers and making it disappear again.

"Isn't that against the rules?" Kat hissed, darting her eyes over to the pub bouncer who wasn't paying them any attention.

Flynn gave a guilty shrug. He'd surrendered other weapons when they came in. Kat had seen him do it. Maybe the bouncer just wasn't on the ball today, which was worrying.

Daisy bustled over with a tray of drinks. They were all different. Some fancier than others.

"I'd appreciate it if you could avoid any trouble, but know this much. The staff will protect you should things get out of hand." She spoke to the air, not making eye contact with anyone.

Kat couldn't help but think the offer was more dangerous than it sounded. There was a definite sense of menace to it. Perhaps they would all end up washing dishes for the next one hundred years.

"That's not a bad idea," said Daisy, winking at Kat as she left the table.

"Um, can elves hear thoughts?" Kat asked the group.

Mr Magus chuckled.

"Only if you're thinking them really loudly."

Kat blushed and concentrated on the drink in front of her. It was smoking slightly. She gingerly sniffed the glass. It smelt of toffee apples and fireworks. She gave it a tentative sip. It tasted like cider, but so much more than that.

"Wow, that's delicious," she said, looking up to tell Amelia all about it when she became aware of a large shadow across their table. Big Al had arrived.

The name was accurate. He was a large man. Not only tall, but broad shouldered and powerfully muscled. He had huge arms and a thick neck, but surprisingly, his face was kind and he had a tangled mane of shaggy brown hair. Behind him stood three companions, one woman who was wiry with a long silvery pony tail and two young men that bore a resemblance to Connor.

"Miss Kritchley?" asked Big Al, his voice deep and rich.

Kat nodded, her throat suddenly dry, unable to speak.

"Please, join us." Mr Magus gestured towards the empty side of the booth, but he made no attempt to rise or extend a hand in greeting.

Kat was appalled by the lack of manners. She bounced upright.

"Yes, call me Kat. It's great to meet you. I've heard so much about you. Thank you for coming." She was aware she was gabbling, but the hand she held out was gently taken and shook by Big Al, and a look of compassion flashed through his eyes.

Once the wolves had settled themselves, there was an awkward silence.

"As you called this meeting, Kat. Perhaps you could illuminate me on why you wanted to talk. Is there..." His eyes flicked briefly towards Mr Magus. "...a favour I can do for you?"

"Ah no. Well. You see, um, there was an attempt on my friend's life. Amelia." Kat pointed. "And we discovered that the poisoned donuts were sent via a young man called Alex, who was working for, er... you. So we wanted to know, um, why exactly you're trying to kill her. Please."

There was a long pause.

Big Al was shaking. At first, Kat thought it was in anger until she realised he was attempting to hide a smile. Laughter exploded from the alpha, although his companions did not join in.

"You've got balls, I'll give you that," he finally said, having laughed so much there were tears in his eyes.

Daisy took this moment to bring drinks over to the table for the wolves, and no one spoke until she was out of earshot again.

"Do you deny it?" asked Kat, feeling more than a little annoyed at being laughed at.

Big Al took a large swig of his drink.

"I do not."

Kat felt Amelia grow rigid next to her.

"But allow me to explain, if you will."

"Talk fast, wolf," hissed Amelia as Kat put a warning hand on her arm.

Big Al barked another laugh.

"Come now, we are all among friends, are we not? I promise I will tell you the whole tale, but first let us break bread and bring my son in from the cold, would you?"

So much for having someone in reserve, thought Kat as Flynn slipped out to get him. It wasn't long before Connor stood in front of the table, tension radiating off him in waves.

"Relax, lad. I'm not going to eat you. Sit. Break bread with your old man."

Connor frowned, his tension turning into disbelief. He slid into the booth next to Kat and murmured a quiet thanks as she shuffled to give him enough space.

No one spoke until food began to arrive from the kitchen.

Chapter 45

Kat stared at the loaf of bread and the salt shaker that had been placed on the table. She knew that Daisy was meant to be intuitive to what you wanted, but Kat was very sure she didn't want plain bread and salt.

"What's this?" she whispered, leaning into Connor a little.

He flinched and bent away, his whole body as stiff as a board, so Kat recoiled too, stung at his unusual reaction.

"This is called breaking bread, Kat. This is what enemies do in a place of peace. You take the loaf," Big Al grabbed it, "and you tear a hunk off." He ripped the end off the loaf effortlessly, but with an underlying menace that made Kat's mouth go dry. "You get the salt and sprinkle some on the bread." The salt shaker looked tiny in his grasp. "Then you eat it." He shoved the bread into his mouth and made short work of it. His eyes darted from person to person on the opposite side of the booth, as if daring them to do it.

Amelia kicked Kat gently in the leg, indicating that she should go first. The pit of Kat's stomach roiled. Surely she wasn't the leader here? It was obviously Mr Magus. She glanced at him for confirmation and he gave a minute nod. Kat reached for the bread and tore a piece off, sprinkled it with salt, and popped it into her mouth.

It was surprisingly delicious, but based on her earlier food experience in the WigWam, Kat wasn't surprised. They were an uneven number at the table, so Mr Magus went next, then a wolf, Amelia, another wolf, Flynn and finally the last visiting wolf. Which left Connor with the heel of the bread. He sprinkled and ate in silence, not looking at anyone.

As soon as he'd finished, Daisy whisked the empty basket away and replaced it with a variety of chips and dips, breadsticks and olives. A mish mash of picky foods that could be easily shared, but nobody made a move to help themselves. The table continued to sit in silence as fresh drinks were brought over and Kat sipped her lemonade gratefully.

"Can I ask you my questions now?" Kat asked, not overly caring if her approach was the right way to do this.

"I don't see why not. Let's say one for one, shall we?" replied Big Al.

"Okay, fine. Why did you send Amelia a box of poisoned donuts?"

"I was fulfilling a contract. How many vampires have you killed?"

Kat was stumped. She didn't actually know how many vampires had been in the car park when her power had gone wild.

"Half a dozen or so." She went for a best guess and tried to appear confident so that Big Al wouldn't challenge her answer. "Who gave you the contract to send the donuts?"

Big Al turned his gaze to Amelia and scrutinised her.

"Her mother," he said finally.

Amelia's hands curled into claws and Kat was sure that if they hadn't been in the WigWam, she would've been sitting next to a dragon right now.

"She's also behind the blood bank thefts and framing those bloodsuckers who are now trapped in the Underbelly." Big Al casually scooped up some salsa on a tortilla chip. "One might say she's on a bit of a power grab. Again." And he popped the chip into his mouth.

"Where's your proof?" snapped Amelia.

"Sorry, little dragon. You don't get to ask any questions. And it's my turn. Where's your father?"

Kat stared at the wolf. Surely he was joking.

"He died. Years ago. I thought in a car accident but…" She glanced at Mr Magus. "I've been recently informed that it was a magical death." Kat took a deep breath to steady herself. "Since when did an Alpha take orders from a lizard?"

That put the wolves on alert. It was veiled, but it was still an insult. Big Al didn't seem to mind. He was laughing again.

"Ha! I like you, kid. She paid me a considerable amount of money. It takes a lot of resources to run a wolf pack these days. Meat's not cheap."

The way he said meat made Kat shiver, but she realised that he was telling the truth. The wolves had no issue with Amelia personally. They were just mercenaries in this situation. She looked to see if Mr Magus had any further questions, but his face was inscrutable.

"Where is your proof? About the blood bank and that." Kat asked.

"Not so fast, young lady. It's my turn. What are your intentions with my son?"

Kat blushed and glanced at Connor, who studiously ignored her presence by his side.

"I… er… not that it's any of your business, but none. I don't have any intentions." Kat hoped she was saying the right thing. She liked Connor, but they hadn't talked about dating or even going for coffee yet. It had just been a bit of light flirting. Hopefully, she wasn't putting him off right now.

"Hmm." Big Al didn't sound convinced. He tilted a

head at one of his underlings, who drew out a thick envelope from their jacket, handing it to Kat. "There's some interesting things in there you should know about."

He stood, causing all the wolves to leap up as well. Kat felt Connor tense beside her, but he didn't stand.

"It's been a pleasure, Miss Kat." Big Al dipped his head in her direction. "Keep killing vampires!" And he laughed as he loped away from them, minions in tow.

Kat waited until she was sure he had left the pub before letting out a huge sigh and dropping her head on her arms on the table. She felt wrung out.

Chapter 46

"I think we need a stiff drink," said Mr Magus, and Kat wholeheartedly agreed.

The envelope Big Al had given her lay heavy in her hands, but nobody else seemed willing to take it, so she slit the envelope open with her thumb and pulled out a thick piece of paper. She began to read.

"To bring a mage back from the dead you require:

> the blood of the damned
>
> the scale of a dragon
>
> the power of an offspring
>
> and the ring of possibility

Combine these items and say the words of release. Beware of the outcome."

She looked up, pale faced, hands shaking.

"What are the words?" asked Mr Magus sharply, but Kat couldn't answer him. She felt frozen.

He leaned over and snatched the parchment out of her hands. She didn't resist. There was nothing else on the paper. She'd read everything aloud.

"The words aren't here. Damn it." He addressed Connor. "The Countess must have given your father this half of the spell so he could collect the items for her. Countess Zandys doesn't like getting her hands dirty. The whole thing has to have been orchestrated. I've been a fool."

Amelia wrapped her arms around Kat and she could feel the warmth radiating from her friend.

"You're like a hot water bottle," Kat managed to say, and Amelia squeezed her tighter.

Their drinks arrived together with unasked for shots. As one, they downed the fiery liquid.

"So, I've been a pawn this whole time. Just a means to an end." Kat didn't know exactly how she felt, but it wasn't great. "Somehow your mother nudged me towards the Agency, made sure I got the job at the solicitors, set you up with that fake admirer, orchestrated the assault triggering your dragonation, planned the attack on me in the car park, stole the blood and framed those poor vampires and, and…" Kat trailed off. Even if Countess Zandys was that good of a master manipulator, and no one was jumping in to argue any of Kat's points, there was no way she had the power to make Dolores hand over her dad's ring. But, Kat had to begrudgingly admit, that was an act of circumstance and if she hadn't got herself in so much trouble, her mum wouldn't have tried to protect her.

"Bitch," she said, half under her breath.

Mr Magus raised his drink.

"I will toast to that."

Although he didn't actually speak the word, the intent was there and everyone followed his lead, toasting the thought.

"Well, it's fair to say that Countess Zandys must know we know her plan now. This meeting with the wolves won't have gone unnoticed. No doubt she has spies everywhere." Mr Magus glanced at Amelia for confirmation. She nodded grimly. "We can expect her to double her efforts. Kat, may I suggest you secure that ring in the Agency's vault? Better safe than sorry."

Kat was lost in thought. She was thinking about the list. Something had been niggling at her.

"Offspring," she said, raising her eyes to lock with Mr Magus. "It doesn't say me. It says offspring."

"Michael!" they both said at the same time before scrambling out of the booth and near running for the

241

exit.

Daisy beat them to the door.

"You can't go out there. It's heaving with wolves. You'll never make it through the carpark in once piece." She gave Kat a sad look. "Even with your gift. There's too many of them."

"Can we use the other exit?" asked Mr Magus, quietly so as not to alert the other patrons of the pub.

Daisy frowned at him.

"You cannot tarry. And you must touch nothing."

"Agreed."

Kat watched the two of them, aware that something more was happening than their simple words suggested. She put out a hand and touched Daisy's shoulder.

"Thank you."

"Oh, don't thank me. There will be a price." Daisy's face looked haunted. "There always is. Quickly, follow me."

Daisy led them to a door in the corner of the pub. Kat hadn't noticed it before. In fact, she would've sworn it hadn't been there five minutes ago. Daisy pushed the door open and ushered everyone through quickly.

Kat stared in wonder. They were standing in a forest. But it wasn't like the straggly bunch of trees in her local park. This was a proper forest. With layers.

"How..?" she began, but Daisy shushed her.

"Try not to talk too much. Touch nothing. Take nothing. Do not leave the path. Continue with your goal firmly in your minds and you will reach another door. Do not leave the path. Anything you see or hear is designed to lure you into the forest, where you will be lost and die a horrible, painful death. I cannot emphasis this enough. Do NOT leave the path."

Mr Magus clasped hands with Daisy.

"Thank you. We'll be safe. See you on the other side."

Daisy nodded sadly. She didn't seem convinced that was going to happen. Kat's whole body shivered and massive goosebumps sprang up all over her arms. Daisy stepped back, closing the door behind her, and the forest drew in. Not exactly menacing, but not exactly friendly either.

"You heard what she said," whispered Mr Magus. "Stick to the path, touch nothing. Take nothing. I shall lead. Flynn, Connor, you bring up the rear. Ladies, stick together." And with that, Mr Magus strode off confidently.

Kat eyed the path they were walking on. It wasn't what she would call a path. For one thing, there was no tarmac or pavement. There was literally an impression upon the forest floor and if you didn't concentrate, it would be so easy to accidentally step off the path. Nervous, she linked arms with Amelia, hoping that the close contact would keep her alert. They set off after Mr Magus. Kat glanced back to see Flynn and Connor just a stride behind. They both flashed her a smile of varying degrees of confidence, but it boosted her anyway. They were the Agency. They could walk through an enchanted forest together without anything bad happening. Couldn't they?

Chapter 47

A giggle escaped. Kat felt lightheaded, like she was almost drunk, but not quite. Tipsy. Another giggle.

"Are you alright, Kat?" whispered Amelia, who was doing a sterling job of keeping her friend upright and moving forward in the right direction.

"This is a magic forest. That we opened a magic door into. A magic door from a magic pub. Owned by a magic elf." Peels of laughter rang out through the forest.

"Just keep her moving, Amelia. Happens sometimes with people new to the craft. Can be somewhat overwhelming." Mr Magus glanced back. "She's handling it well. A little laughter isn't such a bad thing."

"As long as she doesn't attract any unwanted attention," muttered Flynn, too low for his dad to catch, but Amelia heard him and flashed a startled look at him. He just shrugged at her. Could be anything out there.

"I can't sense a presence at the moment, but it might be worth trying to quieten down a little. I'm sure there are things in here we'd rather not come face to face with." Connor looked on edge.

"Wolves?" asked Amelia.

"Maybe. There's nothing stopping one of them from returning to the pub and seeing that we've left. Big Al isn't stupid. He'll know we took a magical exit. And he has contacts. Lots of contacts."

"So even if the wolves don't come after us, something else could."

Connor pressed his lips together in a tight smile and returned to scanning the area, ears on high alert for anything out of the ordinary.

Kat's giggle attack seemed to have passed, but she

still clung to Amelia for support.

"Are you okay?" she whispered.

"I... don't know, really," replied Amelia.

"We just found out your mum wants to kill you. It's okay to be mad or scared."

"I'm not mad." Amelia gave a small smile at the incredulous look on Kat's face. "It's quite normal for dragon parents to kill their offspring. It wasn't just human hunters that did a good job at decimating us. We managed to achieve a lot all on our own."

Kat was shocked.

"Why on earth would dragons want to kill each other? In this day and age, when there are so few of you left."

"It's all about power and control. And wealth. Who has the biggest pile of wealth." Amelia sounded so despondent.

"I take it those things aren't important to you?" asked Kat, giving her friend a one-armed hug.

"I mean, money is nice. It does make life a little easier when you can afford to buy things, but it's not the be all and end all, is it? Money doesn't define a person. You can still have hobbies and cook and make friends and have fun without sitting on a pile of gold." Amelia patted Kat's arm. "I'm not surprised, not really. It's what dragons do to each other. I should've expected it to be honest. After she got rid of my brother and sister. I naively thought she was keeping hold of me. Apparently not."

There was a long silence as Kat digested the fact that Amelia's mother had casually removed Amelia's brother and sister. She was finding it difficult to wrap her head around it.

"Did nobody... complain? Or report her? Or, I don't

know, put her on a watch list? Don't you magic folk have any kind of law enforcement?" asked Kat finally.

"We have the Agency. And the Council. But situations have to be really serious to be reported to the Council. The magical community usually clears up its own messes, and the Agency helps to maintain the balance, keep the non magical world from finding out about us."

"And getting rid of your siblings isn't *really bad*?" Kat was stunned.

Amelia shrugged.

"It's dragony. Plus, my mother is very powerful. She's been around for a long time. She has scales in lots of pies, or whatever the metaphor is."

Kat nodded. She knew what Amelia meant.

"How come I don't know who she is, if she's meant to be that powerful and she's been around forever–how come I've never heard of her? Like, wouldn't she be a celebrity or something? In my world, I mean."

"She likes to lurk. It's never her on the front line, that's always some poor sap she's set up. She is very much the puppet master, the power behind the scenes." Amelia's face twisted, like she'd eaten something bad. "I am surprised at her pulling in the vampires, and the Underbelly, and the wolves, and that teenager lad. It does feel sloppy, like she wanted us to find out it was her."

"We did have to do a fair amount of digging," protested Kat, but not overly strongly. She had been thinking the same thing–it had been relatively easy to find out who was behind things. "Do you suspect it's part of some larger, more elaborate play?"

Amelia considered it for a moment, then shook her head, looking even more sad than before.

"I think she probably left it to her assistant to deal with." Amelia looked up at Kat, her eyes brimming with unshed tears. "I doubt she dealt with any of it directly."

Kat gave her friend another hug as she quietly sobbed. It was one thing to find out your dragon mum was trying to kill you and quite another to realise she'd told her assistant to action it.

"I feel like my head is going to burst," said Kat, pressing one hand to her temple where a massive headache was developing fast. "Anyone else got a bad headache?"

There were shakes and murmured nos, but the pain in Kat's head intensified so much it had her gasping and squinting to be able to see.

"Something's wrong," she managed to say before falling to her knees, her head in her hands. Then her head jerked up and pure white light shot out of her eyes in a massive outpouring of energy.

Chapter 48

"Oh, oh! What do we do?" squealed Amelia.

She was immediately shushed by a very tense Mr Magus.

"Quiet. Control yourself. Remember what Daisy said."

Amelia breathed heavily out of her nose.

"What do you mean, *remember what Daisy said*? Shouldn't we be slightly more worried about what's just happened to Kat?" she snapped.

Flynn and Connor edged closer to Kat, forming a protective ring around her on one side, with Amelia and Mr Magus on the other.

"I think we need to be more concerned about what will be attracted to this much power, so the quieter we can be, the better, yeah?" Flynn spoke in a hushed voice, his gaze darting about, looking for shadows that weren't quite there.

"Shhh. I'm trying to listen." Connor's eyes were closed, his nose scenting the air, ears cocked for the slightest sound. "To your left." He swung around, putting himself directly in front of Kat, who continued to blaze light.

There was a rustling sound and Kat walked out of the forest.

"Oh thank God, I found you. What is going on?"

For a stunned moment, nobody moved. Amelia glanced sideways at the immobile body next to her. That was definitely Kat. They entered the forest with her. She had just been giggling and talking. And yet... that was also Kat. At least it looked a lot like her.

"Guys, seriously. Why are you standing there?"

asked Kat. "That isn't me. We were attacked. They'll be coming back soon. We need to leave now. I found the way out. Hurry! Before they return."

Connor growled low under his breath, muscles coiled, ready to pounce. Flynn stepped around the blazing figure and came and stood next to him.

"What are you talking about? We haven't been attacked. You're not Kat."

"Look out! Behind you!" The Kat in the forest called out a warning.

Everyone turned and saw four elvish archers in the treeline, bows nocked, aimed right at them.

"It's just an illusion," snapped Mr Magus. "Check your feet. Stay on the path."

Amelia glanced down. She was still on the path beside her Kat, but Connor and Flynn were dangerously close to the edge. Suddenly new Kat was standing right next to them. She hadn't moved. One minute she was further away, the next super close. In the blink of an eye.

Everyone had looked down when Mr Magus called out. Everyone had turned their gaze away from the archers. Glancing back up, Amelia saw they were even closer, arrows looking sharper and more deadly.

"Don't avert your gaze. Amelia and I will keep our eyes on the archers. Boys, keep looking at fake Kat and shuffle yourselves back onto the path. Do not engage. Do not look away."

Amelia took heart from the confidence and strength in Mr Magus' voice. She could feel her eyes watering. What would happen if she blinked? Would that count as looking away?

"How long do we have to have this staring match for?" asked Flynn. He sounded closer to Amelia now.

"I don't know. We need to protect Miss Kritchley

until she returns," replied Mr Magus.

"Where has she gone?" asked Amelia. She could just see Connor in the periphery of her vision. He'd sidled himself further back on the path, too.

"I believe she has magically projected herself," said Mr Magus, his voice sounding oddly strained.

"Dad? Are you alright?" Flynn sounded panicked.

"Yes… I… ah… I… achoooooo!" Mr Magus sneezed loudly, closing his eyes in the process.

It was such a loud sneeze, Amelia couldn't help herself. Her eyes darted to make sure he was okay, but they shot back when she felt movement nearby. The Elven archers were within touching distance. Fear trickled down her spine.

"What do we do?" she hissed.

"I can't smell them," said Connor. "I didn't even hear them. Not really. I felt something. I don't believe they're real. They won't release those arrows. Think about it, if they'd wanted to attack us, they would have done it from further away. Why would you shoot an arrow at such close range? It doesn't make sense."

"Tell that to the arrowhead in your face!" Amelia's voice was shrill.

"Amelia, swap with me. I'll look at your archers, you stare at fake Kat. Ready? One, two, three."

Amelia squealed as she turned her head. When she saw that Connor wasn't looking in her direction, she whipped her gaze back. The archers were gone.

"What?"

"It seems Connor was right. Fear gripped us." Mr Magus peered out into the forest, but there was no sign of the archers. "A trick. To make us step off the path."

"Fake Kat is gone too," said Flynn.

"We must stay alert. We don't know what else the

forest will throw at us to make us leave the path. I suggest we hold hands, form a chain around Miss Kritchley, and hope that she returns soon."

Mr Magus held out a hand to Amelia on one side and Flynn on the other. They took them gratefully. Flynn and Connor were a little slower in clasping hands, but they did it without too much scowling. Connected in a circle made everyone feel marginally safer.

"How long will we have to wait?" wondered Amelia.

Chapter 49

Kat rushed through the front door of her house, which stood open. She could hear her mum crying, but she dashed up the stairs to her brother's room. The door hung lopsided on its hinges. The entire room was utterly wrecked. Gone was the precise neatness of Mikey's inner sanctum. Instead, Lego kits had been pulverised to bits and books were scattered across the floor, some with pages loose. Clothes and smellies lay all over the place and the picture frame of the whole family, the one with their dad in as well, was smashed to smithereens in the middle of it all, like some bizarre offering to chaos.

Kat sank to her knees and let out a primal scream of frustration. Pure white light shot out of her eyes and mouth as her back arched and her fingers and arms splayed out. The energy abruptly left her and she slumped to the floor, feeling leaves and twigs beneath her.

"What? What just happened? Where's Mikey?" Kat looked up to see the others standing around her, hands clasped in a protective ring.

"You left your body for a moment, Miss Kritchley. I'm assuming that was your first attempt at transporting yourself. You used far too much energy. I'm surprised that you didn't blow your head off in the process." Mr Magus was mad, but Kat didn't think he was actually cross at her.

"I'm sorry. I didn't mean to freak you all out." She pushed herself up off the ground and dusted off her clothes. "Why are you holding hands?"

"Just being protective. How's your head?" asked Amelia, reluctantly letting go of Connor and Mr Magus.

"My head feels fine. I was so worried about Mikey and it was all I could think about. I kept telling myself we need to be there now. If we can just move quicker, everything will be alright if we get there on time and then, the next thing I knew… I was there."

Kat looked up guiltily, no idea whether she'd broken some kind of magical rule. She barely had any concept of what she should or shouldn't be able to do.

"Probably the additional energy from walking through this enchanted place, feeding into your anxiety, your feelings and boosted by that magical ring–it's a wonder you didn't tear yourself apart," replied Mr Magus.

"He's not there." Kat remembered what she had seen. "Mikey's been taken. And Mum, I didn't see her, I don't know if she's alright or not."

Amelia was wringing her hands.

"This is all my fault," she said, looking miserable.

"How is it your fault?" demanded Kat.

"Well, it's my mother and…"

Kat interrupted.

"We are not responsible for our family. I'm not holding it against you, so you don't need to berate yourself. What you do need to do is think of where your mum would take my brother."

Kat smiled at Amelia, who shakily returned one of her own and then they hugged.

"Thank you," said Amelia in a very small voice.

"I think she'll have taken him to the Underbelly. If they need the blood of the damned vampires, they'd have to go there to get that. Those vamps won't leave the Underbelly. And they still need the dragon aspect." Connor looked expectantly at Amelia.

She looked confused.

"It's almost the end of the month? You're going to change? We did want Cleo wanted. We found out who orchestrated the exile so we can go back and report. You get your underground cavern and we'll guard you."

A mental image of a huge dragon being protected by a wolf and two puny humans with wands in their hands popped into Kat's head. She couldn't help it. She started to laugh and once she started, she couldn't stop.

"Nervous reaction. She's clearly emotionally overwrought. Come on, we can't stay here." Mr Magus surveyed the forest, but all was quiet. "Let's press on before we have any more visitors and go and check on Mrs Kritchley. There might be some evidence at the scene to give us an idea of what else we're facing besides the Countess." Mr Magus sighed. "She doesn't usually do her own dirty work. I really hope it's not your father." He looked at Connor, eyebrow raised.

Connor scuffed his feet on the forest floor. There was every chance that Big Al and his minions had kidnapped Kat's brother while they had dithered in the pub, too chicken to leave by the normal exit.

"What visitors? What happened?" Kat looked around at the group, but nobody was forthcoming.

"It was just a trick." Amelia patted her arm. "A good one. They were trying to get us to leave the path."

"Who's they?" Kat was wide eyed as Amelia shrugged back at her.

"Where does this path lead, anyway?" asked Flynn. "We've been following it, but do we actually know where it's going to kick us out?"

A door appeared at the end of the path.

"That wasn't there a minute ago... was it?" Flynn checked with the others, but Kat and Amelia were still comforting each other and Connor had his head down.

Flynn tutted and strode off towards the door. He turned the handle and stepped into Kat's front room.

"I'll kill you! I'll kill you all!"

Kat pushed past Flynn as everyone crowded into the room, the magical door winking out of existence.

"Mum, Mum! It's me, it's Kat. Here, let me help."

Dolores was lying on the floor, having fallen out of her wheelchair, when someone had clearly tipped it over.

Amelia shushed everyone out into the hallway. Kat was grateful. Dolores hated being watched when she was vulnerable. She helped her mum up into a seated position on the floor.

"Are you okay? What happened?" Kat gave her mum a hug, aware that both their hands were trembling.

There was a faint bruise on the side of Dolores' head and she looked pale and shaken.

"These men burst into the flat. I tried to stop them, but one of them swiped at me and knocked me down. That was me out of the fight. I couldn't do anything. I couldn't stop them." Dolores was sobbing now. "They took your brother, Kat. They took Mikey."

"I know, I know," Kat whispered as she hugged her mum as best as she could. "I'll get him back Mum, I promise." She righted the wheelchair and put the cushion back before gently lifting her mum up.

After settling her mum back into her chair and making sure she was comfortable, Kat went to the kitchen to make her mum a drink, preferably a stiff one, and get her some painkillers. She was visibly shaking with emotion and seemed surprised to see Mr Magus, Amelia, Flynn and Connor filling up the kitchen space.

"What are you all doing in here?" she asked roughly, trying to keep the tears from falling.

Connor wisely opened the back door and let himself,

Flynn, and Mr Magus out into the garden. Amelia hovered, unsure whether she should hug her friend.

"Yes," said Kat, reading her face, and they gave each other a fierce embrace.

As Kat put the kettle on and hunted for some alcohol, Amelia began filling the sink with hot water to do the washing up.

"You don't have to do that," said Kat.

"I know. I'm just keeping my hands busy. So sorry about your mum. Is she badly hurt?"

"A few bumps and bruises, but I think she'll be alright." Kat's voice wobbled. "I can't believe they took Mikey. What am I going to do?"

Amelia grabbed her by the shoulders and stared into her face.

"We're going to kick ass and get him back is what we're going to do. Now, take that to your mum. I'll make sure she's got some food, chocolate, hot water bottle, whatever comforts she needs. You and Connor get up to his room, see what you can see."

Kat nodded and took the drink to her mum. Dolores was pale and looked so small sat in her wheelchair.

"Amelia's going to look after you, Mum. Get you whatever you need. I'm going to go upstairs, yeah?"

Dolores nodded, then gripped Kat's arm painfully.

"You find who did this and you make them suffer!" she hissed.

Kat was a little taken aback at the veracity of her mum's voice, but nodded. Of course, she was going to find Mikey.

Connor met her in the hallway and together they headed upstairs.

"This way, that's my room," said Kat, nodding towards a closed door. "This one…"

As in her weird vision, the door hung on its hinges and the entire room was completely ransacked. It looked like Mikey had put up one hell of a fight.

"Well done, little brother," whispered Kat to herself, but, of course, Connor heard her.

"Kat, I… I'm…"

"If you're going to say you're sorry, save it. I don't need sorry. What I need are clues about who took Mikey and where they're taking him to. If you can't help me, get me someone who can."

Connor didn't reply. He started to pick his way through the room, careful not to disturb too much but at the same time, searching intently for evidence. After a few moments, he pointed to a discarded blackcurrant and liquorice sweet wrapper.

"Does your brother eat these?" he asked.

"No," replied Kat firmly. "He does not."

Connor nodded to himself and came back to the dishevelled doorway.

"You know who took Mikey," declared Kat.

"I do."

Chapter 50

Kat didn't make Connor tell her there and then. Instead, she asked him to go back downstairs while she tidied up. He did, but he soon reappeared with a screwdriver so he could rehang Mikey's door. Kat had no idea where he'd got that from. She wasn't aware they owned a screwdriver.

Whilst annoyed at first that she wasn't alone, Kat began to appreciate having another person there. She didn't have to speak, but Connor brought her black sacks for the wrecked, unfixable things and moved the heavier pieces of furniture back into their place for her. They worked in silence and when she felt she was finished, the room almost looked more broken than before.

All of Mikey's wonderful Lego creations were smashed, so all Kat could do was pile up the Legos and hope Mikey would know how to put them back together again. His clothes had been strewn, not destroyed, so that was something, but several books had lost the fight, with too many pages torn out to be salvageable. Kat hoped that whoever took Mikey had trashed everything after taking her brother out of the room. Initially, she'd thought Mikey had fought back, but now that she'd tidied, it looked more like someone had systematically destroyed things. Maybe to cover their tracks somehow?

After bringing down the rubbish bags and dumping them in the bins outside, Kat and Connor rejoined everyone in the front room. Dolores was looking stronger. She'd finished the hot drink Amelia had brought her and was most definitely holding court. But there were two spots of colour in her cheeks and Kat knew from experience that meant Dolores was mad.

"Thank you, Kat. I know Mikey will appreciate the effort. In his own way."

Kat nodded. She gave Connor a look which she hoped he realised was his cue to tell everyone what he'd discovered.

"Um, I think I know who took Mikey."

The room waited.

"My brother, Callum."

Kat was shocked. Why hadn't Connor mentioned he had a brother before? Of course it made sense that Big Al was behind it all. She felt hot with anger. They'd been so stupid. Running around trying to find out who had sent bloody poisonous donuts and then inviting the enemy to the pub for god's sake. No wonder Big Al had been in such a good mood. They'd all been absolute idiots, walking directly into his trap. He must have been laughing his head off.

"Kat." Mr Magus' tone was warning.

She stared at him and he met her gaze without a flinch, but Kat swore she saw his eyes widen. She looked down at her hands and they were glowing massively again.

"I don't know what you expect me to do about it," she said in irritation.

"I expect you to control yourself," snapped Mr Magus.

Instantly, Kat's power fled and her cheeks reddened.

"Sorry, Mr Magus." Kat felt like she was back at school.

"Connor, can you tell us anything that might be helpful in rescuing Kat's brother?" asked Mr Magus.

Connor shifted his weight, thinking.

"He's not much of a thinker. Does exactly what Big Al tells him to do. So my best guess would be that he's taken Mikey somewhere in the Underbelly. Ready for the ceremony. And seeing as they need dragon scales, I reckon it will be somewhere close to the place Amelia will change."

Kat noticed that Connor didn't call Big Al dad or father or even sir. She wondered exactly why they had fallen out. Connor didn't seem like the other wolves she had met today. They all had a harshness about them. A real sense of danger in that you didn't know if you were safe. Kat felt completely safe with Connor. Even when he had changed in the pub carpark to protect her. Especially then.

Mr Magus clapped his hands together, bringing everyone's attention back to him.

"Right, we know where we've got to go. I suggest we return to the Agency and get ourselves kitted out before heading to the Underbelly. No sense in delaying the inevitable. With any luck, we'll arrive earlier than expected and can extract Mikey before things get too out of hand."

He spoke as if they were going on a simple reconnaissance and not literally walking into the jaws of serious danger and possible death. Kat couldn't help it. A small smile broke out. It was infectious and was soon caught by everyone else, even Dolores.

They all said their goodbyes to Kat's mum and waited outside, giving mother and daughter a moment of privacy. Dolores gave Kat a shaky smile as they embraced again.

"You be careful, you hear me? Yes, I want your brother back, but not at your expense. I'm not losing you."

"Mum, I'll be careful. I'm the last line of defence as it is. I haven't got a clue what I'm doing or how I work."

Kat flapped her hands in her mum's direction, making her smile. "But we'll get him back. I promise."

They sat in silence for a moment.

"He's going to be hard work when he comes home," Kat said finally, remembering how jittery and out of sorts Mikey had been when she was younger and her mum had stayed in hospital overnight. Social Services wouldn't let the two children stay by themselves, so they'd been put into emergency foster care for one night. The place had been nice, and the couple were used to dealing with autistic children, but Mikey took a long time to recover when they'd been sent home. This time, he'd been taken by force by people he didn't know, to a place he didn't know, without any of his things to comfort him. When he came back, he would see his inner sanctum wrecked, despite Kat's best efforts at tidying up–nothing would be in the exact right place and the whole room would likely set him off.

"Yes, he will, but he will be back with us and we will deal with it. He knows we love him." Dolores began to cry. "He used to think this was a safe space." Tears splashed down her cheeks.

"Oh, Mum, don't!" Kat could feel her own tears welling up. She gave her mum another hug. "We'll make it safe for him again, I promise."

Mr Magus cleared his throat outside.

"Mum, I've got to go. I've got to go get Mikey back. Are you going to be alright here on your own?" Kat didn't want to leave her mum alone in this state, but she couldn't very well stay herself.

Dolores visibly pulled herself together.

"I'll be fine. I'll call Monica to come and sit with me. I'll tell her Mikey ran off and you're off finding him."

It had happened before, and Monica had sat with Dolores through it then.

"Okay, that sounds like a good idea. Can I get you anything before I leave?"

Dolores shook her head.

"No, you go. And bring your brother home."

"I will." Kat gave her mum a quick kiss and squeezed her hand before heading out to join the others.

No comment was made about the tears drying on her face as they purposefully walked into town, to the Agency, ready to gear up and save Mikey.

Chapter 51

Gearing up wasn't as exciting as Kat thought it might be. It basically involved Mr Magus meditating in his office with Flynn. She guessed they were doing something magical, but she didn't know what.

Amelia could turn into a dragon and breathe fire– apparently now that she'd dragonfied, and even if she kept her human form, she could still breathe fire. In Kat's mind, there didn't seem to be anything else she needed to worry about, but Amelia was fretting.

The ingredients list said dragon scales, which meant Amelia had to fully transform, something she hadn't done yet.

"But you'll be a dragon," said Kat. "Nobody is going to come anywhere near you."

Amelia looked miserable.

"You say that, but they do. With their pointy sticks, all jabby and stabby. Why do you think there are only a handful of dragons left? Yes, we're massive fire breathers, but we're also massive fire breathers. If you're nimble and swift, I won't be able to manoeuvre out of the way entirely. There are soft spots."

"You sound like you've done it before." Kat was confused. She thought Amelia hadn't triggered her dragoness before.

"Well, I haven't personally, but you know, it runs in my family."

Kat had to give her that. If anyone knew what it was like to dragon, it would be Amelia.

"Perhaps you'd better stand at the back then. You can breathe fire at them over the tops of our heads." Kat was only half joking. "How much longer are they going to be in there?" She glanced at Mr Magus' door, which was still closed. "What are they even doing?"

"They're meditating. Filling up their reserves and clearing out any bad energy. At least, that's what Mr Magus said." A faint blush bloomed on Amelia's cheeks.

"I didn't know you two were… you know, you two." Kat waited for Amelia to spill the beans.

"Oh, it's very on again, off again. Circumstances can make a workplace romance a little awkward but then at times of crisis…" Amelia trailed off, but Kat knew exactly what she meant.

Mr Magus, Xavier, was interested but only motivated when danger threatened. The rest of the time, he had no idea what to do or how to act, which left Amelia not really knowing where she stood. Typical commitment phobe.

"Anyway, what about you and Connor?" Amelia asked, clearly keen to get the spotlight off herself.

Kat started picking invisible lint off her jacket.

"I don't know what you mean," she said, trying to sound as nonchalant as possible.

"Rubbish! There's clearly something going on. Spill the beans."

Kat looked around to make sure Connor wasn't in earshot. He'd disappeared upstairs to *weapons check,* but that didn't mean his enhanced wolf hearing wouldn't catch every word they said.

"I don't know," she whispered to Amelia. "I guess, if all of this hadn't happened, maybe we would have gone on a date or something. There's something there, I think. But you know, it's been a bit awkward. And he was acting so weird at the pub."

"I think that was because of his dad, not you. And you did go skating, very datelike," pointed out Amelia.

"Yeah, we went skating to stake out some kid who tried to kill you. That was a blast." But Kat couldn't help smiling. She'd had fun on the rink.

"Talking about me?" Connor reappeared, making Kat jump and blush furiously.

"No!"

"Okay…"

Kat realised Connor hadn't heard what they said and was joking, but she'd let the cat right out of the bag by reacting so strongly. She wanted to disappear, but there was nowhere to go.

"I'm going to make some tea," declared Amelia, giving Kat a theatrical wink and sashaying out of the office.

Kat gave Connor a half smile and picked up a pen from Amelia's desk to fiddle about with.

"Um, when this is all over…" began Connor.

"Yeah?"

"Maybe we could, you know, go for coffee or something?" asked Connor shyly.

Kat could feel her heart beating out of her chest.

"Uh, are you sure? I thought… well…" Kat stammered, not sure how to ask Connor why he'd been so weird with her earlier.

"There's a lot going on right now and we're both dealing with stuff, but I wanted you to know that, you know, I am interested."

"Okay. Yeah, maybe." Kat tried to play it cool. "That would be nice." She smiled at him, their eyes locking. Kat's stomach swooped and did a loop da loop, making her feel giddy.

Their little moment was interrupted by Mr Magus and Flynn coming out. Flynn's eyes darted from Connor to Kat and back again, making him scowl.

Kat's stomach clenched again, this time not in a good way, but before she had a chance to say anything, Amelia returned with snacks and drinks for them all.

"I thought we should get a bite to eat before battle. We don't know when we'll next have the chance." She smiled, her eyes darting from Flynn to Connor to Kat, knowing she'd missed something.

"Yes, good idea," said Mr Magus, tucking into a sandwich. "We need to strategise."

Kat knew he was right, but she just wanted to go to the Underbelly and rescue Mikey, sod everyone else. She shook her head when Amelia offered her some food. She felt too nauseous to eat, and she wasn't sure all of that was to do with her brother's abduction. Impatiently she listened to Mr Magus outline a plan that might work, but really, they had no clue what they were about to face down there in the Underbelly. Anything could happen.

Chapter 52

It seemed to take forever to get ready. Kat chaffed at the slowness of everyone and when they were finally ready to leave and Mr Magus went to go change his shoes, she couldn't cope anymore. Muttering under her breath, she pushed open the Agency door, not bothering to close it, and stalked outside into the rain.

"Perfect." Kat hunched her shoulders, shoved her hands into her pockets and stood beneath the shop awning next door. She leaned one foot against the wall and sat back, looking like a moody extra from an eighties music video. Fortunately, she didn't have to wait long. The others piled out of the Agency and set off in the opposite direction to where Kat stood.

For a minute she watched them walk away, then quickly pushed off the wall and hurried to catch up.

"Thought you'd gone without us," said Amelia.

"Thought you were about to go without me," said Kat.

They grinned at each other, everything forgiven as the pre-fight nerves settled in.

"We're going to get him back, right?" Kat couldn't keep the uncertainty out of her voice.

"Yep."

Amelia didn't expand. It did not fill Kat with confidence. What were they doing? Why were they walking headlong into what was obviously a trap? Why didn't they have more firepower? Doubt flew around Kat's head and she began picking at the side of her fingers, an old nervous habit she thought she'd broken.

While Kat was lost in her own thoughts, Amelia tapped Mr Magus on the shoulder. He dropped back, and it took Kat a moment to realise she was walking with him and not Amelia.

"Miss Kritchley, might I have a word?"

Kat nodded.

"We go into battle. It's sooner than I had hoped, but I would not want to fight alongside anyone else. In our short time together, you have shown such bravery, such resilience and character. I know your father would be immensely proud of you. And I promise I will do everything in my power to return your brother to you."

It was a good speech and for a moment Kat felt lifted, but Mr Magus had not made any empty promises. He hadn't said he would get Mikey back, only that he would try. And whilst that was great, the realisation wasn't as comforting.

Flynn took over from his dad and began running through the basic spell work he'd been showing Kat.

"I know this," she said.

"I know you do, but it doesn't hurt to practise, especially when you might be fighting for your life in a minute."

And so she went through the motions and made dodgy, flickery orbs of light appear and disappear.

"How is this going to help me rescue my brother?"

Flynn focused his concentration on a pale orb he'd conjured, making it grow brighter and brighter until it burst into flames, at which point he hurled it into the sky. It shot off and was soon lost in the murk of the weather, but the demonstration had the desired effect.

"Fireballs," murmured Kat to herself. She felt she could get the hang of those.

"You'll be amazing," said Flynn.

"Sorry?"

"When you let go and your power releases, it's

amazing. Nothing will be able to withstand that," explained Flynn.

Kat felt a niggle of doubt.

"What if I don't want to let go and destroy everything? What happened with the vampires was an accident. I didn't mean to do that. It's not who I am."

"Yeah, I know that but…" Flynn didn't say anymore.

His attempts at trying to motivate Kat only partly worked. She had been reminded that she did possess uncontrollable power, but also the fact that she possessed uncontrollable power. Kat knew one thing for sure: she did not want to go into the Underbelly and start a war because she accidentally wiped out half the inhabitants.

Connor loped back to walk with her.

"Don't tell me, I'm awesome and I've got this and everything is going to be alright." Kat sounded more than a little snippy.

"Er… no. I was just going to ask how you're doing?"

The softness in his tone made Kat feel instantly bad for being, well, catty.

"Sorry. Had a few pep talks. Feeling a bit overwhelmed."

"And worried. For Mikey." Connor took one of Kat's hands and gave it a squeeze.

Kat held on tight, a bolt of warmth shooting up her arm. She could feel her lip trembling, tears filling her eyes.

"I don't know if he's okay," she said, voice wobbling. "He doesn't like people he doesn't know. He's going to be so scared and alone and he won't know that I'm coming for him. He might never recover from this. Mikey doesn't process things the same way we do."

Connor listened quietly as Kat went on, describing all the things that Mikey didn't like or didn't get on with or struggled with. He let her pour out all her worries and insecurities until she gradually petered out.

"Feel better?" he asked.

Kat took a deep breath. Despite the tears on her face, she did actually feel better. She hadn't spoken about Mikey in that depth for a long, long time. It felt good to get everything off her chest and say some things that she'd never been brave enough to say before. Having an autistic sibling was hard work. There were no two ways around it, but she loved him fiercely, and that was what counted.

"Thank you," she replied.

The others had stopped walking, reaching the midpoint in the cemetery where Amelia had made the opening last time. Mr Magus pricked his finger and allowed a small droplet of blood to fall to the earth. It was a lot less dramatic. Kat realised she was still holding Connor's hand. She had no desire to let go but knowing they were about to enter the Underbelly and face who knows what, she knew she had to release him, reluctantly. He gave her a dazzling grin as she let go, a grin that set off all her butterflies.

The others stood still and, for once, Mr Magus looked a little nervous.

"Is everybody ready? Know what they're doing?"

Flynn nodded and took charge.

"Connor and I will take point. Be the muscle for anyone who wants to fight us as we locate Callum. Xavier, you and Kat will stay behind us and be the magic; defence strategies in the first instance, fire balls in the second. Amelia, you will bring up the rear. Partly for your own protection, and partly so that you can kick ass on any stragglers."

Everyone nodded. They'd discussed this plan and Kat had to agree she thought it was a good one. It kept Amelia away from immediate fighting so she couldn't be snatched for the ceremony.

Callum had been smart when he kidnaped Mikey. He knew Kat would come after him. He knew that one way or the other, he would have the blood he needed and he knew that Amelia would come with Kat. She was her dragon protector. Duty would not have allowed anything different. In fact, it hadn't even been a discussion point when they'd been hammering out the plan. Despite dragon ingredients being needed for the spell, Amelia would go where Kat went.

"Let's go find your brother," said Connor.

"And yours," whispered Kat under her breath.

Chapter 53

Compared to the last time Kat had visited the Underbelly, it was quiet. Eerily so. The area was deserted; no foot shuffling or voices could be heard from the nearby tunnels. No signs of inhabitation. Just seemingly miles and miles of empty pathways.

They were underground, but it wasn't literal tunnels of earth. It looked like a mishmash of abandoned sewage works, old parts of the city and passageways, although exactly where those passages led, Kat had no idea. She saw Mr Magus watching her look around.

"Interesting, isn't it?" he said.

Kat nodded.

"Is every city like this?" she asked.

"More or less. Most people don't realise they live above a honeycomb."

"Is it safe?"

"As long as there aren't any earthquakes," replied Mr Magus with a twinkle in his eye.

Earthquakes were pretty unlikely, so Kat tried to relax, but the fact that they hadn't seen a single person was beginning to give her the heebie jeebies. Surely the Underbelly knew they were coming?

As they turned a corner, she noticed a humming sound. Glancing around, Kat saw the others had heard it too. Was it some kind of machinery or...?

"Get ready to fight. They've massed. Stay in formation," barked Mr Magus, and a bolt of nerves shot through Kat.

As they got closer, Kat realised it was the hum of conversation. A large body of people had gathered. Surely Callum wouldn't try anything in the middle of all those innocent bystanders? Well, as innocent as a bunch of undead people can be.

They entered a large cavern. It was packed with all manner of undead who didn't immediately launch an attack or try to capture them at all. Kat felt very confused. Why were they all here?

"They're here to bear witness," explained Mr Magus. "This fight is not theirs. The Underbelly is just the staging area."

"So is Amelia's mum here?" Kat craned her neck, looking around for the Countess.

"Unlikely. She never gets her hands dirty," said Amelia, pointedly not looking around for her mother.

"I can't see Mikey." There was a hint of desperation in Kat's voice. She had been hoping that once they arrived at the confrontation, she would at least be able to see her brother.

"He's over there," said Connor softly, capable of sensing live ones in a sea of undead. He pointed his head towards the far right side of the cavern. There was a small raised area where a group of muscly men were roaming, one or two wolves dotted amongst them.

"It's all a bit stereotypical, isn't it?" Kat's voice was a little high and full of forced bravado. "I mean, look at them. Big strapping fellows, hulking around. Where are the women? Where are the small and wiry fighters? Who's the underdog?"

"We are," snorted Flynn. "Wolves don't come small and wiry. And you should be relieved the females aren't here to fight. Utterly vicious."

"As are we," said Amelia, putting on a brave face, but Kat could tell she was as anxious as she was.

Mikey lay on the floor in the middle of the wolves. He seemed unconcerned about his surroundings and was pushing a toy train back and forth, making soft train noises. Kat knew that was a coping method to being in a strange place with strange people. He'd completely cut himself off from what was happening around him. She wondered if he'd managed to bring the train with him or whether someone had given it to him.

"Oi, loner!" shouted Callum. He'd finally clocked Connor and the rest of them. "Give us the dragon and you can leave. In one piece."

As threats went, it wasn't that scary. Kat only felt marginally intimidated.

"No. Give us the boy and we'll let you leave," Connor called back.

Kat was surprised at who was talking for a moment, then remembered Mr Magus had suggested Connor speak directly with the wolves. They were more likely to respond positively to him than to a bunch of conjurers. His words, not hers.

"No. You'll have to come and get him." Callum sneered at his brother. "Form up!"

Suddenly, the non-threatening mill of undead people snapped into action and became an aggressive wall of scary ass monsters they had to overcome to reach Mikey and the others.

"Dammit," whispered Mr Magus. He had been hoping the Underbelly would remain impartial and just be the location for the showdown rather than active participants.

"No, look. They're not all against us." Kat had been looking around. Yes, there was a swathe of undead between them and her brother, but there was also a large ring of people not fighting.

"Do I have your word that you are observers only?" called out Mr Magus.

A slight commotion occurred, and the crowd parted to reveal Cleopatra.

"You shall not be attacked from behind," she said with a tiny shrug of her shoulders as if to say, *what more do you want?*

"I guess that's the best we're going to get," replied Mr Magus. "Amelia, watch our backs, please." With a small smile, he flicked his hands forwards, making sure they were free of his suit cuffs, ready to cast.

Chapter 54

What happened next can only be described as pandemonium. The wolves attacked first. There were more of them. Connor morphed immediately, and it was terrifying to watch the giant wolves attacking each other, snarling and biting. Wiping out those unfortunate enough to be too close to whipping tails.

Mr Magus and Flynn began shooting fireballs, singeing fur and keeping the enemy back. Amelia grew. It couldn't be described otherwise. Suddenly, she just inhabited more space. Yes, the undead had claimed they wouldn't attack from the rear, but Amelia was taking no chances. The undead at the front had certainly joined in the melee.

The noise level was deafening and Kat could see Mikey rocking back and forth, his hands clamped across his ears, tears on his face. She had to get to him. It wasn't part of the plan, but everyone else was fully engaged with the enemy, so now seemed like the best idea. Besides, she couldn't conjure anything.

Kat had tried. When the first wolf had bounded towards them, all tooth and claw. She'd tried to access her power. Nothing. She was afraid. Heart pounding, dry mouth, wobbly knees. But she'd been afraid before. Hadn't she? But the magic refused to wake up, so Kat used the fact that everyone around her was pretty distracted to try to sneak past.

Of course, it didn't work. Another wolf lunged for Kat as she sidled out of the protective ring, but Connor got there first, slashing at its muzzle and causing it to whimper and retreat. Several vampires launched themselves towards her only to be met by a sizzling fireball curtesy of Mr Magus, who was firing them like a conductor hitting all the notes. A group of zombies tried to get their hands on her, but Flynn budged Kat out of the way and tackled them head on, literally head butting them to disorientate them and give her the chance to escape their undead clutches.

It was all too much. Too hot, too noisy, too violent. There was blood and fire and yelling. And Mikey was inconsolable, alone, screaming in fear. That's when Kat finally felt her power awaken. Looking at her brother suffering ignited the flame within her and she lit up like a beacon. None of the undead could get anywhere near her. The unlucky ones who were in her way burst into flames and were reduced to ash in minutes.

Mr Magus grabbed Flynn to keep him out of harm's reach. Connor and Amelia retreated to their usual human form, shocked at what was happening. This was more intense than the carpark.

Kat walked slowly towards her brother, not saying a word, just utterly focused on getting to Mikey. Callum had dewolfed and stood blocking her path. She stopped, but the heat rising from her was almost unbearable and the smell of singed clothing and hair hung in the air.

"Move."

Callum took a step backwards, closer to her brother.

"Move."

"I... you can't have him. We need him. The spell. You don't understand. This is a good thing."

You had to give Callum some credit. He was standing his ground as best as he could when faced with a flaming hot, pissed off woman who wanted her brother back.

"You don't get to kidnap someone against their will for a spell they haven't agreed to take part in and say it's a good thing." Kat was getting really angry now. Sparks fired out of her and set off little fires amongst the ranks of undead unlucky enough to be close by. There was a lot of panicked scrambling to put out the flames and get out of range.

"You don't understand," said Callum. "We're resurrecting your father."

Instantly the fire winked out of Kat, she sagged and would have fallen if Connor hadn't dashed forwards to catch her.

"You think I'm an idiot? You think I don't wish every day that my dad could come back? It doesn't work like that. Life doesn't work like that. Magic or no magic. You cannot bring someone back from the dead." Kat was in tears and leaned heavily on Connor. The others had gathered around them, creating a small but determined defensive ring within a sea of the enemy.

"But he's not dead."

Kat went very still.

"What did you say?" There was a dangerous edge to her voice.

"He's not dead. Yes, he was killed. But by magic. But he's not dead and we can bring him back."

Kat looked for Mr Magus, her face searching his for the truth.

"It's semantics," he said to her. "Kieron was killed, here in the Underbelly. He's gone."

"You didn't say dead. You've never said dead. You don't believe he died either. You just can't be bothered to save him. It wasn't because mum asked you to stay away that you never came to see her. You felt guilty. You abandoned him. Bastard!" Kat launched herself at Mr Magus, or at least tried to, but Connor held onto her and Flynn moved to stand between her and his dad.

"That's how it is, huh?" Kat roughly shook off Connor. She stalked away from all of them towards Mikey. The crowd parted, letting her through.

"Hey buddy. It's me. It's Kat." She lowered herself down to the floor and waited for Mikey to acknowledge she was there. It might take a while. He was pretty upset, but if she tried to touch him in this state, she wouldn't get through to him.

Surprisingly, he immediately shuffled over, careful not to touch her but to sit in the same space as her. It was Mikey's version of a hug. Tears sprang into Kat's eyes.

"Save Dad."

"Sorry, what? What did you say?" Kat couldn't believe her ears.

"Save Dad." And Mikey shuffled away again, the closeness too much for him.

Kat sat in stunned silence. What did she do now?

Chapter 55

The Underbelly was milling. No one seemed sure about what to do next. Was the big fight over? The wolves had all humanised, and the undead that had been on their side in the melee had retreated to the background.

Mr Magus and Flynn stood together while Connor and Amelia hovered around Kat, but she refused to look at any of them. Finally, she beckoned Amelia over to her.

"How much would it hurt?" Kat asked.

"How much would what hurt?" replied Amelia.

"If you were to give us a dragon scale."

Amelia's eyebrow raised, and she drew back a little from Kat.

"Who's us?"

Kat shrugged helplessly.

"Me and Mikey. We have to try. If Dad is… we have to."

"But my mother, she's up to something. There's no way she'd put all this effort into resurrecting your father out of the kindness of her heart. We need to keep a really close eye on her."

"We?" Kat smiled as Amelia nodded.

"But I can't give you a scale until I change and that won't be until…" Amelia trailed off. She didn't know when she was going to transform properly, for the first time, into her true dragon form.

"Tonight," said Mikey. "Tonight."

"Tonight?" queried Kat.

Mikey nodded as he rocked, but wouldn't say anything more.

"Do you think it might be tonight?" asked Kat. "Do

you feel… more dragony than usual?"

Amelia gave a short laugh.

"I have no idea! I've never done this before." She sighed a little too dramatically. "All I want to do right now is curl up on a pile of gold and have a lovely snooze. Oh, I say."

The two women grinned at each other.

"Tonight."

"Tonight."

Kat hugged her friend, beyond grateful for her willingness to help.

"So, we're doing this, then?" Connor asked.

Kat turned to look at him.

"That depends. Whose side are you on?" she asked.

"If you're planning on doing a spell with my brother and the rest of the pack, then you need someone to watch your back." He leaned forward so he could whisper in her ear and not be overhead. "Don't trust him. No matter how helpful and charming he might be. The pack will have their own agenda. Wolves don't willingly work for anyone."

Kat stared back at him.

"No matter how helpful and charming. Got it."

Mr Magus cleared his throat.

"I really think you should have the full support of the Agency behind you, Miss Kritchley. If you'll allow us." He gave a small bow, but just hearing him speak made Kat feel mad.

"Yes."

It was Mikey. Speaking up again. Not looking at anyone or interacting directly but clearly following the conversation and choosing to be involved.

Kat felt torn. Her brother rarely interacted like this. And yet here he was, in the midst of a lot of weird strangers, basically holding his own and contributing better than she'd seen him do in a long time. She couldn't ignore it.

"Hey Mikey, are you sure? Do you think it's a good idea?"

"Yes."

He wouldn't be drawn to say more. He wouldn't make eye contact or allow Kat to get any closer to him, shuffling away if she tried. Full credit to the undead who shuffled away from Mikey in turn, giving him the space he needed to feel comfortable.

"Okay then. Do you want to stay?" asked Kat, thinking that she might have time to return him home and give her mum some peace of mind.

"Yes."

As he spoke, Amelia doubled over in pain, letting out a loud gasp.

"It's starting. I think," she called out, and there was a great hubbub in the cavern.

Cleo began barking orders, clearing out the space, ordering most of her undead legion to leave. Before she herself exited, she stalked up to Kat.

"You owe me."

"What?" Kat was confused.

"You killed several members of my kingdom. Nobody comes into the Underbelly and casually kills my people without consequences."

"Then you shouldn't be a party to kidnapping and extortion." Kat refused to back down and stood toe to toe with the ancient mummy.

"You. Owe. Me." Cleo stood her ground. They glared at each other.

Another painful gasp from Amelia reminding Kat that now wasn't really the time.

"Fine," she conceded.

Cleo inclined her head and lurched out with the final stragglers, leaving behind maybe two dozen assorted undead. Presumably to keep an eye on things.

"What can I do?" asked Kat to Amelia, as she hurried over to try to help her friend, who was looking around in a very flustered manner.

"Help me get over there." Amelia pointed to a dark recess. "I can't possibly change in front of all these people. And there's no gold." She was fretting.

"Can you get some gold?" Kat called over to Callum. "After all, you're in charge of all this."

"Er… yeah, actually. We did bring some. It's in sacks over there." He pointed to the part of the cave Amelia was headed towards.

"Do you have goldar?" asked Kat, trying to lighten the mood a little.

Amelia giggled, a little hysterically, but it was a good sound to hear. As they got closer, Kat began to make out the sacks and saw there was a giant dip in the cavern floor, like it knew it was going to be a dragon's nest.

"Let's get emptying," she said, tipping up one of the sacks and pouring the gold coins out. "Where did they even get all these coins?"

"I don't know, but aren't they glorious?" Amelia purred, the gold reflecting in her eyes and her general colouring changing shade to match the coins. "I think I can take it from here. Thank you."

Kat took the hint and hurried out of the way. Already, Amelia was bigger than before. Not dragony yet, but something was definitely happening. She busied herself with the sacks, and Kat pulled herself away. Amelia should have a measure of privacy, at least.

Chapter 56

It turned out that turning into a dragon didn't take that long. Kat had asked the others to keep the wolves away, but to be fair, they were keeping their distance all on their own. Nobody else wished to burn.

Kat was pacing. She really wanted to talk to someone, but she was still too mad to speak to Connor or Flynn and she definitely wasn't going to talk to Mr Magus.

"Callum?" she called over to the wolf.

"Yeah?" He sauntered towards her, trying to play it cool.

"Can I see the spell, please? And what's the plan? How is it all going to work?"

"Ah, I don't have the spell. Only the list of ingredients, sorry." He ducked his head in apology. "We're just the collection team."

"Yes, but where are you taking them? The things you're collecting."

"Nowhere."

Kat was trying hard not to get cross, but Callum was really testing her patience.

"So what are you going to do with everything? Stand around and wait for something to happen?"

"Oh, no."

"Argh!" Kat threw her hands in the air and began pacing again, trying to stay calm.

Connor stepped in and budged his brother in the ribs.

"She wants to know who's collecting the spell ingredients. Where are you delivering them to?"

"Oh, I dunno." Callum quailed under Connor's glare

and pulled a piece of paper out of his pocket. "Er… Big Al gave me the list and said to gather things. I guess here. I suppose they're coming here to collect it. I'm just the gatherer."

"Give me that list," snapped Connor, taking it out of Callum's hand. He pushed his brother away to go stand back with his cronies. He took the hint. Connor looked down at the note in his hands. It was succinct.

Banished vamp blood
A dragon scale
Kieran's kid
Kieran's ring

Kat had come to and look at the piece of paper.

"Says pretty much the same as mine. The one from your dad. I still don't understand why he gave us that information. Isn't he meant to be working for Countess Zandys?"

"He's playing both sides. Always does. He's not even here tonight. Too chicken shit to stand up for what he believes in, if he even believes in anything. So he keeps both sides happy. Always has. It's annoying." Realising that they were standing next to each other, Connor tried to apologise. "Hey, I'm sorry…"

"Don't." Kat wasn't ready for apologies. "How much longer before Amelia's finished?"

~I'm done.~

"Okay, shall I come to you or do you want to come out?" asked Kat.

"Who are you talking to?" Connor gave her a funny look.

"Amelia, of course."

"But she hasn't said anything."

~I'm talking inside your head. It's a dragon thing.~

"Oh. She's talking inside my head. A dragon thing."

285

Kat shrugged. At this point, nothing surprised her. "Hey Mikey, want to come and see a dragon?"

Ignoring Connor and the others, Kat encouraged her brother to walk over to the edge of the cavern, where Amelia had changed, talking to him quietly and not expecting any response. Wanting desperately to hold his hand, but knowing she couldn't.

They came closer and Kat felt warmer. She also began to relax a little. Everything was going to be alright.

Amelia was curled up, as much as a large dragon can. Gloriously golden, emitting warmth and glinting as her scales caught the light.

"Beautiful," said Mikey.

"Yes, you are absolutely gorgeous," said Kat, still not quite able to believe this was her friend.

Amelia lifted her head and gently huffed in their direction. Her breath was warm and spicy on their faces. She had a long, regal looking face with large almond-shaped eyes that sparkled like multi-faceted green jewels. The colours wheeled, making them appear even more exotic and abundantly non-human. She didn't resemble Amelia at all, but somehow her mannerisms were the same.

~You look different.~

"So do you! Can I?" Kat held out a hand, wanting to touch her friend but not wanting to invade her space.

Amelia lowered her head so that her nose was on the same level as Kat and Mikey. Kat gently reached out and placed her hand on the dragon.

"Oh! You're so warm."

She stroked Amelia's snout, marvelling at how smooth and soft the scales felt. Mikey shuffled forwards, bobbing his head, both hands clamped firmly at his side.

He lowered his face so close to Amelia's they almost touched. Closing his eyes, he took a deep breath, then stood up and stepped back.

"Nice."

"Coming from Mikey, that's a huge compliment!" explained Kat, thrilled that her brother had interacted that much. "How do we do this, Amelia? How do we get a dragon scale?"

~Are you going through with the spell?~

"Yes. Everything that's happened since I walked in the Agency door has been leading to this. Everything was planned and I've been prodded from event to event. It's time for me to take charge. They want to resurrect my dad? Well, I'm going to be there. I need to know what's going on. I need answers."

Amelia nodded and began scratching her side with one of her long legs. Like a dog with fleas.

~I do not have fleas.~

"Oh, you can hear my thoughts?" Kat felt slightly panicked.

~No. I just didn't want you to think I had fleas.~

"Do dragons even get fleas?"

~I have no idea!~

Kat chuckled to herself as Amelia finished scratching and shook herself.

~I think I loosened a scale. Go and see.~

It was one thing to stand in front of a dragon and quite another to walk casually down the length of one. Kat knew it was her friend, but couldn't help feeling a little nervous. Heat washed off the dragon's body in waves, bathing her in warmth. There. Glinting on the floor. A golden coin. But it wasn't a coin, it was a dragon scale. Kat picked it up. The scale was as big as her palm and still warm. She flexed it in her hands. It wasn't as rigid as she'd expected.

Coming back to the front of the dragon, she showed Amelia that she'd retrieved the scale.

~That should be enough to count as the scale of a dragon, shouldn't it?~

"I don't see why not. We're certainly not going to skin you," replied Kat.

~Make sure you tell my mother that.~

Kat began to smile, but caught the serious expression on Amelia's face. She meant it.

"What's going on?" asked Connor, and Kat remembered that Amelia had been communicating in her head.

She held up the scale, which glimmered in the light.

"We've got the dragon part. Let's get the blood." Kat flashed a smile at Amelia before heading back over to the remaining undead.

The dragon coiled herself back into her protective space, half hidden by a rocky outcrop, clearly unwilling to be seen. Mikey hung back. Kat hesitated, then figured he'd be just as safe with Amelia the dragon than he would standing by her side.

~Don't worry. I'll look after him.~

Kat nodded to herself, really hoping Amelia wasn't reading her mind. She didn't feel confident about any of this.

Chapter 57

Walking back to the undead meant that Kat had to walk closer to Mr Magus and Flynn. It took everything she had to ignore them. She still felt furious with them. Just being nearby was enough to make her blood boil.

"Where are the banished ones?" she called out, hoping that the exiles were among the undead that had stayed behind.

There was a kerfuffle near the back. Then the small crowd parted and three of the banished vampires came through. They did not look good. Vampires tended to be of the tall and thin variety, but these were spindly, hollow cheeked and grey looking.

"Do you even have any blood to spare?" Kat asked, feeling concerned, but not for the vampires, per se. More because she wouldn't be able to get what she needed for the spell.

"Between us, it should be enough. Do you have a vial?" The strongest of the emaciated vampires asked.

"Er…" Kat knew she was blushing. Of course she didn't have a vial.

"Here." Flynn proffered one. Of course he did.

"Thanks," muttered Kat as she took it off him. Undoing the lid, she held it out to the vampires, expecting them to take it from her.

Instead, the first vampire pressed his thumb into one of the prominent fangs hanging from his mouth. A bead of inky dark blood gradually rose to the surface. The vampire turned his thumb up and over the vial and everyone waited for what seemed like forever for the blood to drop. As soon as it had, the thumb was healed. Even in this state.

The second vampire was able to perform the same act, but the third could barely stand and its fangs were retracted. It got no help from its fellow vamps. Instead, they acted as if they couldn't see him. This vampire was literally the walking dead. Its legs buckled and without thinking about Kat rushed forwards to catch them.

"I'm sorry…" gasped the vampire as they collapsed to the floor.

Kat shot a pleading look at Mr Magus.

"Can't we help them?" she asked.

Sighing, Mr Magus removed his suit jacket, handing it to Flynn. He undid the cufflink and button on his shirtsleeve and smartly rolled it up to his elbow. Then, dropping to one knee, he stuck his wrist beneath the half-dead vampire.

"Come on, I give you permission."

But the vampire turned its head away.

"I… can't. I'm banished. It's forbidden."

"We all know your banishment was illegal. Indeed, I shall speak with Messers Luciano once we leave this place in order to have you reinstated and looked after. What Countess Zandys has done is in direct violation of the balance we are all tasked with maintaining. The Council will be hearing about this."

The sickly vampire looked into Mr Magus eye's with such longing and desperation. Kat was surprised at the depth of compassion in the look he returned to the creature. A gentle nod gave permission again, and the vampire held onto to Mr Magus's wrists for dear life as its fangs gradually descended. Mr Magus stiffened slightly as the vein was punctured, then pulled out his pocket watch with the other hand and began the timer.

The other two vampires looked on greedily and the rest of the undead watched in hushed fascination as Mr

Magus clicked the stopwatch closed.

"That's enough," he said.

Kat waited for nothing to happen and was surprised when the vampire immediately unlatched, releasing Mr Magus's wrist. She had not expected that. Mr Magus touched the puncture marks with his finger, whispering something under his breath and they instantly healed.

From their semi-collapsed position on the floor, the vampire pricked its thumb and proffered the single drop of blood to Kat, who quickly collected it. The sickly vampire didn't look a lick better than before, but clearly something had encouraged its blood to flow enough for her to gather what she needed.

"Thank you," she said, including them all with her words. "I do appreciate it. And we will speak to Luciano's. Get this all cleared up."

The vampires nodded their thanks and sank back into the crowd. The weakest of them now recovered sufficiently to haul themselves up off the floor.

Idly, Kat wondered how long vampires could survive without blood, but her random thoughts were interrupted as Callum held out his hand.

"What do you want?"

"The ingredients. You can give me the ring, too."

"Not bloody likely. I will hold on to everything and you can give me the flipping words of power that need to be said."

Callum bristled and drew himself up, as if to attack when there was a commotion from the far side of the cavern.

~She's here.~

"It's the mother," said Kat quietly, but loud enough for Mr Magus, Flynn and Connor to hear her. She was still mad as hell at them, but she needed them on her side in order to face Countess Zandys.

A wide path was created with wolves scrambling to get out of the way of each other as the Countess walked regally across the cavern floor, shadowed by several burly henchmen.

"Do you have the items?" asked Countess Zandys in withering tones to Callum, but before he could reply, Kat spoke up.

"I do."

Inside she was shaking, especially when Countess Zandys swept her piercing glance up and down Kat.

~You got this.~

"Hmm." It was the only response the Countess made. "Let us begin."

"Just like that?" Kat wasn't sure what she'd expected, but they were about to raise her dad from the dead. Surely it required a degree of ceremony.

"There's no time to waste. We can resurrect your father, but his body won't survive in stasis much longer."

Countess Zandys crooked a finger, which clearly sent some kind of message to people waiting outside the cavern as several minions entered, pushing what looked like a giant incubator. The sort you see premature babies in. This one, too, had various monitors and wires going in and out. It was beeping and ticking, but Kat only had attention for the face within. It was her dad. Her stomach clenched and tears sprang into her eyes. She took half a step forwards but managed to control herself. She hadn't seen him in years, but he looked exactly the same. His chest rose and fell mechanically, machines clearly keeping him alive.

"DAD!"

Kat jumped. She'd forgotten Mikey was here. He ran

full pelt across the cavern, not caring that Countess Zandys was there or her henchman, or her lackeys. Instead, he headed straight for the incubator, thankfully stopping before he barrelled into it.

"Dad," he said again, expecting an answer. "Dad? Dad. Dad." His face pained. He looked Kat right in the eye, wanting an explanation. "Dad?"

"Yes, Mikey. It's Dad, but he's poorly. He needs some medicine. And then he'll wake up." Kat hoped that was true. She couldn't bear to break Mikey's heart and watch him struggle with grief. He had only been a baby when their father died. Then, when he'd been older, Kat and her mum had tried to explain it to him, but he'd had trouble grasping the concept leading to several bad episodes, making him hard to control and exceptionally difficult to deal with.

"Dad," whispered Mikey, seeming to understand that he couldn't reply yet. He fell back to stand with Kat, as close by as he could manage.

"Fine. Let's get on with it. Tell me the words." Kat lifted her chin at Countess Zandys, trying to feel brave.

Countess Zandys clicked her fingers and one of the minions hurried forwards, bobbing their head in deference to Countess Zandys and ignoring Kat completely. They had a drawstring bag in their hands which they opened, spilling some kind of black sand on the floor, walking in a circle around Kat and Mikey.

"Mikey doesn't need to be part of this," began Kat.

"Oh, too late, my dear. He's in the circle now and cannot leave. The ceremony has begun." Countess Zandys curved her lips into a cruel smile.

Kat tried to ignore the bad feeling she had in the pit of her stomach and instead turned to her brother.

"Mikey? Hey, Mikey?" He wouldn't look at her, but

he cocked his head towards her, which meant he was listening. "It's really important that you stay in this circle with me, okay? We mustn't leave the circle."

Mikey nodded imperceptibly. It would have to do.

Chapter 58

The minion finished making the circle and Kat made a mental note to find out exactly what the black sand was. Add it to the massive list of magical things she knew nothing about and needed to learn.

"Do you have the dragon scale?" asked Countess Zandys.

Kat held up the dragon scale and Amelia's mother sniffed. She had made no effort to go and see her daughter on the far side of the cavern. Given that she had orchestrated the blood debt and the catalyst of the change, you'd think she'd at least want to see what kind of dragon her daughter had turned into. Kat felt a momentary pang for her friend. There was no way someone like Countess Zandys would ignore the fact that her offspring had transformed into a literal dragon. She would attempt to weaponise and profit from it, no doubt.

"And the blood?"

Again, Kat held up the item. There wasn't much in the vial, so she hoped it would be enough. Mr Magus looked a little peaky after his generous donation. She supposed she would have to forgive him enough to thank him. But she wasn't there yet.

"I'm assuming that is the ring of power?"

Kat nodded. She assumed so as well. It had definitely amplified her power that night in the carpark. Hopefully, it would do what it was meant to do here. Kat certainly didn't have any ideas on how to wield it.

"Wonderful. Let us begin."

"Before we start... what exactly does the power of an offspring mean?" Kat was worried. Why had the

Countess insisted on Mikey being in the circle? She didn't want anything to happen to him. He didn't have magical powers. And he wasn't wearing the ring, so there was really no need for him to be there. Kat understood there was a protocol to drawing magic circles. Whilst she didn't know much about them, she knew that once they began they had to be completed, so she guessed that whatever was within them when you started had to stay there until the end.

"Let's find out, shall we?" Countess Zandys clicked her fingers and one of her aides brought her a yellowy piece of parchment. The words of release.

What came out of her mouth was utter gibberish and made absolutely no sense to Kat whatsoever, but she felt them take hold. The dragon scale glowed and grew hotter and hotter, almost burning her hand and making her gasp as she dropped it. On touching the floor, the scale flashed golden across the circle, dissolving but leaving a golden layer of dust dancing in the light.

Next to happen was a loud fizzing noise as the blood in the vial begin to bubble and froth.

"I'd uncork that if I were you," said Countess Zandys, smirking at Kat.

She took the advice and quickly opened the vial just in time as the blood foamed up and out of the vial, spiling to the floor where it hissed loudly. It frothed into a dark claret cloud and again filled the full circle, mixing with the golden dust to create a sparkly yet menacing fog that covered Kat and Mikey's feet.

Kat shot a glance at her brother. He seemed okay. His eyes were wide and looking at the fog with concern, but he was standing ramrod still.

"You alright, Mikey?" called Kat softly.

He didn't look at her, but he bobbed his head in a

small yes. Kat could feel a pressure building up inside, making her skin prickle. She looked down at the ring on her finger to see it was glowing. Then her hand, her arm, her entire body followed. She could feel power coursing through her, pulsing with the beat of her heart.

"Argh!" she yelled, unable to stop herself as the power shot out of her, making her whole body arc in pain. It bounced around the circle, hitting an invisible barrier and ping ponging back and forth. Every time the power swooshed back through her, it made her gasp. It wasn't doing it on purpose, but there seemed to be no letup to its mad leaping around.

Mikey clapped his hands and the power suddenly stopped moving. It coalesced into a bright ball and hovered above the sparkly red fog before descending and dissipating, causing little crackles of lighting to spark here and there. Kat's ring stopped glowing and the power pulse cut off instantly.

Kat stared at her brother in surprise. He was back to looking at the floor and not moving. Showing no sign of having done anything or interacted in any way. What had just happened?

"It is finished," intoned Countess Zandys.

"What?" Kat whipped her head back to see Amelia's mum staring at her with a pleased look on her face. "What do you mean, finished? I didn't do anything."

"I know." The self-satisfied smirk in Countess Zandys' voice made Kat take a step forward in anger. "Ah ah ah. Don't break the circle." Her actual smirk grew larger as Kat curled her hands into fists.

"What did you do to my brother?" she seethed.

"Not a thing."

And for a long moment, nothing happened at all. Suddenly, all the alarms went off on the equipment surrounding the adult sized incubator. Kieron's body spasmed again and again as he fitted wildly.

"Where are the medical staff?" yelled Kat, looking around desperately. "Don't you have a paramedic or something?"

Countess Zandys didn't reply. She was fixated on the body, flopping around like it was being electrocuted.

Kat cast a desperate eye on the other members of the Agency, but Mr Magus and Flynn were watching with rapt attention. Only Connor was looking at Kat. He looked as if his heart was breaking for her. She dashed hot tears from her face and glanced back at her brother.

There was a loud bang, liked a clap of thunder that made Kat jump. Instantly, the golden sparkles and the red fog and the lighting forks disappeared. Just like that. One minute they were there, the next gone. As was the black sand circle. Kat wasted no time in rushing towards the incubator, her brother hot on her heels.

The body of her father had stopped fitting. The machines had stopped beeping. One of the Countess' minions began disconnecting wires from the machines, letting them hang down limply, still attached to Kieron's body.

There was a tug on Kat's arm. She turned to see Mr Magus.

"He might…"

Angrily, she pulled her arm away from him.

"He might what?"

"He might not be who you remember. Calling someone back to life is an imprecise art. There's no telling it will even be your father."

The Countess Zandys nodded in satisfaction.

"You!" Kat quivered with rage and pointed her finger in the Countess's face. "You did all this. Why?

Why did you try to drug your daughter? Why kidnap my brother? What's your end game?"

The Countess regarded Kat with a cool gaze, and it seemed for the longest moment that she was not going to answer her. Instead, she held her hand out to one of her minions, who gave her a pair of white gloves, which she preceded to put on slowly.

"My daughter is aware of my feelings on her employee status and if I choose to have her poisoned, then that is a family matter and of no concern to a small being like you. She made the idiotic decision to save your life and then utter an unbreakable oath. Instead of being sensible and killing you, she is choosing to debase her grand lineage and become a human's protector." The Countess shivered in disgust as she spoke those words. "It's a pity the donuts did not do their job on you both. As for the vampires. Well. For a so-called historic institution, they are so very easy to manipulate."

The Countess extended one of her own fingers under Kat's chin and lifted her head, turning it slightly one way, then the other, as if she'd never examined a human before. She let go.

"I am both ancient and powerful, little Katerina. Think carefully before you decide to take me and the might of the Council on. Even with your protector. It's a fight you cannot win. Tell your father I'll be in touch."

The Countess swept out of the cavern with her minions hurrying behind her.

Kat didn't understand why the Countess was leaving. Surely she wanted her father for a particular reason, otherwise why go to all this trouble? She looked back at the incubator. Something was happening. The body in front of her was coming to life. Skin colour was returning to normal, eyes twitching behind closed lids, fingers moving slowly as if remembering how to bend.

The incubator was shut on one side with catches. Kat looked at them in horror.

"Open it! Open it now!" she yelled, scrabbling with the nearest catch. Her father could not wake up in a plastic coffin. It wasn't happening.

Finally, all the catches were undone and, with the help of Connor, Kat lifted the lid open. She waited by the head of the body, barely able to breathe. Waiting for something, anything, to happen.

The body stopped twitching. Then the mouth parted and took in a deep breath. On the exhale, two eyes opened. Kieran Kritchley was back.

~The End~

Kat Kritchley will return...

My Thanks

This book has been a labour of love. Begun several years before I even dreamt of publishing it – *Awaken* has been picked up and put down so many times, but I think this has worked in Kat's favour and she now has the best book I could write to begin her adventures in.

Much loves to my hubby and kids for eating up all my writing time and then being patient with me as I get stroppy playing Taco, Cat, Goat, Cheese, Pizza instead of writing.

As always, my beta readers have been fantastic – their insight invaluable, especially Kev (always my first reader), Eleanor and Donna.

Shout out to my Patreon Super Stars: Andrew Clements and Kitty Bellamy – you guys are still the best!

Finally, thank you to designer Ian Bristow, who created the brilliant cover for *Awaken* working with my garbled notes. You can find out more about his artwork at www.iancbristow.com

Leave A Review

If you enjoyed reading *Awaken*, please consider writing a review. Thank you so much, I really appreciate it.

Sign up for my author newsletter on my website and get a free copy of Rohaven novella, *The Interspecies Poker Tournament*.

Fae are being murdered in Roshaven and the only clue is a shifty moustache.

Jenni the sprite knows more than she's telling and when an interspecies poker tournament is set up to catch the murderer, she does everything in her power to get a seat for her boss Ned Spinks, Chief Thief-Catcher. The cards have been dealt. The stakes are high. Is this the end of the game for Ned or will he come up aces?

www.clairebuss.co.uk

About the Author

Claire Buss is a versatile author whose imagination knows no bounds. With a knack for creating vibrant worlds and compelling characters, she weaves stories across genres, from whimsical fantasy to thought-provoking science fiction. Whether she's penning magical adventures or exploring futuristic landscapes, Claire's writing is known for its wit, heart, and a touch of quirky charm. When she's not writing, she's indulging in her love for books, tea, and all things creative. Follow her journey and dive into her tales, where the ordinary meets the extraordinary.

For regular writing updates, sign up to Claire's author newsletter via her website www.clairebuss.co.uk.

This is Claire's LinkTree where you will find direct links to her website, social media accounts, books and the writing magazine Write On! where she is Deputy Editor.

linktr.ee/clairebuss

www.ingramcontent.com/pod-product-compliance
Lightning Source LLC
Chambersburg PA
CBHW050548190726
48283CB00007B/2050